D0338866

AMONG THE MISSING

AMONG THE MISSING

Dan Chaon

BALLANTINE BOOKS
NEW YORK

A Ballantine Book
Published by The Ballantine Publishing Group

Copyright © 2001 by Dan Chaon

The following stories have appeared,
sometimes in different form, in the following magazines:
Triquarterly: "Among the Missing" and "Falling Backwards"
(originally published under the title "Seven Types of Ambiguity");
Mid-American Review: "Prosthesis";
Witness: "The Illustrated Encyclopedia of the Animal Kingdom";
Ontario Review: "Safety Man";
Other Voices: "Here Is a Little Something to Remember Me By";
Cut Bank: "Passengers, Remain Calm";
Gettysburg Review: "Big Me"; *Epoch:* "I Demand to Know Where You're Taking Me";
PUSHCART PRESS: "The Illustrated Encyclopedia
of the Animal Kingdom" also appeared in *Pushcart Prize 2000:
Best of the Small Presses,* edited by Bill Henderson.

www.randomhouse.com/BB/

Library of Congress Cataloging-in-Publication Data
Chaon, Dan.
Among the missing / Dan Chaon.
p. cm.
ISBN 0-345-44162-1
I. Domestic fiction, American.   I. Title.
PS3553.H277 A8 2001
813'.54—dc21   00-066695

Text design by Holly Johnson

Manufactured in the United States of America

First Edition: July 2001

10   9   8   7   6   5   4   3   2   1

In memory of my parents,
Earl and Teresa Chaon

Whatever this was all about,
it was not a vain attempt—journey.

—RAYMOND CARVER

CONTENTS

ACKNOWLEDGMENTS

It is a pleasure to be able to thank a few people in print: my wife, Sheila Schwartz, best beloved, muse and mentor; my agent, Noah Lukeman, and editor, Dan Smetanka; my good buddy, Steve Lattimore, whose encouragement was invaluable; Reginald Gibbons; Heather Bentoski, Peggy McNally, and Scott Mc-Nulty, who walked through large blocks of this book with me. For their kindness in reading and commenting on early drafts of these stories, I would also like to thank Tom Barbash, Martha Collins, Joan Connor, Tom Gilmore, John Martin, Laura Rhoton McNeal, and Sylvia Watanabe. I also wish to thank the Ohio Arts Council for their generous support during the writing of this book.

SAFETY MAN

Safety Man is all shriveled and puckered inside his zippered nylon carrying tote, and taking him out is always the hardest part. Sandi is disturbed by him for a moment, his shrunken face, and she averts her eyes as he crinkles and unfolds. She has a certain type of smile ready in case anyone should see her inserting the inflator pump into his backside; there is a flutter of protective embarrassment, and when a car goes past she hunches over Safety Man's prone form, sheilding his not-yet-firm body from view. After a time, he begins to fill out—to look human.

Safety Man used to be a joke. When Sandi and her husband, Allen, had moved to Chicago, Sandi's mother had sent the thing. Her mother was a woman of many exaggerated fears, and Sandi and Allen couldn't help but laugh. They took turns reading aloud from Safety Man's accompanying brochure: *Safety Man—the perfect ladies' companion for urban living! Designed as a visual deterrent, Safety Man is a life-size simulated male that appears one hundred*

eighty pounds and six feet tall, to give others the impression that you are pro-
tected while at home alone or driving in your car. Incredibly real-seeming, with
positionable latex head and hands and air-brushed facial highlights, handsome
Safety Man has been field-tested to keep danger at bay!

"Oh, I can't believe she sent this," Sandi had said. "She's really slipping."

Allen lifted it out of its box, holding it by the shoulders like a Christmas gift sweater. "Well," he said. "He doesn't have a penis, anyway. It appears that he's just a torso."

"Ugh!" she said, and Allen observed its wrinkled, bog man face dispassionately.

"Now, now," Allen said. He was a tall, soft-spoken man, and was more amused by Sandi's mother's foibles than Sandi herself was. "You never know when he might come in handy," and he looked at her sidelong, gently ironic. "Personally," he said, "I feel safer already."

And they'd laughed. Allen put his long arm around her shoulder and snickered silently, breathing against her neck while Safety Man slid to the floor like a paper doll.

Now that Allen is dead, it doesn't seem so funny anymore. Now that she is a widow with two young daughters, Safety Man has begun to seem entirely necessary, and there are times when she is in such a hurry to get him out of his bag, to get him unfolded and blown up that her hands actually tremble. Something is happening to her.

There are fears she doesn't talk about. There is an old lady she sees at the place where she often eats lunch. "O God, O

God," the lady will say, "O Jesus, sweet Jesus, my Lord and Savior, what have I done?" And Sandi watches as the old woman bows her head. The old woman is nicely dressed, about Sandi's mother's age, speaking calmly, good posture, her gloved hands clasped in front of her chef's salad.

And there is a man who follows Sandi down the street and keeps screaming, "Kelly!" at her back. He thinks she is Kelly. "Baby," he calls. "Do you have a heart? Kelly, I'm asking you a question! Do you have a heart?" And she doesn't turn, she never gets a clear look at his face, though she can feel his body not far behind her.

Sandi is not as desperate as these people, but she can see how it is possible.

Since Allen died, she has been worrying about going insane. There is a history of it in her family. It happened to her uncle Sammy, a religious fanatic who'd ended his own life in the belief that Satan was planting small packets of dust in the hair behind his ears. Once, he'd told Sandi confidentially, he'd thrown a packet of dust on the floor of his living room, and suddenly the furniture began attacking him. It flew around the room, striking him glancing blows until he fled the house. "I guess I learned my lesson!" he told her. "I'll never do that again!" A few weeks later, he put a shotgun in his mouth and pulled the trigger.

Sandi's mother is not such an extreme case, but she, too, has become increasingly eccentric since the death of Sandi's father. She has become a believer in various causes, and sends Sandi clippings, or calls on the phone to tell her about certain toxic chemicals in the air and water, about the apocalyptic disappearance of frogs from the hemisphere, about the overuse of antibiotics creating a strain of super-resistant viruses, about the dangers of microwave ovens. She accosts people in waiting rooms and supermarkets, digging deep into her purse and bringing up photocopied pamphlets, which she will urge on strangers. "Read this if you don't believe me!" And they will pretend to read it, careful and serious, because they are afraid of her and want her to leave them alone.

But she is functional. At sixty-eight, she still works as a nurse's aide on the neurological ward of the hospital. She'll regale Sandy with the most horrifying stories about her brain-damaged patients. Then she'll say how much she loves her job.

Sandi, too, is functional. Besides Safety Man, there is nothing abnormal about her life. She works, like before, as a claims adjuster at the IRS. She used to have trouble getting up in the morning, but now she wakes before the alarm. She is showered and dressed before her daughters even begin to stir; she has their cereal in the bowls, ready to be doused with milk, their lunches packed, even little loving notes tucked in between bologna sandwiches and juice boxes. She stands at the door as they finish their breakfasts, sipping her coffee, her beige trench coat over her arm. At this very moment, hundreds of women in this exact coat are hurrying down Michigan Avenue. She is no different from them, despite the inflatable man in her tote bag.

The girls love Safety Man. Megan is ten and Molly is eight, and they have decided that Safety Man is handsome. They have been involved in dressing him: their father's old black leather jacket and sunglasses, and a baseball cap, turned backward. They are pleased to be protected by a life-size simulated male guardian, and when she drops them off at school, they bid him farewell. "So long, Jules," they call. They have decided that they would like to have a boyfriend named Jules.

Sandi works all day, picks up the girls, makes dinner, does a few loads of laundry. She doesn't have hallucinations or strange thoughts. She doesn't feel paranoid, exactly, though the odor of accidents, of sudden, inexplicable death is with her always. Most of the time, during the day, her fears seem ridiculous, and even somewhat clichéd. She knows she cannot predict the bad things that lie in wait for her, can never really know. She accepts this, most of the time. She tries not to think about her husband.

Still, when the girls are asleep and the house is quiet, Sandi feels certain that he will appear to her. He is here somewhere, she thinks. The most supernatural thing she can imagine is the idea that he has truly ceased to exist, that she will never see him again.

At night, she goes down to the kitchen, which is where he passed away. He had been standing at the counter, making coffee. No one else was awake, and when she found him he was sprawled on the tile, not breathing. She called 911, then pressed her mouth to his lips, thrust her palms against his chest, trying to remember high school CPR. But he had been dead for a while.

She finds herself standing there in the kitchen, waiting. She imagines that he will walk in, a translucent hologram of himself, like ghosts on TV—that loping, easygoing tall man's walk he had, a sleepy smile on his face. But she would be satisfied even with something less than that—a blurry shape in the door frame like a smudge on a photo negative, or a bobbing light passing through the hall. Anything, anything. She can remember how badly she once wanted to believe in ghosts, how much she'd wanted, after her father died, to believe that he was watching over her— "hovering above us," as her mother said.

But she never felt any sort of presence, then or now. There is nothing but Safety Man, sitting in the window facing the street, his positionable hands clutching a book, his positionable head bent toward it in thoughtful repose, a Milan Kundera novel that she'd found among Allen's books, a passage he'd underlined: "Chance and chance alone has a message for us. Everything that occurs out of necessity, everything expected, repeats day in and day out, is mute. Only chance can speak to us. We read its messages much as gypsies read the images made by coffee grounds at the bottom of a cup." Alone beside the standing lamp, Safety Man considers the passage as Sandi sleeps. Because he has no legs, his jeans hang flaccidly from his waist. He reads and reads, a lonely figure.

Most of the time, Sandi is okay. Everything feels anesthetized. The worst part is when her mother calls. Sandi's mother still lives on the outskirts of Denver, in the small suburb where Sandi grew up; her voice on the phone is boxy and distant. Mostly, Sandi's mother wants to talk about her job, her patients, whom Sandi has come to know like characters in a book—Brad, the comatose boy who'd been in a bicycle accident, and whose thick, beautiful hair her mother likes to comb; Adrienne, who had drug-induced brain damage, and who compulsively hides things in her bra; little old Mr. Hudgins, who suffers from confusion after a small stroke. Sometimes he feels certain that Sandi's mother is his wife. But the cast of her mother's stories is always changing, and Sandi has learned not to become too attached to any one of them. Once, when she asked after a patient that her mother had talked about frequently, her mother had sighed forgetfully. "Oh, didn't I tell you?" she said. "He passed away a couple of weeks ago."

Sometimes, Sandi's mother likes to talk about death or other philosophical issues. One night after dinner, while Sandi is drinking tea at the kitchen table and the girls are watching music videos on television, Sandi's mother calls to ask whether she believes in an afterlife.

"I realized," Sandi's mother says. "I don't know this about you."

Sandi sighs. "I don't know, Mom," she says. "I really haven't given it much thought."

"Oh, you must have some opinion!" her mother says. She has that bright, nursely twinkle in her voice that makes Sandi cringe.

"Really," Sandi says. "It's not something I want to talk about. I mean, I *hope* that there's some part of us that lives on. That's about as far as I've imagined at this point."

"Hmm ..." her mother says thoughtfully. "I'm undecided, myself. I don't think most people are interesting enough to have souls." And her voice takes on a musing quality that Sandi recognizes with grim resignation. "Do you know that the living now outnumber the dead? You understand what I'm saying? It's the result of the global population boom. There are six billion people alive on this planet, and that's more than have died in all of recorded history! It's a fact."

"Where did you hear that?" Sandi asks. "That doesn't seem accurate."

"Oh, it's true," Sandi's mother says brightly. "I read it!" Then she sighs. "Oh, Sandi," she says. "I wish your father and I had given you kids some religious training when you were young. Religion would be very helpful to you right now."

"Oh, really?" Sandi says. She thinks of Uncle Sammy and his packets of devil dust.

"Well, you are that type of person, sweetheart," her mother says firmly. "You've always been that way, ever since you were little. I'm very comfortable with doubt, and I thought you'd be the same way, because you're my child. But you're not that way at all!"

Sandi doesn't know what to say to her. "Comfortable with doubt?" What does that mean? Where has her mother picked up language like that? "Okay," Sandi says passively. She has been reading a lot of self-help books with the same tone. They spoke like this—"coping," "coming to terms," "finding closure." As if such a thing is possible.

At the IRS, sometimes people are threatened. The woman in the next cubicle, Janice, has been getting letters from a man who wants to kill and eat her. It's not funny, Sandi feels, though Janice often pretends it is. She reads his letters aloud—gruesome descriptions of what this person would like to do to her—and her voice takes on a dry, comic quality, as if it is nothing more than an anecdote. "It's like something out of a movie!" Janice exclaims. And Sandi loves Janice's easy, unfrightened confidence.

Still, when she and Janice go out to lunch, Sandi wonders if the letter-writer might be watching, following them. As they pass through the lobby of the building where they work, Sandi watches the faces. The man will look outwardly normal, Sandi feels. She lets her eyes rest on the lecherous security guards at the front desk, the skinny one and the handsome one. She scans over the heavy-set man who sits before his open briefcase, eating a sandwich; beyond him, three young men in identical suits and haircuts burst into laughter; through the window behind them, Sandi can see the figures of people walking by on the sidewalk, their shapes hazy in the windblown snow, the small cadre of secretaries huddled against the side of the building, smoking cigarettes.

Once, not long ago, she walked past the standing ashtray they convene around. She remembers looking down. There, among the slender, lipstick-stained cigarette butts, which stood up in the gravel like dead trees, she saw a tooth—a human tooth, lying there. She stood staring at it. What's happening to the world? she thought.

She wishes she could tell this story to Allen. What would he say? she wonders.

She has noticed that when she imagines speaking to him, she can clearly hear his voice. She can carry on long conversations in her head, and it seems very real. For a while, she'd had the same experience after her father died. Then the voice faded away.

Most of the time, she imagines Allen laughing his baritone

laugh. "You've really built a big thing out of this, haven't you?" he says. He would tease her into smiling about it. "You're a trooper with the big stuff, but you obsess over the details," he says. "You're funny that way."

Once, he told her that he thought she tended to "displace her emotions." She didn't mind it when he would use this kind of jargon, though she kidded him about it. He had been a psychology major in college, had become an insurance salesman. She didn't think he could help himself. It was something she'd loved about him, that mix of irony and kindly officiousness.

"*Displaced emotion*," she'd said, rolling her eyes. "Oh, please. What does that mean, exactly?"

He smiled a little, as if he knew more than he was willing to say. They were washing dishes, and he handed her a plate to dry. "It means," he said, "that you're not worried about what you *think* you're worried about."

Which is something she worries about, nowadays. What should she be worried about? What are the things she tries not to think about?

Well, there's this: Sometimes, she sleeps with Safety Man. The thought of someone knowing this actually makes her blush, so she tries not to let it cross her mind. It's no one's business— probably it's perfectly natural, perfectly normal to want to fill that empty spot in their bed with a body, even an artificial one.

But what about that one night, when she'd stayed up late, drinking? In bed, she'd boozily cuddled against Safety Man, legless though he was. She'd even kissed him.

No, she doesn't think about that. She doesn't think about

the way, in crowds, she sees Allen's face, or her mother, or her daughters, and her heart will crackle like a product being freeze-dried. She doesn't think about the janitor who resembles Safety Man, disappearing around the corner of a hallway as she walks from her cubicle to the restroom to pat water on her face. She doesn't think about her mother, clutching her at Allen's funeral. "You know, honey," her mother said, "you're never going to find another man who loves you as much as Allen did." Her mother sighed. "It's a real tragedy," she said, and put a hand to her throat, as if to constrict a sob.

Sometimes, such thoughts seem unbearable.

But she is functional. She maneuvers through her day, despite the cannibal letter-writers, despite teeth in ashtrays, despite Safety Man janitors steering their wheeled mop buckets past her workstation. When she begins to feel a wave of grief or terror washing over her, she likes to visualize a line of cheer-leaders in her mind's eye. They jump and do splits and wave their pom-poms: "Push it back! Push it back! Push it wa-a-ay back!" they chant, and it seems to work. She thinks of how much Allen would like these mental cheerleaders. How he would laugh.

Sandi's daughters, Megan and Molly, seem to be coping fairly well. Sandi knows that she doesn't think about them as much as she should, but she is there for them. She makes nice desserts, she helps them with their homework. She sits in the TV room with them for a while, trying to watch what they are watching.

"What is this?" she asks, and Megan shrugs, her eyes blank, reflecting light.

"I don't know," Megan says. "It's something like, *I Eat Your Flesh*, or something like that. It's not scary. They don't show anything," she says with disappointment, and Sandi nods.

"Mom," Molly says. "Put your arm around me." And Sandi does. Molly leans against her as, on screen, a woman opens a basement door. The woman peers down the dark stairs, and the lightbulb fizzles and goes out as the music begins to build.

"This doesn't seem like it's appropriate," Sandi says, though she's hypnotized as the woman begins to descend the stairs into darkness.

She is thinking of her mother. "You sound depressed," her mother had said, earlier, and Sandi had sighed.

"Not really," Sandi said. "Not especially, under the circumstances."

"Mmm," her mother said, in the same suspicious voice she used once, when Sandi would say she was too sick to go to school. "You know something, sweetie?" her mother said at last, thoughtfully. "I'll tell you. I don't pity the dead. The ones I feel sorry for are those poor children. I think about them all the time, the little doomed things. You and I, Sandi, we probably won't live long enough to see the end of things, but they will. They'll see the beginning of the end, at least. It's going to be so hard on them, and I just keep thinking, what can we do to prepare them and make it easier on them? I don't know, honey. It's inevitable, now. There's no turning back."

Sandi had closed her eyes tightly while her mother was talking, and when she opened them, she saw that her hands were folded on the kitchen table, limp as gloves. "Mother," she said. "I have no idea what you're talking about."

• • •

But she does. That's the worst thing. She knows now, as they sit watching TV, and she will know later, when the girls are asleep, when the house is quiet: There are terrible forces at work in the world. She will sit in front of the television, but even with the volume up she will hear the noises as the house settles, creaks, sighs. She'll be aware of the sudden movement of shadows; she'll slip into the girls' bedroom, hovering over their beds, feeling their breath. Once, as she leaned over Molly's bed, the child stirred. "Dad?" she murmured, sleepily, and when Sandi touched her she relaxed. She even smiled vaguely, and Sandi knew that in the child's dream, her father's fingers were against her cheek. A feeling shot through Sandi's hand.

Perhaps there are times such as this for everyone, Sandi thinks, times when we draw closer to the spirit world, to the other lives. Allen himself had said as much, having grown up in a funeral parlor, with dead bodies always downstairs from his bedroom. "I don't discount *anything*," Allen had told her. "I've seen too much to think that death is really just *death*."

At the same time, it seems to Sandi that most people, normal people, would recoil from such intimations. Schizophrenia is merely intuition gone awry—intuition metastasizing and growing malignant. Sandi can feel it sometimes, and as she sits in front of the television, she can hear her husband's laugh among the audience that responds to a late-night talk show host's punch line. "Allen?" she whispers, and Safety Man seems to glow in the moonlight as he sits by the window. He says nothing.

• • •

"So, who's the guy?" says Janice one afternoon, while they are eating lunch. Across the room, the praying lady is solemnly bending over her salad, and for a moment Sandi is so lost in watching, so lost in thought, that she doesn't know what Janice is talking about.

"Guy?" she says blankly.

"The man I saw you with," Janice says, smiling. "He was riding with you in your car." She arches her eyebrows, gently suggestive. "He looked cute, from a distance."

What can she say? "Oh," she says. "No, it's . . . just someone I know."

"That's a start," Janice says. "Knowing someone, I mean." She shakes her head thoughtfully, and her bobbed hair sways from side to side. "You know," she says. "I just wanted to say that . . . I don't know anyone who has gone through the kind of personal tragedy you've gone through, and I just want you to know how much I admire you. You really are a together person, and it's such an inspiration to me. I wanted you to know that. I mean, you're seeing people, and you're getting on with your life, and I'm just really glad for you."

Sandi thinks for a moment: a myriad of things. "Thank you," she says at last, and Janice briefly touches her hand.

"You're a real role model for me," Janice says earnestly. "I'm sorry, I just wanted to tell you that."

The old woman across the room has stopped praying. She now appears to be sobbing silently.

• • •

Sandi used to have a normal life. Didn't she? She remembers
thinking so, when they first moved to Chicago. She'd loved the
big north suburban house they'd bought—so old, so much history! She loved that there was a little park right around the corner, and not far beyond was a row of small quaint shops, and
beyond that was the girls' school, everything comfortably arranged. She was away from her crazy family at last, away from
the small-town restrictions of her former life.

So it had seemed. But now, as she feels more and more unsettled, she can't help but worry that this comfort is only an
illusion. Earlier that week, as she stood on the playground, waiting to pick her girls up after school, a thin, shrill woman—
another parent, apparently—had harangued her about the harmones that were being injected into chicken and cattle. These
harmones were affecting the children, the woman said. The girls
are having their periods earlier and earlier, sometimes as young
as nine and ten! And the boys, the woman continued. Had Sandi
noticed how aggressive they'd become? "Doesn't it frighten you?"
the woman asked, glaring, and Sandi had nodded, somewhat
dizzily.

"I saw a tooth," Sandi confided. "A human tooth, outside
the building where I work. In an ashtray!" And the woman had
looked at her warily, silent. After a moment, she walked away, as
if Sandi had somehow offended her.

She must have seemed like a crazy person, Sandi thinks now
as she sits at her desk. She frowns, moving her cursor along a
line of numbers on her computer screen. Somewhere, over the
tops of the thin-walled maze of cubicles, she can hear Janice
laughing her flirtatious laugh, and she has to swallow down the
presentiment that Janice will die soon, that Janice will, in fact,

be murdered. She slides the arrow of her mouse, points and clicks as the janitor who looks like Safety Man passes by and salutes cheerfully when she glances up. I am an insane person, Sandi thinks. They will all recognize it, eventually. She can't go on like this much longer. Sooner or later, they'll begin to realize that she is not really one of them; that she is in a different place entirely.

But she continues on: weeks pass, months, and yet here she is, driving through the flow of traffic, humming to a tune on the radio, and Safety Man smiles serenely beside her, gazing forward like a noble sea captain.

"You're doing fine," Safety Man tells her. "Everyone thinks so. You can go on like this for a very long time, and no one will notice. You keep thinking you're going to hit some sort of bottom, but I'm here to tell you: There is no bottom."

"Yes," she murmurs to herself. "Yes, that's true."

And maybe it is. Despite everything, she and her daughters arrive in the parking lot across from their apartment building. Despite everything, there is dinner to be made, and homework to be done, and storybooks to be read. Sandi almost hates to let the air out of Safety Man, but she does nevertheless. She deflates and folds him up, so they can all walk with dignity across the street, to their door. Later, after the girls are put to bed, she will reinflate him, so he can sit in the window while they sleep. But now, as she lays him out on the backseat, as his comforting face begins to shrivel and sag, as he gasps and sighs, she can't help but feel a pang.

"Poor Jules," Molly says. "He's passing away."

"Hush," Sandi says. She presses the flat of her hand against Safety Man's plastic skin. "Shh," she says, as if comforting him, and he replies back: "Shhhhh . . ." It's all right. The street lights are beginning to click on above her, and the city sky glows above the silhouette edges of the rooftops. Far away, her mother is leaning over the bed of a comatose child, combing his beautiful hair; far away, a man suddenly shudders as he rounds a dark corner, whispering, "Kelly? . . ." uncertainly; in the distance, Allen's spirit pauses for a moment, midflight, and listens.

"It's all right," she says, and she smiles as the last bit of air goes out of Safety Man. Megan and Molly are standing behind her, solemnly, as she begins to fold him neatly into a square. They watch her hopefully.

"It's all right," Sandi says again. As if she means it.

I Demand to Know
Where You're Taking Me

Cheryl woke in the middle of the night and she could hear the macaw talking to himself—or laughing, rather, as if he had just heard a good joke. "Haw, haw, haw!" he went. "Haw, haw, haw": a perfect imitation of her brother-in-law Wendell, that forced, ironic guffaw.

She sat up in bed and the sound stopped. Perhaps she had imagined it? Her husband, Tobe, was still soundly asleep next to her, but this didn't mean anything. He had always been an abnormally heavy sleeper, a snorer, and lately he had been drinking more before bed—he'd been upset ever since Wendell had gone to prison.

And she, too, was upset, anxious. She sat there, silent, her heart quickened, listening. Had the children been awakened by it? She waited, in the way she had when they were infants. Back then, her brain would jump awake. Was that a baby crying?

No, there was nothing. The house was quiet.

• • •

The bird, the macaw, was named Wild Bill. She had never especially liked animals, had never wanted one in her home, but what could be done? Wild Bill had arrived on the same day that Tobe and his other brothers, Carlin and Randy, had pulled into the driveway with a moving van full of Wendell's possessions. She'd stood there, watching, as item after item was carried into the house, where it would remain, in temporary but indefinite storage. In the basement, shrouded in tarps, was Wendell's furniture: couch, kitchen set, bed, piano. There were his boxes of books and miscellaneous items, she didn't know what. She hadn't asked. The only thing that she wouldn't allow were Wendell's shotguns. These were being kept at Carlin's place.

It might not have bothered her so much if it had not been for Wild Bill, who remained a constant reminder of Wendell's presence in her home. As she suspected, the bird's day-to-day care had fallen to her. It was she who made sure that Wild Bill had food and water, and it was she who cleaned away the excrement-splashed newspaper at the bottom of his cage.

But despite the fact that she was his primary caretaker, Wild Bill didn't seem to like her very much. Mostly, he ignored her—as if she were some kind of *wife*, a negligible figure whom he expected to serve him. He seemed to like the children best, and of course they were very attached to him as well. They liked to show him off to their friends, and to repeat his funny sayings. He liked to ride on their shoulders, edging sideways, lifting his wings lightly, for balance.

Occasionally, as they walked around with him, he would

laugh in that horrible way. "Haw, haw, haw!" he would squawk, and the children loved it.

But she herself was often uncomfortable with the things Wild Bill said. For example, he frequently said, "Hello, sexy," to their eight-year-old daughter, Jodie. There was something lewd in the macaw's voice, Cheryl felt, a suggestiveness she found troubling. She didn't think it was appropriate for a child to hear herself called "sexy," especially since Jodie seemed to respond, blushing—flattered.

"Hello, sexy," was, of course, one of Wendell's sayings, along with "Good God, baby!" and "Smell my feet!" both of which were also part of Wild Bill's main repertoire. They had subsequently become catchphrases for her children. She'd hear Evan, their six-year-old, out in the yard, shouting "Good God, baby!" and then mimicking that laugh. And even Tobe had picked up on the sophomoric retort "Smell my feet!" It bothered her more than she could explain. It was silly, but it sickened her, conjuring up a morbid fascination with human stink, something vulgar and tiring. They repeated it and repeated it until finally, one night at dinner, she'd actually slammed her hand down on the table. "Stop it!" she cried. "I can't stand it anymore. It's ruining my appetite!"

And they sat there, suppressing guilty grins. Looking down at their plates.

How delicate she was! How ladylike! How prudish!

But there was something else about the phrase, something she couldn't mention. It was a detail from the series of rapes that had occurred in their part of the state. The assaulted women had been attacked in their homes, blindfolded, a knife pressed against their skin. The first thing the attacker did was to force the women to kneel down and lick his bare feet. Then he moved on to more brutal things.

These were the crimes that Wendell had been convicted of, three months before. He had been convicted of only three of the six rapes he was accused of, but it was generally assumed that they had all been perpetrated by the same person. He was serving a sentence of no less than twenty-five years in prison, though his case was now beginning the process of appeals. He swore that he was innocent.

And they believed him—his family, all of them. They were all determined that Wendell would be exonerated, but it was especially important to Tobe, for Tobe had been Wendell's lawyer. Wendell had insisted upon it—"Who else could defend me better than my brother?" he'd said—and Tobe had finally given in, had defended Wendell in court, despite the fact that he was a specialist in family law, despite the fact that he had no experience as a criminal attorney. It was a "no-brainer," Tobe had said at the time. "No jury would believe it for a second." She had listened, nodding, as Tobe called the case flimsy, "a travesty," he said, "a bumbled investigation."

And so it was a blow when the jury, after deliberating for over a week, returned a guilty verdict. Tobe had actually let out a small cry, had put his hands over his face, and he was still in a kind of dizzied state. He believed now that if he had only recused himself, Wendell would have been acquitted. It had affected him, it had made him strange and moody and distant. It frightened her—this new, filmy look in his eyes, the drinking, the way he would wander around the house, muttering to himself.

She felt a sort of hitch in her throat, a hitch in her brain. Here he was, laughing with Jodie and Evan, his eyes bright with amusement as she slammed her hand down. She didn't understand it. When the bird croaked, "Smell my feet," didn't Tobe make the same associations that she did? Didn't he cringe? Didn't he have the same doubts?

Apparently not. She tried to make eye contact with him, to plead her case in an exchange of gazes, but he would have none of it. He smirked into his hand, as if he were one of the children.

And maybe she was overreacting. A parrot! It was such a minor thing, wasn't it? Perhaps not worth bringing up, not worth its potential for argument. He stretched out in bed beside her and she continued to read her book, aware of the heaviness emanating from him, aware that his mind was going over and over some detail once again, retracing it, pacing around its circumference. In the past few months, it had become increasingly difficult to read him—his mood shifts, his reactions, his silences.

Once, shortly after the trial had concluded, she had tried to talk to him about it. "It's not your fault," she had told him. "You did the best you could."

She had been surprised at the way his eyes had narrowed, by the flare of anger, of pure scorn, which had never before been directed at her. "Oh, really?" he said acidly. "Whose fault is it, then? That an innocent man went to prison?" He glared at her, witheringly, and she took a step back. "Listen, Cheryl," he'd said. "You might not understand this, but this is my brother we're talking about. My little brother. Greeting card sentiments are not a fucking comfort to me." And he'd turned and walked away from her.

He'd later apologized, of course. "Don't ever talk to me that way again," she'd said, "I won't stand for it." And he agreed, nodding vigorously, he had been out of line, he was under a lot of stress and had taken it out on her. But in truth, an unspoken rift had remained between them in the months since. There was something about him, she thought, that she didn't recognize, something she hadn't seen before.

Cheryl had always tried to avoid the subject of Tobe's brothers. He was close to them, and she respected that. Both of Tobe's parents had died before Cheryl met him—the mother of breast cancer when Tobe was sixteen, the father a little more than a decade later, of cirrhosis—and this had knit the four boys together. They were close in an old-fashioned way, like brothers in Westerns or gangster films, touching in a way, though when she had first met them she never imagined what it would be like once they became fixtures in her life.

In the beginning, she had liked the idea of moving back to Cheyenne, Wyoming, where Tobe had grown up. The state, and the way Tobe had described it, had seemed romantic to her. He had come back to set up a small law office, with his specialty in family court. She had a degree in educational administration, and was able, without much trouble, to find a job as a guidance counselor at a local high school.

It had seemed like a good plan at the time. Her own family was scattered: a sister in Vancouver; a half sister in Chicago, where Cheryl had grown up; her father, in Florida, was remarried to a woman about Cheryl's age and had a four-year-old son, whom she could hardly think of as a brother; her mother, now divorced for a third time, lived alone on a houseboat near San Diego. She rarely saw or spoke to any of them, and the truth was that when they'd first moved to Cheyenne, she had been captivated by the notion of a kind of homely happiness—family and neighbors and garden, all the mundane middle-class clichés, she knew, but it had secretly thrilled her. They had been happy for quite a while. It was true that she found Tobe's family a little backward. But at the time, they had seemed like mere curiosities, who made sweet, smart Tobe even sweeter and smarter, to have grown up in such an environment.

She thought of this again as the usual Friday night family gathering convened at their house, now sans Wendell, now weighed with gloom and concern, but still willing to drink beer and play cards or Monopoly and talk drunkenly into the night. She thought back because almost ten years had now passed, and she still felt like a stranger among them. When the children had been younger, it was easier to ignore, but now it seemed more and more obvious. She didn't belong.

She had never had any major disagreements with Tobe's family, but there had developed, she felt, a kind of unspoken animosity, perhaps simple indifference. To Carlin, the second-oldest, Cheryl was, and would always remain, merely his brother's wife. Carlin was a policeman, crew-cut, ruddy, with the face of a bully, and Cheryl couldn't ever remember having much of a conversation with him. To Carlin, she imagined, she was just another of the womenfolk, like his wife, Karissa, with whom she was often left alone. Karissa was a horrid little mouse of a woman with small, judgmental eyes. She hovered over the brothers as they ate and didn't sit down until she was certain everyone was served; then she hopped up quickly to offer a second helping or clear a soiled plate. There were times, when Karissa was performing her duties, that she regarded Cheryl with a glare of pure, self-righteous hatred. Though of course, Karissa was always "nice"—they would talk about children, or food, and Karissa would sometimes offer compliments. "I see you've lost weight," she'd say, or: "Your hair looks much better, now that you've got it cut!"

Cheryl might have liked Tobe's next brother, Randy—he was a gentle soul, she thought, but he was also a rather heavy drinker, probably an alcoholic. She'd had several conversations with Randy that had ended with him weeping, brushing his hand "accidentally" across the small of her back or her thigh, wanting to hug. She had long ago stopped participating in the Friday night card games, but Randy still sought her out, wherever she was trying to be unobtrusive. "Hey, Cheryl," he said, earnestly pressing his shoulder against the door frame. "Why don't you come and drink a beer with us?" He gave her his sad grin. "Are you being antisocial again?"

"I'm just enjoying my book," she said. She lifted it so he could see the cover, and he read aloud in a kind of dramatized way.

"The House of Mirth," he pronounced. "What is it? Jokes?" he said hopefully.

"Not really," she said. "It's about society life in old turn-of-the-century New York."

"Ah," he said. "You and Wendell could probably have a conversation about that. He always hated New York!"

She nodded. No doubt Wendell would have read *House of Mirth* and would have an opinion of it that he would offer to her in his squinting, lopsided way. He had surprised her, at first, with his intelligence, which he masked behind a kind of exaggerated folksiness and that haw-hawing laugh. But the truth was, Wendell read widely, and he could talk seriously about any number of subjects if he wanted. She and Wendell had shared a love of books and music—he had once stunned her by sitting down at his piano and playing Debussy, then Gershwin, then an old Hank Williams song, which he sang along with in a modest, reedy tenor. There were times when it had seemed as if they could have been friends—and then, without warning, he would turn on her. He would tell her a racist joke, just to offend her; he would call her "politically correct" and would goad her with his far-right opinions, the usual stuff—gun control, feminism, welfare. He would get a certain look in his eyes, sometimes right in the middle of talking, a calculating, shuttered expression would flicker across his face. It gave her the creeps, perhaps even more now than before, and she put her hand to her mouth as Randy stood, still wavering, briefly unsteady, in the doorway. In the living room, Tobe and Carlin suddenly burst into laughter, and Randy's eyes shifted.

"I miss him," Randy said, after they had both been silently thoughtful for what seemed like a long while; he looked at her softly, as if she, too, had been having fond memories of Wendell. "I really miss him bad. I mean, it's like this family is cursed or something. You know?"

"No," she said, but not so gently that Randy would want to

be patted or otherwise physically comforted. "It will be all right," she said firmly. "I honestly believe everything will turn out for the best."

She gave Randy a hopeful smile, but she couldn't help thinking of the way Wendell would roll his eyes when Randy left the room to get another beer. "He's pathetic, isn't he?" Wendell had said, a few weeks before he was arrested. And he'd lowered his eyes, giving her that look. "I'll bet you didn't know you were marrying into white trash, did you?" he said, grinning in a way that made her uncomfortable. "Poor Cheryl!" he said. "Tobe fakes it really well, but he's still a stinky-footed redneck at heart. You know that, don't you?"

What was there to say? She was not, as Wendell seemed to think, from a background of privilege—her father had owned a dry-cleaning store. But at the same time, she had been comfortably sheltered. None of her relatives lived in squalor, or went to prison, or drank themselves daily into oblivion. She'd never known a man who got into fistfights at bars, as Tobe's father apparently had. She had never been inside a home as filthy as the one in which Randy lived.

But it struck her now that the trial was over, now that Randy stood, teary and boozy in her bedroom doorway. These men had been her husband's childhood companions—his brothers. He loved them. He *loved* them, more deeply than she could imagine. When they were together, laughing and drinking, she could feel an ache opening inside her. If he had to make a choice, who would he pick? Them or her?

•   •   •

In private, Tobe used to laugh about them. They were "charac-ters," he said. He said, "You're so patient, putting up with all of their bullshit." And he kissed her, thankfully.

At the same time, he told her other stories. He spoke of a time when he was being abused by a group of high school bul-lies. Randy and Carlin had caught the boys after school, one by one, and "beat the living shit out of them." They had never bothered Tobe again.

He talked about Randy throwing himself into their mother's grave, as the casket was lowered, screaming "Mommy! Mommy!" and how the other brothers had to haul him out of the ground. He talked about how, at eleven or twelve, he was feeding the infant Wendell out of baby-food jars, changing his diapers. "Then, after Mom got cancer, I practically raised Wendell," he told her once, proudly. "She was so depressed—I just remember her laying on the couch and telling me what to do. She wanted to do it herself, but she couldn't. It wasn't easy, you know. I was in high school, and I wanted to be out partying with the other kids, but I had to watch out for Wendell. He was a sickly kid. That's what I remember most. Taking care of him. He was only six when Mom finally died. It's weird. I probably wouldn't have even gone to college if I hadn't had to spend all that time at home. I didn't have anything to do but study."

The story had touched her, when they'd first started dating. Tobe was not—had never been—a very emotional or forthcoming person, and she'd felt she discovered a secret part of him.

Was it vain to feel a kind of claim over these feelings of Tobe's? To take a proprietary interest in his inner life, to think: "I am the only one he can really talk to." Perhaps it was, but they'd had what she thought of as a rather successful marriage, up until the time of Wendell's conviction. There had been an easy, friendly camaraderie between them; they made love often enough; they both loved their children. They were normally happy.

But now—what? What was it? She didn't know. She couldn't tell what was going on in his head.

Winter was coming. It was late October, and all the forecasts predicted cold, months of ice and darkness. Having grown up in Chicago, she knew that this shouldn't bother her, but it did. She dreaded it, for it always brought her into a constant state of predepressive gloom, something Scandinavian and lugubrious, which she had never liked about herself. Already, she could feel the edges of it. She sat in her office, in the high school, and she could see the distant mountains out the window, growing paler and less majestic until they looked almost translucent, like oddly shaped thunderheads fading into the colorless sky. A haze settled over the city. College Placement Exam scores were lower than usual. A heavy snow was expected.

And Tobe was gone more than usual now, working late at night, preparing for Wendell's appeal. They had hired a new lawyer, one more experienced as a defense attorney, but there were still things Tobe needed to do. He would come home very late at night.

She hoped that he wasn't drinking too much, but she suspected that he was. She had been trying not to pay attention, but she smelled alcohol on him nearly every night he came to bed; she saw the progress of the cases of beer in the refrigerator, the way they were depleted and replaced.

What's wrong? she thought, waiting up for him, waiting for the sound of his car in the driveway. She was alone in the kitchen, making herself some tea, thinking, when Wild Bill spoke from his cage.

"Stupid cunt," he said.

She turned abruptly. She was certain that she heard the words distinctly. She froze, with the kettle in her hand over the burner, and when she faced him, Wild Bill cocked his head at her, fixing her with his bird eye. The skin around his eye was bare, whitish wrinkled flesh, which reminded her of an old alcoholic. He watched her warily, clicking his claws along the perch. Then he said, thoughtfully: "Hello, sexy."

She reached into the cage and extracted Wild Bill's food bowl. He was watching, and she very slowly walked to the trash can. "Bad bird!" she said. She dumped it out—the peanuts and pumpkin seeds and bits of fruit that she'd prepared for him. "Bad!" she said again. Then she put the empty food bowl back into the cage. "There," she said. "See how you like that!" And she closed the cage with a snap, aware that she was trembly with anger.

It was Wendell's voice, of course: his words. The bird was merely mimicking, merely a conduit. It was Wendell, she thought, and she thought of telling Tobe; she was wide awake when he finally came home and slid into bed, her heart was beating heavily, but she just lay there as he slipped under the covers—he smelled of liquor, whiskey, she thought. He was already asleep when she touched him.

Maybe it didn't mean anything: Filthy words didn't make

someone a rapist. After all, Tobe was a lawyer, and he believed that Wendell was innocent. Carlin was a policeman, and he believed it, too. Were they so blinded by love that they couldn't see it?

Or was she jumping to conclusions? She had always felt that there was something immoral about criticizing someone's relatives, dividing them from those they loved, asking them to take sides. Such a person was her father's second wife, a woman of infinite nastiness and suspicion, full of mean, insidious comments about her stepdaughters. Cheryl had seen the evil in this, the damage it could do.

And so she had chosen to say nothing as Wendell's possessions were loaded into her house, she had chosen to say nothing about the macaw, even as she grew to loathe it. How would it look, demanding that they get rid of Wendell's beloved pet, suggesting that the bird somehow implied Wendell's guilt? No one else seemed to have heard Wild Bill's foul sayings, and perhaps the bird wouldn't repeat them, now that she'd punished him. She had a sense of her own tenuous standing as a member of the family. They were still cautious around her. In a few brief moves, she could easily isolate herself—the bitchy city girl, the snob, the troublemaker. Even if Tobe didn't think this, his family would. She could imagine the way Karissa would use such stuff against her, that perky martyr smile as Wild Bill was remanded to her care, even though she was allergic to bird feathers. "I'll make do," Karissa would say. And she would cough, pointedly, daintily, into her hand.

Cheryl could see clearly where that road would lead.

•　　•　　•

But she couldn't help thinking about it. Wendell was everywhere—
not only in the sayings of Wild Bill, but in the notes and papers
Tobe brought home with him from the office, in the broody
melancholy he trailed behind him when he was up late, pacing
the house. In the various duties she found herself performing for
Wendell's sake—reviewing her own brief testimony at the trial,
at Tobe's request; going with Tobe to the new lawyer's office on
a Saturday morning.

Sitting in the office, she didn't know why she had agreed to
come along. The lawyer whom Tobe had chosen to replace him,
Jerry Wasserman, was a transplanted Chicagoan who seemed
even more out of place in Cheyenne than she did, despite the
fact that he wore cowboy boots. He had a lilting, iambic voice,
and was ready to discuss detail after detail. She frowned, touching her finger to her mouth as Tobe and his brothers leaned forward intently. What was she doing here?

"I'm extremely pleased by the way the appeal is shaping
up," Wasserman was saying. "It's clear that the case had some
setbacks, but to my mind the evidence is stronger than ever in
your brother's favor." He cleared his throat. "I'd like to outline
three main points for the judge, which I think will be quite—
quite!—convincing."

Cheryl looked over at Karissa, who was sitting very upright
in her chair, with her hands folded and her eyes wide, as if she
were about to be interrogated. Carlin shifted irritably.

"I know we've talked about this before," Carlin said gruffly.
"But I still can't get over the fact that the jury that convicted him
was seventy-five percent female. I mean, that's something we ought
to be talking about. It's just—it's just wrong, that's my feeling."

"Well," said Wasserman. "The jury selection is something

we need to discuss, but it's not at the forefront of the agenda. We have to get through the appeals process first." He shuffled some papers in front of him, guiltily. "Let me turn your attention to the first page of the document I've given you, here . . ."

How dull he was, Cheryl thought, looking down at the first page, which had been photocopied from a law book. How could he possibly be more passionate or convincing than Tobe had been, in the first trial? Tobe had been so fervent, she thought, so certain of Wendell's innocence. But perhaps that had not been the best thing.

Maybe his confidence had worked against him. She remembered the way he had declared himself to the jury, folding his arms. "This is a case without evidence," he said. "Without *any* physical evidence!" And he had said it with such certainty that it had seemed true. The crime scenes had yielded nothing that had connected Wendell to the crimes; the attacker, whoever he was, had been extremely careful. There was no hair, no blood, no semen. The victims had been made to kneel in the bathtub as the attacker forced them to perform various degrading acts, and afterwards, the attacker had left them there, turning the shower on them as he dusted and vacuumed. There wasn't a single fingerprint.

But there was this: In three of the cases, witnesses claimed to have seen Wendell's pickup parked on a street nearby. A man matching Wendell's description had been seen hurrying down the fire escape behind the apartment of one of the women.

And this: The final victim, Jenni Martinez, had been a former girlfriend of Wendell's. Once, after they'd broken up, Wendell got drunk and sang loud love songs beneath her window. He'd left peaceably when the police came.

"Peaceably!" Tobe noted. These were the actions of a romantic, not a rapist! Besides which, Wendell had an alibi for the night the Martinez girl was raped. He'd been at Cheryl and Tobe's house, playing cards, and he'd slept that night on their sofa. In order for him to have committed the crime, he'd have had to feign sleep, sneaking out from under the bedding Cheryl had arranged for him on the living room sofa, without being noticed. Then, he'd have had to sneak back into the house, returning in the early morning so that Cheryl would discover him when she woke up. She had testified: He was on the couch, the blankets twisted around him, snoring softly. She was easily awakened; she felt sure that she would have heard if he'd left in the middle of the night. It was, Tobe told the jury, "a highly improbable, almost fantastical version of events."

But the jury had believed Jenni Martinez, who was certain that she'd recognized his voice. His laugh. They had believed the prosecutor, who had pointed out that there had been no more such rapes since Jenni Martinez had identified Wendell. After Wendell's arrest, the string of assaults had ceased.

After a moment, she tried to tune back in to what Wasserman was saying. She ought to be paying attention. For Tobe's sake, she ought to be trying to examine the possibility of Wendell's innocence more rationally, without bias. She read the words carefully, one by one. But what she saw was Wendell's face, the way he'd looked as one of the assaulted women had testified: bored, passive, even vaguely amused as the woman had tremulously, with great emotion, recounted her tale.

Whatever.

• • •

That night, Tobe was once again in his study, working as she sat on the couch, watching television. He came out a couple of times, waving to her vaguely as he walked through the living room, toward the kitchen, toward the refrigerator, another beer.

She waited up. But when he finally came into the bedroom he seemed annoyed that she was still awake, and he took off his clothes silently, turning off the light before he slipped into bed, a distance emanating from him. She pressed her breasts against his back, her arms wrapped around him, but he was still. She rubbed her feet against his, and he let out a slow, disinterested breath.

"What are you thinking about," she said, and he shifted his legs.

"I don't know," he said. "Thinking about Wendell again, I suppose."

"It will be all right," she said, though she felt the weight of her own dishonesty settle over her. "I know it." She smoothed her hand across his hair.

"You're not a lawyer," he said. "You don't know how badly flawed the legal system is."

"Well," she said.

"It's a joke," he said. "I mean, the prosecutor didn't prove his case. All he did was parade a bunch of victims across the stage. How can you compete with that? It's all drama."

"Yes," she said. She kissed the back of his neck, but he was already drifting into sleep, or pretending to. He shrugged against her arms, nuzzling into his pillow.

•   •   •

One of the things that had always secretly bothered her about Wendell was his resemblance to Tobe. He was a younger, and—yes, admit it—sexier version of her husband. The shoulders, the legs; the small hardness of her husband's mouth that she had loved was even better on Wendell's face, that sly shift of his gray eyes, which Wendell knew was attractive, while Tobe did not. Tobe tended toward pudginess, while Wendell was lean, while Wendell worked on mail-order machines, which brought out the muscles of his stomach. In the summer, coming in from playing basketball with Tobe in the driveway, Wendell had almost stunned her, and she recalled her high school infatuation with a certain athletic shape of the male body. She watched as he bent his naked torso toward the open refrigerator, looking for something to drink. He looked up at her, his eyes slanted cautiously as he lifted a can of grape soda to his lips.

Stupid cunt. It gave her a nasty jolt, because that was what his look said—a brief but steady look that was so full of leering scorn that her shy fascination with his muscled stomach seemed suddenly dirty, even dangerous. She had felt herself blushing with embarrassment.

She had not said anything to Tobe about it. There was nothing to say, really. Wendell hadn't *done* anything, and in fact he was always polite when he spoke to her, even when he was confronting her with his "beliefs." He would go into some tirade about some issue that he held dear—gun control, or affirmative action, et cetera, and then he would turn to Cheryl, smiling: "Of course, I suppose there are differences of opinion," he would say, almost courtly. She remembered him looking at her once, during one of these discussions, his eyes glinting with some withheld emotion. "I wish I could think like you, Cheryl," he said. "I guess I'm just a cynic, but I don't believe that people are good, deep down. Maybe that's my problem." Later, Tobe told her not to take him seriously. "He's young," Tobe would say, rolling his eyes. "I don't know where he comes up with this asinine stuff. But he's got a good heart, you know."

Could she disagree? Could she say, no, he's actually a deeply hateful person?

But the feeling didn't go away. Instead, as the first snow came in early November, she was aware of a growing unease. With the end of daylight savings time, she woke in darkness, and when she went downstairs to make coffee, she could sense Wild Bill's silent, malevolent presence. He ruffled his feathers when she turned on the light, cocking his head so he could stare at her with the dark bead of his eye. By that time, she and Tobe had visited Wendell in prison, once, and Tobe was making regular, weekly phone calls to him. On Jodie's birthday, Wendell had sent a handmade card, a striking, pen-and-ink drawing of a spotted leopard in a jungle, the twisted vines above him spelling out, "Happy Birthday, sweet Jodie." It was, she had to admit, quite beautiful, and must have taken him a long time. But why a leopard? Why was it crouched as if hunting, its tail a snakelike whip? There was a moment, going through the mail, when she'd seen Jodie's name written in Wendell's careful, spiked cursive, that she'd almost thrown the letter away.

There was another small incident that week. They were sitting at dinner. She had just finished serving up a casserole she'd made, which reminded her, nostalgically, of her childhood. She set Evan's plate in front of him and he sniffed at the steam that rose from it.

"Mmmm," he said. "Smells like pussy."

"Evan!" she said. Her heart shrank, and she flinched again when she glanced at Tobe, who had his hand over his mouth, trying to hold back a laugh. He widened his eyes at her.

"Evan, where on earth did you hear something like that?" she said, and she knew that her voice was too confrontational, because the boy looked around guiltily.

"That's what Wild Bill says when I give him his food," Evan said. He shrugged, uncertainly. "Wild Bill says it."

"Well, son," Tobe said. He had recovered his composure, and gave Evan a serious face. "That's not a nice thing to say. That's not something that Wild Bill should be saying, either."

"Why not?" Evan said. And Cheryl had opened her mouth to speak, but then thought better of it. She would do more damage than good, she thought.

"It's just something that sounds rude," she said at last.

"Dad," Evan said. "What does 'pussy' mean?"

Cheryl and Tobe exchanged glances.

"It means a cat," Tobe said, and Evan's face creased with puzzlement for a moment.

"Oh," Evan said at last. Tobe looked over at her and shrugged.

Later, after the children were asleep, Tobe said, "I'm really sorry, honey."

"Yes," she said. She was in bed, trying hard to read a novel, though she felt too unsettled. She watched as he chuckled, shaking his head. "Good God!" he said with amused exasperation. "Wendell can be such an asshole. I thought I would die when Evan said that." After a moment, he sat down on the bed and put his fingers through his hair. "That stupid *Playboy* stuff," he said. "We're lucky the bird didn't testify."

He meant this as a joke, and so she smiled. Oh, Tobe, she thought, for she could feel, even then, his affection for his younger brother. He was already making an anecdote to tell to Carlin and Randy, who would find it hilarious. She closed her eyes as Tobe put the back of his fingers to her earlobe, stroking.

"Poor baby," he said. "What's wrong? You seem really depressed lately."

After a moment, she shrugged. "I don't know," she said. "I guess I am."

"I'm sorry," he said. "I know I've been really distracted, with Wendell and everything." She watched as he sipped thoughtfully from the glass of beer he'd brought with him. Soon, he would disappear into his office, with the papers he had to prepare for tomorrow.

"It's not you," she said, after a moment. "Maybe it's the weather," she said.

"Yeah," Tobe said. He gave her a puzzled look. For he knew that there was a time when she would have told him, she would have plunged ahead, carefully but deliberately, until she had made her points. That was what he had expected.

But now she didn't elaborate. Something—she couldn't say what—made her withdraw, and instead she smiled for him. "It's okay," she said.

•   •   •

Wild Bill had begun to molt. He would pull out his own feathers distractedly, and soon his gray, naked flesh was prominently visible in patches. His body was similar to the Cornish game hens she occasionally prepared, only different in that he was alive and not fully plucked. The molting, or something else, made him cranky, and as Thanksgiving approached, he was sullen and almost wholly silent, at least to her. There were times, alone with him in the kitchen, that she would try to make believe that he was just a bird, that nothing was wrong. She would turn on the television, to distract her, and Wild Bill would listen, absorbing every line of dialogue.

They were alone again together, she and Wild Bill, when Wendell telephoned. It was the second day in less than two weeks that she'd called in sick to work, that she'd stayed in bed, dozing, until well past eleven. She was sitting at the kitchen table, brooding over a cup of tea, a little guilty because she was not really ill. Wild Bill had been peaceful, half-asleep, but he ruffled his feathers and clicked his beak as she answered the phone.

At first, when he spoke, there was simply an unnerving sense of dislocation. He used to call her, from time to time, especially when she and Tobe were first married. "Hey," he'd say, "how's it going?" And then a long silence would unravel after she said, "Fine," the sound of Wendell thinking, moistening his lips, shaping unspoken words with his tongue. He was young back then, barely twenty when she was pregnant with Jodie, and she used to expect his calls, even look forward to them, listening as he hesitantly began to tell her about a book he'd read, or asked her to listen as he played the piano, the tiny sound blurred through the phone line.

This was what she thought of at first, this long ago time when he was still just a kid, a boy with, she suspected, a kind of crush on her. This was what she thought of when he said, "Cheryl?" hesitantly, and it took her a moment to calibrate her mind, to span the time and events of the last eight years and realize that here he was now, a convicted rapist, calling her from prison. "Cheryl?" he said, and she stood over the dirty dishes in the sink, a single Lucky Charm stuck to the side of one of the children's cereal bowls.

"Wendell?" she said, and she was aware of a kind of watery dread filling her up—her mouth, her nose, her eyes. "Where are you?" she said, and he let out a short laugh.

"I'm in jail," he said. "Where did you think?"

"Oh," she said, and she heard his breath through the phone line, could picture the booth where he was sitting, the little room that they'd sat in when they'd visited, the elementary school colors, the mural of a rearing mustang with mountains and lightning behind it.

"So," he said. "How's it going?"

"It's going fine," she said—perhaps a bit too stiffly. "Are you calling for Tobe? Because he's at his office. . . ."

"No," Wendell said, and he was silent for a moment, maybe offended at her tone. She could sense his expression tightening, and when he spoke again there was something hooded in his voice. "Actually," he said, "I was calling for you."

"For me?" she said, and her insides contracted. She couldn't imagine how this would be allowed—that he'd have such freedom with the phone—and it alarmed her. "Why would you want to talk to me?" she said, and her voice was both artificially breezy and strained. "I . . . I can't do anything for you."

Silence again. She put her hand into the soapy water of the sink and began to rub the silverware with her sponge, her hands working as his presence descended into her kitchen.

"I've just been thinking about you," he said, in the same hooded, almost sinuous way. "I was . . . thinking about how we used to talk, you know, when you and Tobe first moved back to Cheyenne. I used to think that you knew me better than anybody else. Did you know that? Because you're smart. You're a lot smarter than Tobe, you know, and the rest of them—Randy, Carlin, that stupid . . . moron, Karissa. Jesus! I used to think, *What is she doing here? What is she doing in this family?* I guess that's why I've always felt weirdly close to you. You were the one person—" he said, and she waited for him to finish his sentence, but he didn't. He seemed to loom close, a voice from nearby, floating above her, and she could feel her throat constricting. What? she thought, and she had an image of Jenni Martinez, her wrists bound, tears leaking from her blindfold. He would have spoken to her in this way, soft, insidious, as if he were regretfully blaming her for his own emotions.

"Wendell," she said, and tried to think of what to say. "I think . . . it must be very hard for you right now. But I don't know that . . . I'm really the person. I certainly don't think that I'm the *one* person, as you say. Maybe you should talk to Tobe?"

"*No,*" he said, suddenly and insistently. "You just don't understand, Cheryl. You don't know what it's like—in a place like this. It doesn't take you long to sort out what's real and what's not, and to know—the right person to talk to. Good

God!" he said, and it made her stiffen because he sounded so much like Wild Bill. "I remember so much," he said. "I keep thinking about how I used to give you shit all the time, teasing you, and you were just so ... calm, you know. Beautiful and calm. I remember you said once that you thought the difference between us was that you really believed that people were good at heart, and I didn't. Do you remember? And I think about that. It was something I needed to listen to, and I didn't listen."

She drew breath—because she *did* remember—and she saw now clearly the way he had paused, the stern, shuttered stare as he looked at her, the way he would seek her out on those Friday party nights, watching and grinning, hoping to get her angry. Her hands clenched as she thought of the long, intense way he would listen when she argued with him. She worked with high school boys who behaved this way all the time—why hadn't she seen? "Wendell," she said. "I'm sorry, but ..." And she thought of the way she used to gently turn away certain boys—*I don't like you in that way. I just want to be friends....* It was ridiculous, she thought, and wondered if she should just hang up the phone. How was it possible that they could let him call her like this, unmonitored? She was free to hang up, of course, that's what the authorities assumed. But she didn't. "I'm sorry," she said again. "Wendell, I think ... I think ..."

"No," he said. "Don't say anything. I know I shouldn't say this stuff to you. Because Tobe's my brother, and I *do* love him, even if he's a shitty lawyer. But I just wanted to hear your voice. I mean, I never would have said anything to you if it wasn't for being here and thinking—I can't help it—thinking that things would be different for me if we'd ... if something had happened, and you weren't married. It could have been really different for me."

"No," she said, and felt a vaguely nauseated, surreal wavering passing through the room. A bank of clouds uncovered the sun for a moment, and the light altered. Wild Bill edged his clawed toes along his perch. "Listen, Wendell. You shouldn't do this. You were right to keep this to yourself, these feelings. People think these things all the time, it's natural. But we don't act on them, do you see? We don't—"

She paused, pursing her lips, and he let out another short laugh. There was a raggedness about it that sent a shudder across her.

"Act!" he said. "Jesus Christ, Cheryl, there's no *acting* on anything. You don't think I'm fooling myself into thinking this appeal is going to amount to anything, do you? I'm stuck here, you know that. For all intents and purposes, I'm not going to see you again for twenty years—if I even live that long. I just—I wanted to talk to you. I guess I was wondering if, considering the situation, if I called you sometimes. Just to talk. We can set ... boundaries, you know, if you want. But I just wanted to hear your voice. I think about you all the time," he said. "Day and night."

She had been silent for a long time while he spoke, recoiling in her mind from the urgency of his voice and yet listening steadily. Now that he had paused she knew that she should say something. She could summon up the part of herself that was like a guidance counselor at school, quick and steady, explaining to students that they had been expelled, that their behavior was inappropriate, that their SAT scores did not recommend college, that thoughts of suicide were often a natural part of adolescence but should not be dwelled upon. She opened her mouth, but this calm voice did not come to her, and instead she merely held the phone, limp and damp against her ear.

"I'll call you again," he said. "I love you," he said, and she heard him hang up.

In the silence of her kitchen, she could hear the sound of her pulse in her ears. It was surreal, she thought, and she crossed her hands over her breasts, holding herself. For a moment, she considered picking up the phone and calling Tobe at his office. But she didn't. She had to get her thoughts together.

She gazed out the window uncertainly. It was snowing hard now; thick white flakes drifted along with the last leaves of the trees. Something about Wendell's voice, she thought restlessly, and the fuzzy lights of distant cars seemed to shudder in the blur of steady snow. Her hands were shaking, and after a time, she got up and turned on the television, flicking through some channels: a game show, a talk show, an old black-and-white movie.

She could see him now very clearly, as a young man, the years after they'd first moved back to Wyoming—the way he would come over to their house, lolling around on the couch in his stocking feet, entertaining the infant Jodie as Cheryl made dinner, his eyes following her. And the stupid debates they used to have, the calculated nastiness of his attacks on her, the way his gaze would settle on her when he would play piano and sing. Wasn't that the way boys acted when they were trying not to be in love? Could she really have been so unaware, and yet have still played into it? *What is she doing in this family?* Wendell had said. She tried to think again, but something hard and knuckled had settled itself in her stomach. "My God," she said. "What am I going to do?" Wild Bill turned from the television, cocking his head thoughtfully, his eyes sharp and observant.

"Well?" she said to him. "What *am* I going to do?"

He said nothing. He looked at her for a little longer, then lifted his pathetic, molting wings, giving them a shake. "What a world, what a world," he said, mournfully.

This made her smile. It was not something she'd heard him say before, but she recognized it as a quote from *The Wizard of Oz*, which Wendell used to recite sometimes. It was what the Wicked Witch of the West said when she melted away, and a heaviness settled over her as she remembered him reciting it, clowning around during one of the times when they were just making conversation—when he wasn't trying to goad her. There were those times, she thought. Times when they might have been friends. "Yes," she said to Wild Bill. "What a world."

"Whatever," Wild Bill said; but he seemed to respond to her voice, or to the words that she spoke, because he gave a sudden flutter and dropped from his perch onto the table—which he would sometimes do for the children, but never for her, not even when she was eating fruit. She watched as he waddled cautiously toward her, his claws clicking lightly. She would have scolded the children: *Don't let that bird on the table, don't feed him from the table,* but she held out a bit of toast crust, and he edged forward.

"It's not going to work," she told Wild Bill as he nipped the piece of toast from her fingers. "It's not," she said, and Wild Bill observed her sternly, swallowing her bread. He opened his beak, his small black tongue working.

"What?" she said, as if he could advise her, but he merely cocked his head.

"Stupid cunt," he said gently, decisively, and her hand froze over her piece of toast, recoiling from the bit of crust that she'd been breaking off for him. She watched the bird's mouth open again, the black tongue, and a shudder ran through her.

"No!" she said. "No! Bad!" She felt her heart contract, the weight hanging over her suddenly breaking, and she caught Wild Bill in her hands. She meant to put him back in his cage, to throw him in, without food or water, but when her hands closed over his body he bit her, hard. His beak closed over the flesh of her finger and he held on when she screamed; he clutched at her forearm with his claws when she tried to pull back, and she struck at him as he flapped his wings, her finger still clutched hard in his beak.

"You piece of filth!" she cried. Tears came to her eyes as she tried to shake loose, but he kept his beak clenched, and his claws raked her arm. He was squawking angrily, small feathers flying off him, still molting as he beat his wings against her, the soundtrack of some old movie swelling melodramatically from the television. She slapped his body against the frame of the kitchen door, and he let loose for a moment before biting down again on her other hand. "Bastard!" she screamed, and she didn't even remember opening the door until the cold air hit her. She struck him hard with the flat of her hand, flailing at him, and he fell to the snow-dusted cement of the back porch, fluttering. "Smell my feet!" he rasped, and she watched as he stumbled through the air, wavering upward until he lit upon the bare branch of an elm tree in their backyard. His bright colors stood out against the gray sky, and he looked down on her vindictively. He lifted his back feathers and let a dollop of shit fall to the ground. After a moment, she closed the back door on him.

• • •

It took a long time for him to die. She didn't know what she was thinking as she sat there at the kitchen table, her hands tightened against one another. She couldn't hear what he was saying, but he flew repeatedly against the window, his wings beating thickly against the glass. She could hear his body thump softly, like a snowball, the tap of his beak. She didn't know how many times. It became simply a kind of emphasis to the rattle of the wind, to the sound of television that she was trying to stare at.

She was trying to think, and even as Wild Bill tapped against the glass, she felt that some decision was coming to her—that some firm resolve was closing its grip over her even as Wild Bill grew quiet. He tapped his beak against the glass, and when she looked she could see him cocking his eye at her, a blank black bead peering in at her—she couldn't tell whether he was pleading or filled with hatred. He said nothing, just stared as she folded her arms tightly in front of her, pressing her forearms against her breasts. She was trying to think, trying to imagine Tobe's face as he came home from work, the way he would smile at her and she would of course smile back, the way he would look into her eyes, long and hard, inscrutably, the way Wild Bill was staring at her now. Are you okay, he would say, and he wouldn't notice that Wild Bill was gone, not until later. I don't know, she would say. I don't know what happened to him.

The rich lady on television was being kidnapped as Wild Bill slapped his wings once more, weakly, against the window. Cheryl watched intently, though the action on the screen seemed meaningless. "How dare you!" the rich lady cried as she was hustled along a corridor. Cheryl stared at the screen as a thuggish actor pushed the elegant woman forward.

"I demand to know where you're taking me," the elegant woman said desperately, and when Cheryl looked up, Wild Bill had fallen away from his grip on the windowsill.

"You'll know soon enough, lady," the thug said. "You'll know soon enough."

BIG ME

It all started when I was twelve years old. Before that, everything was a peaceful blur of childhood, growing up in the small town of Beck, Nebraska. A "town," we called it. Really, the population was just less than two hundred, and it was one of those dots along Highway 30 that people didn't usually even slow down for, though strangers sometimes stopped at the little gas station near the grain elevator, or ate at the café. My mother and father owned a bar called The Crossroads, at the edge of town. We lived in a little house behind it, and behind our house was the junkyard, and beyond that were wheat fields, which ran all the way to a line of bluffs and barren hills, full of yucca and rattlesnakes.

Back then I spent a lot of time in my mind, building a city up toward those hills. This imaginary place was also called Beck, but it was a metropolis of a million people. The wise though cowardly mayor lived in a mansion in the hills above the interstate, as did the bullish, Teddy Roosevelt–like police commissioner, Winthrop Golding. There were other members of the rich and powerful who lived in enormous old Victorian houses along the bluffs, and many of them harbored dreadful secrets, or were involved in one way or another with the powerful Beck underworld. One wealthy, respectable citizen, Mr. Karaffa, turned out to be a lycanthrope who preyed on the lovely, virginal junior high school girls, mutilating them beyond recognition, until I shot him with a silver bullet. I was the city Detective, though I was often underappreciated, and, because of my radical notions, in danger of being fired by the cowardly mayor. The police commissioner always defended me, even when he was exasperated by my unorthodox methods. He respected my integrity.

I don't know how many of my childhood years existed in this imaginary city. Already by the age of eight I had become the Detective, and shortly thereafter I began drawing maps of the metropolis. By the time we left Beck, I had a folder six inches thick, full of street guides and architecture and subway schedules. In the real town, I was known as the strange kid who wandered around talking to himself. Old people would find me in their backyard garden and come out and yell at me. Children would see me playing on their swing sets, and when they came out to challenge me, I would run away. I trapped people's cats and bound their arms and legs, harshly forcing confessions from them. Since no one locked their doors, I went into people's houses and stole things, which I pretended were clues to the mystery I was trying to solve.

Everyone real also played a secret role in my city. My parents, for example, were the landlord and his wife, who lived downstairs from my modest one-room flat. They were well-meaning but unimaginative people, and I was polite to them. There were a number of comic episodes in which the nosy landlady had to be tricked and defeated. My brother, Mark, was the district attorney, my nemesis. My younger sister, Debbie, was my secretary, Miss Debbie, whom I sometimes loved. I would marry her if I weren't such a lone wolf.

My family thought of me as a certain person, a figure I knew well enough to act out on occasion. Now that they are far away, it sometimes hurts to think that we knew so little of one another. Sometimes I think: If no one knows you, then you are no one.

In the spring of my twelfth year, a man moved into a house at the end of my block. The house had belonged to an old woman who had died and left her home fully furnished but tenantless for years, until her heir had finally gotten around to having the estate liquidated, the old furniture sold, the place cleared out and put up for sale. This had been the house I took cats to, the hideout where I extracted their yowling confessions. Then finally the house was emptied and the man took up residence.

I first saw the man in what must have been late May. The lilac bush in his front yard was in full bloom, thick with spade-shaped leaves and clusters of perfumed flowers. The man was mowing the lawn as I passed, and I stopped to stare.

It immediately struck me that there was something familiar about him—the wavy dark hair and gloomy eyes, the round face and dimpled chin. At first I thought he looked like someone I'd seen on TV. And then, as I looked at him, I realized: He looked like me! Or rather, he looked like an older version of me—me grown up. As he got closer with his push lawn mower, I was aware that our eyes were the same odd, pale shade of gray, that we had the same map of freckles across the bridge of our nose, the same stubby fingers. He lifted his hand solemnly as he reached the edge of his lawn, and I lifted my opposite hand, so that for a moment we were mirror images of one another. I felt terribly worked up and began to hurry home.

That night, considering the encounter, I wondered whether the man actually *was* me. I thought about all that I'd heard about time travel, and considered the possibility that my older self had come back for some unknown purpose—perhaps to save me from some mistake I was about to make, or to warn me. Maybe he was fleeing some future disaster, and hoped to change the course of things.

I suppose this tells you a lot about what I was like as a boy, but these were among the first ideas I considered. I believed wholeheartedly in the notion that time travel would soon be a reality, just as I believed in UFOs and ESP and Bigfoot. I used to worry, in all seriousness, whether humanity would last as long as the dinosaurs had lasted. What if we were just a brief, passing phase on the planet? I felt strongly that we needed to explore other solar systems and establish colonies. The survival of the human species was very important to me.

Perhaps it was because of this that I began to keep a journal. I had recently read *The Diary of Anne Frank*, and had been deeply moved by the idea that a piece of you, words on a page, could live on after you were dead. I imagined that, after a nuclear holocaust, an extraterrestrial boy might find my journal, floating among some bits of meteorite and pieces of buildings and furniture that had once been Earth. The extraterrestrial boy would translate my diary, and it would become a bestseller on his planet. Eventually, the aliens would be so stirred by my story that they would call off the intergalactic war they were waging and make a truce.

In these journals I would frequently write messages to myself, a person whom I addressed as Big Me, or The Future Me. Rereading these entries as the addressee, I try not to be insulted, since my former self admonishes me frequently. *"I hope you are not a failure,"* he says. *"I hope you are happy,"* he says.

I'm trying to remember what was going on in the world when I was twelve. My brother, Mark, says it was the worst year of his life. He remembers it as a year of terrible fights between my parents. "They were drunk every night, up till three and four in the morning, screaming at each other. Do you remember the night Mom drove the car into the tree?"

I don't. In my mind, they seemed happy together, in the bantering, ironic manner of sitcom couples, and their arguments seemed full of comedy, as if a laugh track might ring out after their best put-down lines. I don't recall them drunk so much as expansive, and the bar seemed a cheerful, popular place, always full, though they would go bankrupt not long after I turned thirteen.

Mark says that was the year that he tried to commit suicide, and I don't recall that either, though I do remember that he was in the hospital for a few days. Mostly, I think of him reclining on the couch, looking regal and dissipated, reading books like *I'm Okay, You're Okay*, and taking questionnaires that told him whether he was normal or not.

The truth is, I mostly recall the Detective. He had taken an interest in the mysterious stranger who had moved in down the block. The Stranger, it turned out, would be teaching seventh-grade science; he would be replacing the renowned girl's basketball coach and science teacher, Mr. Karaffa, who'd had a heart attack and died right after a big game. The Stranger was named Louis Mickleson, and he'd moved to Beck from a big city: Chicago, or maybe Omaha. "He seems like a lonely type of guy," my mother commented once.

"A weirdo, you mean?" said my father.

I knew how to get into Mickleson's house. It had been my hide-out, and there were a number of secret entrances: loose windows, the cellar door, the back door lock, which could be dislodged with the thin, laminated edge of my library card.

He was not a very orderly person, Mr. Mickleson, or perhaps he was simply uncertain. The house was full of boxes, packed and unpacked, and the furniture was placed randomly about the house, as if he'd merely left things where the moving men had set them down. In various corners of the house were projects he'd begun and then abandoned—tilting towers of stacked books next to an empty bookcase, silverware organized in rows along the kitchen counter, a pile of winter coats left on the floor near a closet. The boxes seemed to be carefully classified. Near his bed, for example, were socks—underwear—white T-shirts—each in a separate box, neatly folded near a drawerless dresser. The drawers themselves lay on the floor and contained reams of magazines that he'd saved, *Popular Science* in one, *Azimov's Science Fiction* magazine in another, *Playboy* in yet another, though the dirty pictures had all been fastidiously scissored out.

You can imagine that this was like a cave of wonders for me, piled high with riches, with clues, and each box almost trembled with mystery. There was a collection of costume jewelry, and old coins and keys; here were his old lesson plans and grade books, the names of former students penciled in alongside their attendance and grades and small comments ("messy"; "lazy"; "shows potential!") racked up in columns. Here were photos and letters: a gold mine!

One afternoon, I was kneeling before his box of letters when I heard the front door open. Naturally, I was very still. I heard the front door close, and then Mr. Mickleson muttering to himself. I tensed as he said, "Okay, well, never mind," and read aloud from a bit of junk mail he'd gotten, using a nasal, theatrical voice: " 'A special gift for you enclosed!' How lovely!" he mocked. I crouched there over his cardboard box, looking at a boyhood photo of him and what must have been his sister, circa 1952, sitting in the lap of an artificially bearded Santa. I heard him chuckling as he opened the freezer and took something out. Then he turned on the TV in the living room, and voices leapt out at me.

It never felt like danger. I was convinced of my own powers of stealth and invisibility. He would not see me because that was not part of the story I was telling myself: I was the Detective! I sensed a cool, hollow spot in my stomach, but I could glide easily behind him as he sat in his La-Z-Boy recliner, staring at the blue glow of the television, watching the news. He didn't shudder as the dark shape of me passed behind him. He couldn't see me unless I chose to be seen.

I had my first blackout that day I left Mickleson's house, not long after I'd sneaked behind him and crept out the back door. I don't know whether "blackout" is the best term, with its redolence of alcoholic excess and catatonic states, but I'm not sure what else to say. I stepped into the backyard and I remember walking cautiously along a line of weedy flower beds toward the gate that led to the alley. I had taken the Santa photo and I stared at it. It could have been a photograph of me when I was five, and I shuddered at the eerie similarity. An obese calico cat was hurrying down the alley in front of me, disappearing into a hedge that bordered someone else's backyard.

A few seconds later, I found myself at the kitchen table eating dinner with my family. I was in the process of bringing an ear of buttered corn to my mouth and it felt something like waking up, only faster, as if I'd been transported in a blink from one place to another. My family had not seemed to notice that I was gone. They were all eating silently, grimly, as if everything were normal. My father was cutting his meat, his jaw firmly locked, and my mother's eyes were on her plate, as if she were watching a small round television. No one seemed surprised by my sudden appearance.

It was kind of alarming. At first, it just seemed odd—like,

"Oh, how did I get here?" But then, the more I thought about it, the more my skin crawled. I looked up at the clock on the kitchen wall, a grinning black cat with a clock face for a belly and a pendulum tail and eyes that shifted from left to right with each tick. I had somehow lost a considerable amount of time— at least a half hour, maybe forty-five minutes. The last thing I clearly recalled was staring at that photo—Mr. Mickleson or myself, sitting on Santa's knee. And then, somehow, I had left my body. I sat there, thinking, but there wasn't even a blur of memory. There was only a blank spot.

Once, I tried to explain it to my wife.

"A *blank* spot?" she said, and her voice grew stiff and concerned, as if I'd found a lump beneath my skin. "Do you mean a blackout? You have *blackouts*?"

"No, no," I said, and tried to smile reassuringly. "Not exactly."

"What do you mean?" she said. "Listen, Andy," she said. "If I told you that I had periods when I . . . lost time . . . wouldn't you be concerned? Wouldn't you want me to see a doctor?"

"You're blowing this all out of proportion," I said. "It's nothing like that." And I wanted to tell her about the things that the Detective had read about in the weeks and months following the first incident—about trances and transcendental states, about astral projection and out-of-body travel. But I didn't.

"There's nothing wrong with me," I said, and stretched my arms luxuriously. "I feel great," I said. "It's more like daydreaming. Only—a little different."

But she still looked concerned. "You don't have to hide any-thing from me," she said. "I just care about you, that's all."

"I know," I said, and I smiled as her eyes scoped my face. "It's nothing," I said, "just one of those little quirks!" And that is what I truly believe. Though my loved ones sometimes tease me about my distractedness, my forgetfulness, they do so affec-tionately. There haven't been any major incidents, and the only times that really worry me are the times when I am alone, when I am driving down one street and wake up on another. And even then, I am sure that nothing terrible has happened. I sometimes rub my hands against the steering wheel. I am always intact. There are no screams or sirens in the distance. It's just one of those things!

But back then, that first time, I was frightened. I remember asking my mother how a person would know if he had a brain tumor.

"You don't have a brain tumor," she said irritably. "It's time for bed."

A little later, perhaps feeling guilty, she came up to my room with aspirin and water.

"Do you have a headache, honey?" she said.

I shook my head as she turned off my bedside lamp. "Too much reading of comic books," she said, and smiled at me exag-geratedly, as she sometimes did, pretending I was still a baby. "It would make anybody's head feel funny, little man!" She touched my forehead with the cold, dry pads of her fingertips, looking down into my eyes, heavily. She looked sad, and for a moment lost her balance slightly as she reached down to run a palm across my cheek. "Nothing is wrong," she whispered. "It will all seem better in the morning."

That night, I sat up writing in my diary, writing to Big Me: *I hope you are alive,* I wrote. *I hope that I don't die before you are able to read this.*

That particular diary entry always makes me feel philosophical. I'm not entirely sure of the person he is writing to, the future person he was imagining. I don't know whether that person is alive or not. There are so many people we could become, and we leave such a trail of bodies through our teens and twenties that it's hard to tell which one is us. How many versions do we abandon over the years? How many end up nearly forgotten, mumbling and gasping for air in some tenement room of our consciousness like elderly relatives suffering some fatal lung disease?

Like the Detective. As I wander through my big suburban house at night, I can hear his wheezing breath in the background, still muttering about secrets that can't be named. Still hanging in there.

My wife is curled up on the sofa, sipping hot chocolate, reading, and when she looks up she smiles shyly. "What are you staring at?" she says. She is used to this sort of thing, by now—finds it endearing, I think. She is a pleasant, practical woman, and I doubt that she would find much of interest in the many former selves that tap against my head like moths.

She opens her robe. "See anything you like?" she says, and I smile back at her.

"Just peeking," I say brightly. My younger self wouldn't recognize me, I'm sure of that.

•   •   •

Which makes me wonder: What did I see in Mickleson, beyond the striking resemblance? I can't quite remember my train of thought, though it's clear from the diary that I latched whole-heartedly on to the idea. Some of it is obviously playacting, making drama for myself, but some of it isn't. Something about Mickleson struck a chord.

Maybe it was simply this—*July 13: If Mickleson is your future, then you took a wrong turn somewhere. Something is sinister about him! He could be a criminal on the lam! He is crazy. You have to change your life now! Don't ever think bad thoughts about Mom, Dad, or even Mark. Do a good deed every day.*

I had been going to his house fairly frequently by that time. I had a notebook, into which I had pasted the Santa photo, a sample of his handwriting, and a bit of hair from a comb. I tried to write down everything that seemed potentially signifi-cant: clues, evidence, but evidence of what, I don't know. There was the crowd of beer cans on his kitchen counter, sometimes arranged in geometric patterns. There were the boxes, unpacked then packed again. There were letters: "I am tired, unbelievably tired, of going around in circles with you," a woman who signed herself Kelly had written. "As far as I can see, there is no point in going on. Why can't you just make a decision and stick to it?" I had copied this down in my detective's notebook.

In his living room, there was a little plaque hanging on the wall. It was a rectangular piece of dark wood; a piece of parch-ment paper, burned around the edges, had been lacquered to it. On the parchment paper, in careful, calligraphy letters, was written:

> I wear
> the chain
> I forged
> in life.

Which seemed like a possible secret message. I thought maybe he'd escaped from jail.

From a distance, behind a hedge, I watched Mickleson's house. He wouldn't usually appear before ten o'clock in the morning. He would pop out his front door in his bathrobe, glancing quickly around as if he sensed someone watching, and then he would snatch up the newspaper on his doorstep. At times, he seemed aware of my eyes.

I knew I had to be cautious. Mickleson must not guess that he was being investigated, and I tried to take precautions. I stopped wearing my favorite detective hat, to avoid calling attention to myself. When I went through his garbage, I did it in the early morning, while I was fairly certain he was still asleep. Even so, one July morning I was forced to crawl under a thick hedge when Mickleson's back door unexpectedly opened at eight A.M. and he shuffled out to the alley to dump a bag into his trash can. Luckily I was wearing brown and green and blended in with the shrubbery. I lay there, prone against the dirt, staring at his bare feet and hairy ankles. He was wearing nothing but boxer shorts. I could see that his clothes had been concealing a large quantity of dark, vaguely sickening body hair; there was even some on his back! I had recently read a Classics Illustrated comic book version of *Dr. Jekyll and Mr. Hyde,* and I recalled the description of Hyde as "something troglodytic," which was a word I had looked up in the dictionary and now applied as Mickleson dumped his bag into the trash can. I had just begun to grow a few hairs on my own body, and was chilled to think I would end up like this. I heard the clank of beer cans, and then he walked away and I lay still, feeling uneasy.

At home, after dinner, I would sit in my bedroom, reading through my notes, puzzling. I would flip through my lists, trying to find clues I could link together. I'd sift through the cigar box full of things I'd taken from his home: photographs, keys, a Swiss army knife, a check stub with his signature, which I'd compared against my own. But nothing seemed to fit. All I knew was that he was mysterious. He had some secret.

Once, one late night that summer, I thought I heard my parents talking about me. I was reading, and their conversation had been mere background, rising and falling, until I heard my name. "Andrew ... how he's turning out ... not fair to anybody!" Words, rising through the general mumble, first in my father's, then my mother's voice. Then, loudly: "What will happen to him?"

I sat up straight, my heart beating heavily, because it seemed that something must have happened, they must have discovered something. I felt certain that I was about to be exposed: my spying, my breaking and entering, my stealing. I was quiet, frightened, listening, and then after a while I got up and crept downstairs.

My mother and father were at the kitchen table, speaking softly, staring at the full ashtray that sat between them. My mother looked up when I came in and clenched her teeth. "Oh, for God's sake," she said. "Andy, it's two-thirty in the morning! What are you doing up?"

I stood there in the doorway, uncertainly. I wished that I were a little kid again, to tell her that I was scared. But I just hovered there. "I couldn't sleep," I said.

My mother frowned. "Well, try harder, God damn it," she said.

I stood there a moment longer. "Mom?" I said.

"Go to bed!" She glared.

"I thought I heard you guys saying something about that man that just moved in down the block. He didn't say anything about me, did he?"

"Listen to me, Andrew," she said. Her look darkened. "I don't want you up there listening to our conversations. This is grown-up talk and I don't want you up there snooping."

"He's going to be the new science teacher," I said.

"I know," she said, but my father raised his eyebrows.

"Who's this?" my father said, raising his glass to his lips. "That weirdo is supposed to be a teacher? That's a laugh."

"Oh, don't start!" my mother said. "At least he's a customer! You better God damn not pick a fight with him. You've driven enough people away as it is, the way you are. It's no wonder we don't have any friends!" Then she turned on me. "I thought I told you to go to bed. Don't just stand there gaping when I tell you something! My God, I can't get a minute's peace!"

Back in my bedroom, I tried to forget what my parents had said—it didn't matter, I thought, as long as they didn't know anything about me. I was safe! And I sat there, relieved, slowly forgetting the fact that I was really just a strange twelve-year-old boy, a kid with no real playmates, an outsider even in his own family. I didn't like being that person, and I sat by the window, awake, listening to my parents' slow-arguing voices downstairs, smelling the smoke that hung in a thick, rippling cloud over their heads. Outside, the lights of Beck melted into the dark fields, the hills were heavy, huddled shapes against the sky. I closed my eyes, wishing hard, trying to will my imaginary city into life, envisioning roads and streetlights suddenly sprouting up through the prairie grass. And tall buildings. And freeways. And people.

It has been almost twenty years since I last saw Beck. We left the town in the summer before eighth grade, after my parents had gone bankrupt, and in the subsequent years we moved through a blur of ugly states—Wyoming, Montana, Panic, Despair—while my parents' marriage dissolved.

Now we are all scattered. My sister, Debbie, suffered brain damage in a car accident when she was nineteen, out driving with her friends. She now lives in a group home in Denver, where she and the others spend their days making Native American jewelry to sell at truck stops. My brother, Mark, is a physical therapist who lives on a houseboat in Marina del Rey, California. He spends his free time reading books about childhood trauma, and every time I talk to him, he has a series of complaints about our old misery: At the very least, surely I remember the night that my father was going to kill us all with his gun, how he and Debbie and I ran into the junkyard and hid in an old refrigerator box? I think he's exaggerating, but Mark is always threatening to have me hypnotized so I'll remember.

We have all lost touch with my mother. The last anyone heard, she was living in Puerto Vallarta, married to a man who apparently has something to do with real estate development. The last time I talked to her, she didn't sound like herself: A Caribbean lilt had crept into her voice. She laughed harshly, then began to cough, when I mentioned old times.

For a time before he died, I was closest to my father. He was working as a bartender in a small town in Idaho, and he used to call me when I was in law school. Like me, he remembered Beck fondly: the happiest time of his life, he said. "If only we could have held on a little bit longer," he told me. "It would have been a different story. A different story entirely."

Then he'd sigh. "Well, anyway," he'd say. "How are things going with Katrina?"

"Fine," I'd say. "Just the usual. She's been a little distant lately. She's very busy with her classes. I think med school takes a lot out of her."

I remember shifting silently because the truth was, I didn't really have a girlfriend named Katrina. I didn't have a girlfriend, period. I made Katrina up one evening, on the spur of the moment, to keep my dad from worrying so much. It helped him to think that I had a woman looking after me, that I was heading into a normal life of marriage, children, a house, et cetera. Now that I have such things, I feel a bit guilty. He died not knowing the truth. He died waiting to meet her, enmeshed in my made-up drama—in the last six months of his life, Katrina and I came close to breaking up, got back together, discussed marriage, worried that we were not spending enough time together. The conversations that my father and I had about Katrina were some of the best we ever had.

• • •

I don't remember much about my father from that summer when I was twelve. We certainly weren't having conversations that I can think of, and I don't ever recall that he pursued me with a gun. He was just there: I walked past him in the morning as he sat, sipping coffee, preparing to go to work. I'd go into the bar, and he would pour me a glass of Coke with bitters "to put hair on my chest." I'd sit there on the bar stool stroking Suds, the bar's tomcat, in my lap, murmuring quietly to him as I imagined my detective story. My father had a bit part in my imagination, barely a speaking role.

But it was at the bar that I saw Mr. Mickleson again. I had been at his house that morning, working through a box of letters, and then I'd been out at the junkyard behind our house. In those unenlightened times, it was called The Dump. People drove out and pitched their garbage over the edge of a ravine, which had become encrusted with a layer of beer cans, broken toys, bedsprings, car parts, broken glass. It was a magical place, and I'd spent a few hours in the driver's seat of a rusted-out Studebaker, fiddling with the various dashboard knobs, pretending to drive it, to stalk suspects, to become involved in a thrilling high-speed chase. At last I had come to the bar to unwind, to drink my Coke and bitters and re-create the day in my imagination. Occasionally, my father would speak to me and I would be forced to reluctantly disengage myself from the Detective, who was brooding over a glass of bourbon. He had become hardened and cynical, but he would not give up his fight for justice.

I was repeating these stirring lines in my mind when Mr.

Mickleson came into the bar. I felt a little thrum when he entered. My grip tightened on Suds the cat, who struggled and sprang from my lap.

Having spent time in The Crossroads, I recognized drunkenness. I was immediately aware of Mickleson's flopping gait, the way he settled heavily against the lip of the bar. "Okay, okay," he muttered to himself, then chuckled. "No, just forget it, never mind," he said cheerfully. Then he sighed and tapped his hand against the bar. "Shot o'rum," he said. "Captain Morgan, if you have it. No ice." I watched as my father served him, then flicked my glance away when Mickleson looked warily in my direction. He leveled his gaze at me, his eyes heavy with some meaning I couldn't decipher. It was part friendly, that look, but part threatening, too, in a particularly intimate way— as if he recognized me.

"Oh, hello," Mr. Mickleson said. "If it isn't the staring boy! Hello, Staring Boy!" He grinned at me, and my father gave him a stern look. "I believe I know you," Mr. Mickleson said jauntily. "I've seen you around, haven't I?"

I just sat there, blushing. It occurred to me that perhaps, despite my precautions, Mr. Mickleson had seen me after all. "Staring Boy," he said, and I tried to think of when he might have caught me staring. How many times? I saw myself from a distance, watching his house but now also being watched, and the idea set up a panic in me that was difficult to quell. I was grateful that my father came over and called me son. "Son," he said, "why don't you go on outside and find something to do? You may as well enjoy some of that summer sunshine before school starts."

"All right," I said. I saw that Mickleson was still grinning at me expectantly, his eyes blank and unblinking, and I realized that he was doing an imitation of my own expression—Staring Boy, meet Staring Man. I tried to step casually off the bar stool, but instead stumbled and nearly fell.

"Oopsie-daisy!" Mr. Mickleson said, and my father gave him a hard look, a careful glare that checked Mr. Mickleson's grin. He shrugged.

"Ah, children, children," he said confidingly to my father as I hurried quickly to the door. I heard my father start to speak sharply as I left, but I didn't have the nerve to stick around to hear what was said.

Instead, I crept along the outside of the bar; I staked out Mickleson's old Volkswagen and found it locked. There were no windows into the bar, and so I pressed myself against the wall, trying to listen. I tried to think what I would write in my notebook: that look he'd given me, his grinning mimicry of my stare. I believe I know you, he'd said: What, exactly, did he know?

And then I had a terrible thought. Where was the notebook? I imagined, for a moment, that I had left it there, on the bar, next to my drink. I had the horrifying image of Mr. Mickleson's eyes falling on it, the theme book cover, which was decorated with stylized question marks, and on which I'd written: ANDY O'DAY MYSTERY SERIES #67: THE DETECTIVE MEETS THE DREADFUL DOUBLE! I saw him smiling at it, opening it, his eyes narrowing as he saw his photo pasted there on the first page.

But it wasn't in the bar. I was sure it wasn't, because I remembered not having it when I went in. I didn't have it with me, I knew, and I began to backtrack, step by step, from the

Studebaker to lunchtime to my bedroom and then I saw it, with the kind of perfect clarity my memory has always been capable of, despite everything.

I saw myself in Mickleson's living room, on my knees in front of a box of his letters. I had copied something in the notebook and put it down on the floor. It was right there, next to the box. I could see it as if through a window, and I stood there observing the image in my mind's eye, as my mother came around the corner, into the parking lot.

"Andy!" she said. "I've been calling for you! Where the hell have you been?"

She was in one of her moods. "I am so sick of this!" she said, and gave me a hard shake as she grabbed my arm. "You God damn lazy kids just think you can do as you please, all the God damn day long! This house is a pigsty, and not a one of you will bend a finger to pick up your filthy clothes or even wash a dish." She gritted her teeth, her voice trembling, and she slammed into the house, where Mark was scrubbing the floor and Debbie was standing at the sink, washing dishes. Mark glared up at me, his eyes red with crying and self-pity and hatred. I knew he was going to hit me as soon as she left. "Clean, you brats!" my mother cried. "I'm going to work, and when I get home I want this house to shine!" She was in the frilly blouse and makeup she wore when she tended bar, beautiful and flushed, her eyes hard. "I'm not going to live like this anymore. I'm not going to live this kind of life!"

"She was a toxic parent," Mark says now, in one of our rare phone conversations. "A real psycho. It haunts me, you know, the shit that we went through. It was like living in a house of terror, you know? Like, you know, a dictatorship or something. You never knew what was next, and that was the scariest part. There was a point, I think, where I really just couldn't take it anymore. I really wanted to die." I listen as he draws on his cigarette and then exhales, containing the fussy spitefulness that's creeping into his voice. "Not that you'd remember. It always fell on me, whatever it was. They thought you were so cute and spacy, so you were always checked out in La-La Land while I got the brunt of everything."

I listen but don't listen. I'm on the deck behind my house with my cell phone, reclining, watching my daughters jump through the sprinkler. Everything is green and full of sunlight, and I might as well be watching an actor portraying me in the happy ending of a movie of my life. I've never told him about my blackouts and I don't now, though they have been bothering me again lately. I can imagine what he would come up with: fugue states, repressed memories, multiple personalities. Ridiculous stuff.

"It all seems very far away to me," I tell Mark, which is not true exactly, but it's part of the role I've been playing for many years now. "I don't really think much about it."

This much is true: I barely remember what happened that night. I wasn't even there, among the mundane details of children squabbling and cleaning and my mother's ordinary unhappiness. I was the Detective!—driving my sleek Studebaker through the streets of Beck, nervous though not panicked, edgy and white-knuckled but still planning with steely determination: the notebook! The notebook must be retrieved! Nothing else was really happening, and when I left the house I was in a state of focused intensity.

It must have been about eleven o'clock. Mark had been especially evil and watchful, and it wasn't until he'd settled down in front of the television with a big bowl of ice cream that I could pretend, at last, to go to bed.

Outside, out the door, down the alley: It seems to me that I should have been frightened, but mostly I recall the heave of adrenaline and determination, the necessity of the notebook, the absolute need for it. It was my story.

The lights were on at Mickleson's house, a bad sign, but I moved forward anyway, into the dense and dripping shadows of his yard, the crickets singing thickly, my hand already extended to touch the knob of his back door.

Which wasn't locked. It didn't even have to be jimmied, it gave under the pressure of my hand, a little electrical jolt across my skin, the door opening smooth and uncreaking, and I passed like a shadow into the narrow back foyer that led to the kitchen. There was a silence in the house, and for a moment I felt certain that Mickleson was asleep. Still, I moved cautiously. The kitchen was brightly fluorescent and full of dirty dishes and beer cans. I slid my feet along the tile, inching along the wall. Silence, and then Mickleson's voice drifted up suddenly, a low mumble and then a firmer one, as if he were contradicting himself. My heart shrank. Now what? I thought as I came to the edge of the living room.

Mickleson was sitting in his chair, slumping, his foot jiggling with irritation. I heard the sail-like snap of a turning page, and I didn't even have to look to know that the notebook was in his hands. He murmured again as I stood there. I felt light-headed. The notebook! I thought, and leaned against the wall. I felt my head bump against something, and Mr. Mickleson's plaque tilted, then fell. I fumbled for a moment before I caught it.

But the sound made him turn. There I was, dumbly holding the slice of wood, and his eyes rested on me. His expression seemed to flicker with surprise, then terror, then annoyance—before settling on a kind of blank amusement. He cleared his throat.

"I believe I see a little person in my house," he said, and I might have fainted. I could feel the Detective leaving me, shriveling up and slumping to the floor, a suit of old clothes; the city of Beck disintegrated in the distance, streets drying up like old creek beds, skyscrapers sinking like ocean liners into the wheat fields. I was very still, his gaze pinning me. "A ghostly little person," he said, with satisfaction. He stood up for a moment, wavering, and then stumbled back against the chair for support, a look of affronted dignity freezing on his face. I didn't move.

"Well, well," he said. "Do I dare assume that I am in the presence of the author of this—" and he waved my notebook vaguely "—this document?" And he paused, thumbing through it with an exaggerated, mimelike gesture. "Hmm," he murmured, almost crooning. "So—imaginative! And—there's a certain—*charm*—about it—I think." And then he leaned toward me. "And so at last we meet, Detective O'Day!" he said, in a deep voice. "You may call me Professor Moriarty!" He made a strange shape with his mouth and laughed softly—not sinister exactly, but musing, as if he'd just told himself a good joke and I was somehow in on it.

"Why so quiet?" he exclaimed, and waggled the notebook at me. "Haven't you come to find your future, young Detective?" I watched as he pressed his fingers to his temples, like a stage medium. "Hmm," he said, and began to wave his arms and fingers with a seaweedlike floating motion, as if casting a magic spell or performing a hula dance. "Looking for his future," he said. "What lies in wait for Andy O'Day? I ask myself that question frequently. Will he grow up to be ..." —and here he read aloud from my journal— "... 'troglodytic' and 'sinister'? Will he ever escape the sad and lonely life of a Detective, or will he wander till the end of his days through the grim and withering streets of Beck?"

He paused then and looked up from my journal. I thought for a moment that if I leapt out, I could snatch it from him, even though the things I had written now seemed dirty and pathetic. I thought to say, "Give me back my notebook!" But I didn't really want it anymore. I just stood there, watching him finger the pages. He leaned toward me, wavering, his eyes not exactly focused on me, but on some part of my forehead or shoulder or hair. He smiled, made another small effort to stand, then changed his mind. "What will happen to Andy O'Day?" he said again, thoughtfully. "It's such a compelling question, a very lovely question, and I can tell you the answer. Because, you see, I've come through my time machine to warn you! I have a special message for you from the future. Do you want to know what it is?"

"No," I said at last, my voice thick and uncertain.

"Oh, Andy," he said, as if very disappointed. "Andy, Andy. Look! Here I am!" He held his arms out wide, as if I'd run toward them. "Your Dreadful Double!" I watched as he straightened himself, correcting the slow tilt of his body. "I know you," Mr. Mickleson said. His head drooped, but he kept one eye on me. "You must be coming to me—for *something?*"

I shook my head. I didn't know. I couldn't even begin to imagine, and yet I felt—not for the last time—that I was standing in a desolate and empty prairie, the fields unraveling away from me in all directions. The long winds ran through my hair.

"Don't you want to know a secret?" he said. "Come over here, I'll whisper in your ear."

And it seemed to me, then, that he did know a secret. It seemed to me that he would tell me something terrible, something I didn't want to hear. I watched as he closed my notebook and placed it neatly on the coffee table, next to the *TV Guide*. He balanced himself on two feet, lifting up and lurching toward me. "Hold still," he murmured. "I'll whisper."

I turned and ran.

I once tried to explain this incident to my wife, but it didn't make much sense to her. She nodded, as if it were merely strange, merely puzzling. Hmmm, she said, and I thought that perhaps it *was* odd to remember this time so vividly, when I remembered so little else. It *was* a little ridiculous that I should find Mr. Mickleson on my mind so frequently.

"He was just a drunk," my wife said. "A little crazy, maybe, but ..." And she looked into my face, her mouth pursing. "He didn't ... *do* anything to you, did he?" she said awkwardly, and I shook my head.

"No—no," I said. And I explained to her that I never saw Mr. Mickleson again. I avoided the house after that night, of course, and when school started he wasn't teaching Science 7. We were told, casually, that he had an "emergency," that he had been called away, and when, after a few weeks, he still didn't return, he was replaced without comment by an elderly lady substitute, who read to us from the textbook—*The World of Living Things*—in a lilting, storybook voice, and who whispered "My God," as she watched us later, dissecting earthworms, pinning them to corkboard and exposing their many hearts. We never found out where Mr. Mickleson had gone.

"He was probably in rehab," my wife said sensibly. "Or institutionalized. Your father was right. He was just a weirdo. It doesn't seem that mysterious to me."

Yes. I nodded a little, ready to drop the subject. I couldn't very well explain the empty longing I felt, the eager dread that would wash over me, going into the classroom and thinking that he might be sitting there behind the desk, waiting. It didn't make sense, I thought, and I couldn't explain it, any more than I could explain why he remained in my mind as I crisscrossed the country with my family, any more than I could explain why he seemed to be there when I thought of them, even now: Mark, fat and paranoid, on his houseboat; my mother in Mexico, nodding over a cocktail; Debbie, staring at a spider in the corner of her room in the group home, her eyes dull; my father, frightened, calling me on the phone as his liver failed him, his body decomposing in a tiny grave in Idaho that I'd never visited. How could I explain that Mickleson seemed to preside over these thoughts, hovering at the edge of them like a stage director at the back of my mind, smiling as if he'd done me a favor?

I didn't know why he came into my mind as I thought of them, just as I didn't know why he seemed to appear whenever I told lies. It was just that I could sense him. *Yes,* he whispered as I told my college friends that my father was an archaeologist living in Peru, that my mother was a former actress; *Yes,* he murmured as I lied to my father about Katrina; *Yes,* as I make excuses to my wife, when I say I am having dinner with a client when in fact I am tracing another path entirely—following a young family as they stroll through the park, or a whistling old man who might be my father, if he'd gotten away, or a small, brisk-paced woman, who looks like Katrina might, if Katrina weren't made up. How can I explain that I walk behind this Katrina woman for many blocks, living a different life, whistling my old man tune?

I can't. I can't explain it, no more than I can admit that I still have Mickleson's plaque, just as he probably still has my notebook; no more than I can explain why I take the plaque out of the bottom drawer of my desk and unwrap the tissue paper I've folded it in, reading the inscription over, like a secret message: "I wear the chains I forged in life." I know it's just a cheap Dickens allusion, but it still seems important.

I can hear him say, "Hold still. I'll *whisper.*"

Hmmm, my wife would say, puzzled and perhaps a bit disturbed. She's a practical woman, and so I say nothing. It's probably best that she doesn't think any more about it, and I keep to myself the private warmth I feel when I sense a blackout coming, the darkness clasping its hands over my eyes. It's better this way—we're all happy. I'm glad that my wife will be there when I wake, and my normal life, and my beautiful daughters, looking at me, wide-eyed, staring.

"Hello?" my wife will say, and I'll smile as she nudges me. "Are you there?" she'll whisper.

PRODIGAL

Mine is the typical story: I used to despise my father, and now that he is dead I feel bad about despising him. There's not much more to say about that.

When I was young, I used to identify with those precociously perceptive child narrators one finds in books. You know the type. They always have big dark eyes. They observe poetic details, clear-sighted, very sensitive: the father's cologne-sweet smell, his lingering breath of beer and cigarettes, his hands like ____. Often farm animals are metaphorically invoked, and we see the dad involved in some work—hunched over the gaping mouth of a car, straightening the knot in his salesman's tie, pulling himself into the cab of his semi-truck, on his hands and knees among the rosebushes. We'll see a whole map of his wasted, pathetic life in the squeal of his worn-out brakes, in the wisping smokestacks of the factory where he works, in the aching image of him rising before dawn to turn up the thermostat. The mom will peer from behind a curtain as he drives away. Her hands tremble as she folds clothes, washes dishes, makes you a sandwich. Something you don't quite understand is always going on, and you press close to the bathroom door she is locked behind. You'll probably hear her weeping.

Now that I have children of my own, this bothers me. This type of kid. Sometimes, when I feel depressed and stare out the window while my kids pester me for attention, or when I lose my temper and throw a plate or whatever, or when I'm in a good mood and I'm singing some song from the radio too loudly and too off-key, I think of that gentle, dewy-eyed first person narrator and it makes my skin crawl. It doesn't matter what you do. In the end, you are going to be judged, and all the times that you're not at your most dignified are the ones that will be recalled in all their vivid, heartbreaking detail. And then of course these things will be distorted and exaggerated and replayed over and over, until eventually they turn into the essence of you: your cartoon.

My father is a good example. My father used to whistle merry little tunes when he was happy and soft, minor key ones when he was sad. I can't remember when exactly this began to annoy me, but by the time I was eleven or twelve, I could do a pretty amazing parody of it. I'd see him coming, loping along with his hands behind his back and his eyes downcast, whistling some dirge, and I could barely contain my private laughter.

Once, when he was visiting, he began to whistle in an elevator, completely oblivious of the obvious codes of silence and anonymity that govern certain public places. The second the doors slid shut, he abruptly puckered his lips, like a chaste kiss, and began to trill, filling the air with melody, accenting the tune with grace notes and a strange, melodramatic vibrato at the climactic parts, until everyone nearby was turned to stone with horror and embarrassment, staring straight ahead and pretending they couldn't hear it.

He was on his last legs by that point—"last legs," he said, as if he had more than one pair. I didn't believe him at the time, in part because those words seemed so trite and goofy. I felt that any person really facing death would conceive of it in much grander terms. Even my father.

One time my father hit my mother. I wish you could've seen his face: the bared teeth and bulged eyes, the mottled redness of the cheeks and forehead, the skin seeming to shine like a lacquered surface. If someone had been there to take a photograph, to freeze the expression in the moment before his hand lurched up to grab my mom by the neck, in a purely objective picture, you would not be able to identify the emotion in that look as rage. You might assume that it was pain or terror. There's a great photo from the Vietnam war—you know the one, of the guy screaming as he's shot through the head. That's what my dad looked like at that moment.

I never saw him look like that, before or after. But if I close my eyes I can see that face as clearly as I can picture the school portraits of my children on the coffee table, or the blue LeSabre that is waiting for me in the garage, or my first and only dog, Lucky, who, on the night of my parents' fight lay under the table in the kitchen, his long snout resting warily on his paws.

I'm sure that my father never realized how easily I could graft that face over his gentle one, how much more easily I could conjure up that image instead of some thought of his good qualities. It probably would have made him cry. He wept easily in his last years. I recall seeing him sitting in his easy chair, touching his fingers to his moist eyes as he watched a news special about poor orphans in Romania. When he and my mother had their fiftieth wedding anniversary, and he stood up to make a speech, his voice broke. "This woman," he said, and he choked back a sob. "This woman is the first and only love of my life."

I don't know. It's hard to decide if the waver in his voice was authentic or not. Who knows what he was really thinking as he spoke, as he stood there with my mother beaming, glistening-eyed, up at him—whether that strangled "love of my life" was tinged with regret, self-pity, whether it was because he was standing in front of all those people who knew that he and my mom hadn't had the most pleasant of lives together. But it also might be that he said it with true, honest feeling. In the end, there probably isn't much difference between being in love and acting like you're in love.

I don't mean this as a put-down either. I really don't believe that it's possible to be in love all of the time, any more than it's possible to always be good. So you must go with the next best thing. You try to pretend.

There are times when I would do anything to be a good person. But I'm not. Deep down, most of the time, I'm not.

What can you do? You have a flash of goodness and you try to hold on to it, ride it for all it's worth.

There was this one time that my kids and I were playing with clay, the three of us together. I don't know why this moment was special, but it was. We were all quiet, concentrated on our work, our fingers kneading and shaping. We were making an elephant, and I remember how excited they were when I rolled out its trunk, a careful snake between my palm and the surface of the table. My youngest was about three at the time, and I remember how he rested his cheek against my arm, watching me. I remember how soft and warm that cheek felt. The older one was pounding out a flap for the ear, and I can recall my voice being gentle and perfect when I told him how great it was. He gave it to me; I pressed it to the elephant's head.

But it didn't last for long, that moment. I am sure that neither of them remember it as I do, for pretty soon they started arguing, whining about who had more clay and so on. It was a jolt; I could actually feel the goodness moving out of me, the way you can feel blood moving when you blush or grow pale. "Come on, guys," I said, "let's not fight. This is fun, isn't it? Let's have fun." But my gentle voice was just an imitation, I was mimicking the tone of those enlightened parents you see sometimes, the kind who never seem to raise their voice beyond the steady monotone of kind patience, like the computer in that movie *2001: A Space Odyssey*.

But even parents like that won't be forgiven, you know. My wife's friend is a psychologist, and she spent her life explaining things in the most calm, reasonable voice you can imagine. She never raised her voice. Even when her kid was two years old, she was out there saying things like, "Please don't run in the street, because, even though you're excited and it's hard to pay attention, some people drive their cars too fast and they might not see you," et cetera. Now, naturally, her adult son won't talk to her. At all. He finds her unbearably manipulative. Repressive. Repulsive. Good words like that.

I recall when my wife's friend first told us about this. How old was I? Twenty-three or twenty-four maybe, and the son might have been twenty. I was sitting at the kitchen table across from this old, heavy, smooth-talking gal, the leader of some women's group thing my wife went to, and I was holding my sweet, sleeping baby in my arms. I can recall giving her that stern, bored stare I used to reserve for people I thought of as adults. She was almost my father's age, and her angry son was only a few years younger than I. She was a failure, I thought then. I stared down at my sleeping baby's face, the long-lashed eyes, the softly parted lips that moved slightly, as if he dreamed of nursing, and I thought: That will never happen to me. I will never let them hate me.

Now, as they are growing older, I am aware that hatred is a definite possibility at the end of the long tunnel of parenthood, and I suspect that there is little one can do about it.

Not long ago, when I insisted that he come down to dinner, my youngest son called me a "stupid idiot." I did not spank him, or wash his mouth out with soap, as my own father might have done; I simply set him up on the "time-out" stool—our preferred method of punishment—and scolded him while he kicked his legs and sang defiantly. His eyes sparked at me, and I could clearly see the opening of a vortex I would eventually be sucked into, against my will.

Once, I recall, when my oldest son was about five years old, he asked me if he could have my skeleton when I was dead. He told me that when he was grown up, he wanted to own a haunted house. He would cover my remains with spider webs and charge people five dollars to look at them.

"Sure," I said. "Whatever." I even smiled, as if it were cute. I did not act as if I was offended. But the truth is, my throat tightened. You'll be sorry, I wanted to say. You'll be sorry when I'm gone!

Do you know how sorry I was? You should have seen me at my father's funeral. I look back on this with some embarrassment, because I truly lost control. I wailed and tore at my hair. My children may have been too young to remember seeing this.

When my grandfather died, my father wept silently. Tears ran out of his nose, and I remember that it took me a long time to figure out that he didn't simply have a cold. At the funeral, he stared straight ahead, rigid, almost glaring, his jaw set.

One time, I remember, we were at the county fair. We were walking back to our car through the parking lot, when a group of older teenagers began to make fun of us. This was in the early seventies, and the teens were what we then called "hippies"—shaggy, raggedly dressed, full of secrets. As a child, I was warned to stay away from them, as they might kidnap me in one of their Volkswagen vans and force me to smoke marijuana.

In any case, they were amused by us. We must have looked ridiculously corny to them, and I remember one of them calling out, "Look! Here comes Mother, Father, and the Children!" And the others joined in: "Hello, Mother! Hello, Father! Hello, little Wally!"

My father acted as if they weren't there, though his face became stiff and his eyes fixed harshly on some point in the distance. He just kept plodding forward, as if he couldn't hear them. That was the look, I thought, that he had at the funeral.

The times in my childhood that I remember seeing him cry, they were always because of music. He was frequently brought to tears by some old, unbearably sentimental song. I remember this one called "Scarlet Ribbons," and another that went:

O my Papa!
To me he was so wonderful!
O my Papa!
To me he was so good!

This song, in particular, used to drive me crazy, and when he would play it I would leave the room, if possible. It wasn't only because of the maudlin tremor in the singer's voice, or because of my father's solemn canonizing of my grandfather, a man who had once burned my father's arm with a red-hot fork, leaving a scar which still remained. ("It taught me a lesson," my father said. He was being punished for having cruelly burned his younger sister with a match.)

It wasn't the hypocrisy that repelled me. It was simply that I understood the implications of the line: "To me, he was so wonderful." By which the singer meant, "No matter what, my father seemed wonderful to me." And I knew that my father wasn't weeping because he was extending this grace to his own father. No: He was weeping because he was wishing it for himself. He hoped that I would someday sing "O My Papa!" He cried for himself, and each tear said, "Someday you will love me unconditionally. Someday you will forgive me. Someday you will be sorry."

Which was something I didn't want to hear at the time.

I've suffered a little. Along with his sentimental side came a nasty temper. I got my share of what my father called "lickings," a term which, even in the extremity of my punishment, would cause me to smirk into my hand. I was beaten with a wire brush, a belt, a length of hose. And I was the victim of verbal and emotional abuse. I don't know whether I mentioned this or not, but once my father hit my mother. I stood by watching.

Nowadays, I meet a lot of people who were never beaten when they were children. They never witnessed any sort of violence in the home and the idea of striking a child is so aberrant to them that I enjoy shocking them with tales of my abuse—most of which are quite true.

My father would have been just as outraged to hear of a parent who *didn't* use corporal punishment. You couldn't really reason with a child, he would have said, but you had to make sure they obeyed. They had to learn to respect before they learned to think. The idea of a world filled with unspanked children would have made him frown grimly. For what would become of society, once these children grew up? The children would be spoiled, and the world would be filled with rude, disrespectful, dishonest, shiftless adults.

He worried about me being spoiled. By "spoiled," he didn't

mean what my mother means when she says that she can hardly wait to see her grandchildren at Christmastime. "I'll spoil them rotten," she says devilishly, and I say, "Oh, they're already so spoiled it's not funny." And we laugh.

To my father, the word still retained a large part of its older, more serious connotations: "Spoiled" meant "ruined," and the act of *spoiling* had flickers of its archaic meaning—to pillage, to plunder. In my father's estimation, a man who spoiled his children was robbing them, for a spoiled child would never be capable of the higher emotions: love, patriotism, self-sacrifice, honor, duty. Though he wept when the father made the son shoot the pet deer in *The Yearling*, he felt that the father did the right thing. We got into a heated argument about this one night about a year before he died. "It had to be done!" my father had insisted, and his voice rose, almost cracking with emotion. "That's how it was back then, damn it!"

"Well, do you know how it is now?" I said—I immediately saw the opening I'd been waiting years for, my chance to educate him. "Do you know what would happen to a man who burned his child with a red-hot fork? He would be jailed and his children would be taken by the state!"

My father could not help but look at his scar—the tattoo of his father that he would still be wearing as he lay in his casket.

(I saw it there—I pushed up the sleeve of his jacket, smoothing my fingers over that paper-dry corpse skin, and there it was. I touched the scar, and that was the last time I touched my father.)

My father stared at the four smooth lines the fork had left

just above the wristband of his watch. "Do you think my dad loved me any less than you love your kids?" he said. "Is that what you think?"

And we were both silent.

I don't know the answer, even now. Maybe love, like suffering, is relative. My wife's psychologist friend once told me, judgmentally, that sarcasm is more damaging to a child's spirit than a slap across the face. Emerson once said that the civilized person actually suffers more than those primitive people who are inured to hardship because the genteel person is more acutely aware of pain. I used to call this Emerson's Princess and the Pea Theory, but maybe it's true. We all require a certain amount of pain to justify ourselves later, and if we aren't lucky enough to have parents who beat us and force us to shoot our beloved pets, the stab of an unkind word or a neglectful shrug of the shoulders will do just as well.

Still, sometimes when I hear the stories of other people, I feel a little ashamed for complaining. I once knew a girl whose father raped her, regularly, when she was between the ages of two and six. Another of my friends, a guy from Cambodia, lost his mother and four brothers to the Khmer Rouge; his own father informed on them. Listening to such stuff, I feel like an anorexic in a country of starving people. Why was I so angry at my father? What's the point of my complaint? I've suffered very little, relatively speaking, so why do I feel so bad, so maudlin?

I'm not even sure I'm going to die right away. I might easily—75 percent chance—recover. According to the books, "the five-year survival rate for patients with localized disease is 75 percent." But I could live twenty more years. Or fifty! What's the point in even wondering?

That's what my father used to say when I asked him about death: There's no point in wondering, in worrying about it. It will come to all of us, sooner or later, he said, very solemn and sagelike, though I was thinking, "Duh—I *know* that." You could get hit by a truck tomorrow, he continued, and I sort of shut him off after that, his thoughtful droning. Why had I even bothered to ask?

Actually, I do remember one other thing he said—though whether he said it that time or another I can't recall.

"Our children relive our lives for us," he said. "That's the only kind of afterlife I believe in, just that we live on through our children. I don't know whether that makes any sense. It probably doesn't now, but it will. You try different things, you make different choices, but it's still all the same person. You. Me. Your grandpa. We get mostly the same raw material, just recycled. We're more alike than different, you know."

At the time, the thought seemed ridiculous. I'm not you, I thought. I knew for a fact that I was much smarter and more capable than he'd ever be.

I wonder how my own children would react if I told them my father's theory. I doubt that it would make any more sense to them than it did to me, though they are not old enough yet to be repulsed by the idea, I don't think.

Still, it's hard to guess what they imagine I am. I doubt that they think of it much; I am "Dad," that's all. It's strange how easily we fall into those roles—the form-fitting personalities that my children think of as "Mom" and "Dad." As they've grown, we have increasingly given over pieces of our lives to these caricatures, until the "Dad" part of me casts a shadow over what I think of as my "real" self. I feel like an old soap opera actor who, after years of playing the same part, begins to feel the character taking on a presence in his soul. My wife and I have not yet taken to calling one another Mom and Dad, as my parents used to, but much of the time, this is how we think of one another. We are already lost, even to ourselves. We slip helplessly into parody.

There is no way for my sons to know this, no possible way. They don't even really believe that the world existed before they were born. They know it intellectually, of course, but at the same time it's as unfathomable as infinity, or zero.

I start my chemotherapy tomorrow, and they don't know that either. They know that I am going to the hospital, but very little else. We have decided, my wife and I, that it would be too much for them to handle. And so they go on with their everyday lives: playing outside, squabbling at the dinner table, watching some cartoon on television and laughing uproariously, interrupting me as I talk on the phone to the doctor. I turn to my youngest fiercely, cupping my hand over the receiver. "Will you shut up! Can't you see I'm on the phone?" And in that moment, I see him blanch, hurt and resentment flickering across his face. One more piece of me disappears.

Later, standing at the edge of their bedroom, watching as they play checkers, I want to tell them. I want to say: "I might die soon." I want to shake them. "Can't you see me? Can't you see that I'm real?" But what I say is, "Hey, bud, I'm sorry I was sharp with you when I was talking on the phone. I didn't mean to snap like that."

He shrugs his shoulders, absorbed in his game. "S'okay," he says. He doesn't look up.

Once, my father hit my mother and I stood by watching, smirking into my hand. For a long time in my life, every bad thing that happened seemed bitterly hilarious. I felt that I had a heightened sense of the absurd. When my father was dying—dying of the same cancer I now have, if you want the truth—I was almost giddy with the terrible irony of it, the sarcasm of God. It was about two months after the retirement he'd been talking about, hoping for; for years he had been planning to buy a Winnebago, to go traveling across the country with my mother. He was diagnosed shortly after he'd purchased the thing.

That time he hit my mother, they had been arguing for a long while. I don't remember what it was about. It must have been very important to them at the time, but I saw how minuscule it was, how little it mattered in the grand scheme of things. What could I do but try to contain my private laughter? Back then, I believed that I had no connection to these strangers, these two foolish people who didn't realize that they were already summed up. Their lives were already over, I thought then. Nothing they ever did could change things.

And so, in giddy and adrenaline-fueled shock, I clamped my hand over my mouth. I saw my father's face twist as he turned to me, and I wonder what he thought I was thinking. His eyes widened and his mouth moved. We looked at one another; I think now that he hoped that I could save him.

Why do we think that, we parents? Why do I think it even now, standing in the dark, watching my sons sleeping? Save me, save me, I think. And yet they can't, of course. Already I am halfway gone. Even from the beginning, when their infant's eyes begin to focus on your floating face, the way a cat will watch the moon, already you are a ghost of yourself.

He must have known that, too, my father. He must have seen it in my face as I stared back at him. I sit down on my youngest son's bed, as my father might have sat on my bed late one night when I was a child. We look down, we touch the child's ear, watching him stir a little.

But no matter how hard we try, we are disappearing. Oh, my child, you will never save me. You will never be what I wanted to be, you will never love me in the way I need you to, you will never give me myself back.

And yet, I forgive you. You won't know this until a long time later, my little narrator, my wide-eyed camera. You won't know it, but I forgave you a long time ago.

Passengers, Remain Calm

Here is a snake with a girl in his mouth. She is a little blond girl, about four years old, and he is a rare albino anaconda, pink and white, about three feet long—just a baby, really. Nevertheless, he is trying to eat the child; her hand and forearm have disappeared down his throat, and he has coiled the rest of his body around her bicep, trying to constrict it. His wide mouth gives the impression of gloating merriment; she, of course, is screaming, and Hollis and his young nephew draw closer to the small circle of bystanders who have formed around her. "It's all right," the owner of the Reptile Petting Zoo tells the gathering as he tries to unwind the snake's coils. "Everything is under control." The girl is apparently the owner's daughter. "Just calm down," he says. "Didn't Daddy tell you that you should always wash your hands after playing with the gerbils? Now Rosario thinks that you are a gerbil!"

"I hate Rosario!" the little girl wails.

"There, there," her father soothes. "No you don't." He speaks in a soft voice, but he grunts with exertion as he attempts to untangle his daughter's arm from the snake, whose tail whips wildly when it is disengaged. "Damn, damn," the man whispers, sweating.

"My God!" says a woman in the audience. "Kill the thing! Kill it!"

"Please!" the father cries, struggling to maintain his jovial, showman's voice. "Stand back, everyone! Everything is under control!"

For a moment, Hollis wonders whether his nephew ought to be watching. But then a uniformed security officer arrives, and with the officer's help, the girl is pried free. There is a smattering of applause. The girl's hand is red, a bit swollen, but not bleeding. Hollis watches as the owner returns the snake to its glass cage. The owner presses the snake's snout into a dish of water. "Here," the man says. "Have a drink." He holds the snake's head underwater for a few moments, and though the man's voice sounds placid, even gentle, Hollis can see his jaw tighten with rage.

Hollis has noticed that he always seems to witness these weird little incidents more than other people.

This is at the town's yearly carnival, which, along with the Reptile Petting Zoo, features the usual menagerie—a hay ride, a carousel, a Ferris wheel, a few scary rides, like the Octopus and the Hammerhead. There are a series of game booths, at which children gamble for stuffed animals and plastic trinkets. At two in the afternoon, there is a pet show; at five, there is a raffle for a brand-new Kawasaki motorcycle; at dusk, there will be fireworks. Hollis's nephew is deeply engrossed, running purposefully from exhibit to exhibit, and Hollis follows thoughtfully, still occupied with the image of the girl and the snake, which he plans to write about in his journal.

Hollis has been spending a lot of time with his nephew lately. Hollis is twenty-two years old, and the boy, F. D., is eight, but Hollis generally finds the child good company. It gives him a chance to do things he wouldn't otherwise, like going to matinees or ice-cream parlors.

F. D.'s father, Wayne, has been gone for over a month now. Wayne is Hollis's older brother, and though Hollis had known that Wayne was unhappy, he'd never expected him to do something so drastic. No one knew where Wayne had gone—their mother had gotten a postcard, and so had Wayne's wife, Jill, but Wayne had offered no explanation, only a kind of vague apology. "Everything is okay," he'd written to their mother. "Sorry for any worry, will contact you ASAP. xxxooo Wayne."

Hollis hasn't seen the postcard that Wayne had sent Jill, but he suspects that she knows more about Wayne's disappearance than she's told anyone. She's been in an odd state since Wayne left—not outraged, not hysterical, not desperate and furious, as Hollis might have expected—but subdued, moody, distracted. Hollis thinks that she might be taking some sort of drug. Her eyes have that floating, somewhere-else look, and on weekends she never seems to get out of her pajamas. Her beautiful dark hair wants cutting, and she has been biting her nails.

But she appears to be getting by: She goes to her job at the supermarket, and F. D. and his little sister Hanna are clean and make it every day to the school bus, but it's clear that things aren't going well. Last Friday night, Hollis went through and collected all the dirty dishes that were lying around, empty cereal bowls in the living room, half-full coffee cups on various surfaces, plates still left on the table from two or three suppers back. He gathered up all the dishes in the sink and washed them.

"You're a nice guy, Hollis," Jill had said to him as he stood there at the sink, and he'd shrugged, a little embarrassed. The truth was, he felt a little guilty and ashamed of his brother's behavior. Somebody had to act like a decent person, he'd thought, though he didn't say this. "You *are*," she said. "You're a nice guy." He'd just shaken his head.

"Not really," he said, and after a moment she put her hand on the small of his back, low, right above the slope of his buttock. Her hand seemed to tingle, and the air was heavy with the idea that she might kiss him, or he might kiss her. Then she backed away.

"Hollis," she said. "Let's forget I did that, okay?"

He nodded, and she'd looked into his eyes in a way he found inexplicable. He knew then that there were a lot of things she wasn't telling him and that Wayne hadn't told him either. "Okay," he'd said, but it wasn't as if he could really forget it, either. That night, he'd written about it in his journal, just a little paragraph. He doesn't write about his feelings or thoughts in the journal. He just describes stuff.

F. D. does not know what is going on. The whole family, including Jill, seems to be colluding to keep it from the boy. Hollis thinks it is wrong, but he hasn't been given any official say in the matter. The story that F. D. has been given is that Wayne has gone on a long trip, and will be back soon. ("Will he be back by my birthday?" F. D. had asked, and everyone agreed, *yes, certainly by F. D.'s birthday*, which is October 31, and which is now beginning to loom ominously.) It is criminal, Hollis sometimes feels, to play with the boy's mind in such a way. F. D. must know that something is wrong, Hollis thinks.

But if so, he never asks. He seems, as far as Hollis can tell, pretty cheerful, pretty normal.

Still, Hollis thinks of this as they sit on the hay ride, listening to the horses clop heavily along the pathways of the park. They are being driven around the circumference of the carnival. They pass by booths of politicians and county agencies: people running for city council or school board; people who represent the county recycling effort, giving demonstrations on how to create a compost heap; people representing the Department of Human Services, handing out pamphlets that tell of how to avoid abusing your children. The fire department is handing out Rescue Me stickers for the childrens' windows, fluorescent circles that will identify their rooms should their houses ever catch afire. He recognizes a few of the men, from the brief time he'd worked at the fire department, but he doesn't wave.

But the people on the hay ride do, and the people below wave back, smiling. "Hello! Hello!" the children call. F. D. occupies himself with this for a while, solemnly lifting his hand over his head in a way that makes Hollis sad. F. D. is holding tightly to a small stuffed animal, a furry blue snake with a wide, red felt mouth and google-eyes, about six inches long. F. D. had won it by throwing a dart at a corkboard wall lined with a row of balloons. When a balloon had popped, he'd crowed with triumph and did a little dance. "All *right!*" he'd said, pumping his fists as athletic champions did on television.

Now, F. D. dotes over the toy snake thoughtfully, smoothing its polyester fur. "You know," F. D. says, "someday, I'd like to have a real snake as a pet. That's one of my dreams."

"Yeah," Hollis says. "That would be cool. As long as the snake didn't try to eat you."

F. D. snorts. "That little girl was an idiot," he says with distaste. "I felt more sorry for the snake than I did for her."

"Well," Hollis says. "She was just little."

"I suppose," F. D. says. "But she should have listened to what that man told her, that's all. Most snakes are a friend to Man." He looks solemnly across the hay ride to where the woman sits who had earlier shouted, "Kill the thing! Kill it!" in the Reptile Petting Zoo. She is a plump, round-faced woman with shoulder-length reddish blond hair, bobbed in a fashion that is popular among women of her age and social class, and like F. D., Hollis takes an instinctive dislike to her.

"I see what you mean," Hollis says.

I see what you mean. It was funny, because this was something he would often say when he was talking to Wayne. Wayne was a convincing talker, and Hollis, who was five years younger, would find himself frequently swayed by Wayne's views. It was Wayne who had said, for example, "Never assume that you know what goes on inside a marriage. Because I'm telling you, no matter how close you think you are, you will never know those people like they know each other. It's like a closed system. The weather inside a marriage is always different from the weather of everything around it." Hollis had nodded slowly, considering this. They had been talking about their parents that night, and Hollis had said that he felt certain that neither one of them had ever had an affair. Hollis had said that he couldn't understand why people would do that to their spouses. It didn't make sense, he said, and then Wayne swept in with his metaphors of weather. "I'm not saying that I've had an affair, either," Wayne said. "I'm just saying that you can never assume to know."

"I see what you mean," Hollis said.

He and Wayne had been sitting out in the garage, near the woodstove, in lawn chairs. It was winter, and they were feeding logs into the fire, drinking beers out of a cooler that sat between them. It was their Friday night ritual. Hollis would come over for dinner, and then they would sit in the garage and drink beer, sometimes smoking a little pot, talking. Wayne read a lot, and he always had something interesting to say. Wayne had hoped to be a lawyer, before Jill became pregnant.

Sometimes, Hollis felt that his brother was his best friend, and he would go to sleep on Wayne and Jill's couch with a feeling that there was one person on earth who understood him, one person who would always recognize him. Other times, less frequently, he would find himself driving home, his feelings hurt, driving even though he was drunk and afraid of being pulled over, or getting into an accident, and Wayne did not stop him.

Once he'd told Wayne that he thought more weird things happened to him than to normal people, and he'd described that feeling he had, that the world seemed full of strange little incidents. He had expected Wayne to agree wholeheartedly.

But instead Wayne had looked at him sternly. "It's not the world, Hollis," he'd said, "it's you. I mean, you're an intelligent guy and all, but you're sort of emotionally retarded." Hollis was surprised by the irritation in Wayne's tone of voice. "It's like, do you remember the time Dad had a heart attack? And we were going to the hospital and you looked out the car window and saw a dog with a missing leg? All you wanted to talk about was that stupid dog, and you couldn't believe that the rest of us didn't see it. But we were normal, Hollis. We weren't looking out the window and noticing goofy shit. We were mentally focused on something serious, which you seldom are."

Hollis was stunned, as he always was, though he probably should have been used to it. Sometimes, for no reason, Wayne would attack, treating him like a criminal he was cross-examining during a trial. It didn't make sense. What had he said, to bring this on? He had the sensation of shrinking.

"I didn't know that Dad had a heart attack," he said, after a moment, quietly. "Nobody told me."

"Hollis," Wayne said. He passed his hand, hard, through his bangs, an old gesture that meant, essentially: I can't believe my brother is so stupid. "Hollis," he said. "You never bothered to find out what was wrong. There's a difference."

Now, thinking of this, Hollis gets a hollow feeling in his stomach. He can't believe that Wayne didn't send him a postcard. It makes him feel tricked. But by whom? Wayne, or himself? He thinks that he should know why Wayne left, but he doesn't.

F. D. looks like the paternal side of his family. More specifically, he looks a lot like Hollis himself, which Hollis has always found secretly thrilling. In his personality, F. D. is more like Wayne. There is an austere confidence that Hollis recognizes, an expectation that what he has to say is true and important, a certain way his gray eyes cloud with confidence, a way his mouth moves in judgment of other people's ignorance. *Most snakes are a friend to Man.*

Hollis thinks of this as he and F. D. are sitting at a picnic table, eating nachos. F. D. eats heartily and Hollis mostly watches. They have recently purchased three raffle tickets, five dollars each, and F. D. is talking about the possibility of winning the motorcycle.

"Well," Hollis says. "I don't usually win stuff."

"But if you did," F. D. says. "What would you do?"

"If I win," Hollis says, "I'll give it to you. When you're sixteen, you can drive it, and until you're old enough I'll give you rides on it. We'll go on a trip on our motorcycle. Like to Washington, D.C., or something. Haven't you always wanted to see the Smithsonian, and the Washington Monument, and all that?"

"And the White House?" says F. D. enthusiastically. At that moment, F. D. and Hollis love each other unconditionally.

"Yeah," Hollis says. "All of it." He smiles. "And when I'm old, you can take me for rides on it. We'll have to buy helmets."

"Gold ones," F. D. says. "That's the kind I like. Metallic."

"Yeah," Hollis says. And they both drift into separate imaginings.

When Wayne wanted to analyze Hollis, he would say that Hollis was a dreamer, not a doer. "You don't seem to have any plans for your life," Wayne said in a thoughtful voice that was meant to be constructive criticism. "You just seem to drift from one thing to the next." And Hollis sat there, nodding, as Wayne talked about making up a Five-Year Plan, setting some goals.

This was after Hollis quit the job he'd taken on with the fire department, and Wayne was disappointed. Wayne had liked the idea of Hollis's job, and Hollis had, too, at first. But then he'd actually started going to accident sites with the emergency crew and he changed his mind. He had thought about telling Wayne this, but then didn't. He didn't want to talk about it.

There was one accident that he remembered. This was about midnight on a Thursday night, and he had been working for a month by then. It was a collision: This kid had rear-ended the back of a stalled semi out on the highway, and the kid's truck had burst into flames on impact. The kid was about twenty or so, he found out later, and must have been going around seventy miles per hour when he crashed. That was it for him, of course. "A boom and a flash," said one of the firemen, Larry. "The fat lady sings." By the time they arrived, there wasn't much left, and even Larry said it was bad, very bad. He and Larry had tried to get the kid's corpse out of the truck and onto the stretcher, but the body just fell apart, "like a chicken that got burned up on the barbecue," Larry said later: cinders, ash, cooked meat. Hollis began to have nightmares, after that, and finally he went to see a therapist that the fire department had hired, whom the firemen could talk to, for free.

"You know," the therapist said. "You show signs of being susceptible to posttraumatic stress disorder." The man had a slow, affectless voice, as if he'd recently smoked marijuana. "If you'd gone to Vietnam, you'd probably have become a schizophrenic. Of course, no one can predict. You may become inured to it, after this. It's hard to tell."

Shortly after, he'd resigned. The other men at the fire station had known the reason, and he thought they respected the decision. He hadn't explained the whole thing to Wayne, which was why Wayne became annoyed. But he didn't know if he could make Wayne understand. He hadn't even written about it in his journal.

Beyond the tent where he and F. D. are eating nachos, he can hear the voice of the operator of the Hammerhead, a tinny voice through a microphone, giving the ride a hard sell. "Passengers, remain calm," he says ominously, as if he is a pilot announcing an engine failure. "Hold tight to your loved ones. Prepare yourself. Try not to scream."

"This guy's good," Hollis said to F. D.

"What guy?"

And Hollis waved his hand, pointing to the air so F. D. would know to listen.

"This is what it feels like to be in a plane that is going down," the operator of the Hammerhead crows. "Do you dare to experience it? Can you take it? Can you take this trip without screaming in horror?"

He grins at F. D., and F. D. grins back: They're not going on the Hammerhead, they agree, in a brief exchange of glances.

Someday, Hollis thinks, he will tell F. D. about the kid's body that fell apart when he tried to lift it. F. D. would understand. "Passengers, remain calm," the man calls in the distance, and Hollis feels for a moment as if he has half glimpsed a secret, some hidden aspect of the world, something he didn't want to know. He can hear Wayne saying, "It's not the world. It's *you*." He can hear Jill saying, "You're a nice guy, Hollis." He looks over to where F. D. is sitting, munching tortilla chips. His heart aches.

To a certain extent, he has a life of his own. He now has a job in a factory that makes paper tube products, and it pays pretty well. He has friends his own age, with whom he goes out to bars and such. He has girlfriends, too, though he has noticed that date number three always seems like the end, that things almost always peter out after that.

But the truth is, he had always felt most comfortable with Wayne and Jill and F. D.—just hanging out, as if he were somehow one of them, as if that was where he really belonged. He has the image of the four of them, sitting in the living room, watching TV. Wayne and Jill are on the couch and he is in the recliner and F. D. is in his pajamas, tucked into a sleeping bag on the floor. They are watching a comedy movie, something he's seen before, but he's enjoying it anyway. He likes to listen to them laugh. He feels safe and welcome: happy. It's awful, because he now feels certain that this moment isn't true.

There is a line at the bathroom and they wait quietly, shuffling slowly toward a single blue Port-O-Potty. They are both silent and, after a time, Hollis smiles down at F. D. "What are you thinking, buddy?"

F. D. shrugs. "Nothing," he says. He is thoughtful, and he hesitates for a moment. "Uncle Hollis," he says at last. "Have you ever seen the movie *Alien*?"

"I think so," Hollis says. "I don't remember."

"I've been wanting to see it for my whole life," says F. D. "But Mom thinks it's too scary. And I was thinking that maybe we could rent it and watch it at your house sometime. I promise I wouldn't tell Mom. I wouldn't get scared, either."

"Well," Hollis says. "I don't know. That sounds kind of sneaky."

F. D. shrugs. "Not *bad* sneaky," he says. "It wouldn't hurt anybody."

"I don't know," Hollis says. "I'll have to think about it."

"Okay," F. D. says. His eyes rest on Hollis seriously, a long, searching, hopeful look. After a minute, F. D. says, "I wish I lived with you."

Hollis doesn't say anything. He thinks it would be okay to say, "So do I, buddy," but he's not sure. It might also be wrong.

They walk along a row of game booths, toward the rides. Out of the corner of his eye, Hollis can see a tent with a sign that says PSYCHIC READINGS. A lady is sitting there at a card table, with her hands folded, waiting—a woman in her late forties, with a long, solemn face, stoically wearing a shiny turban, as if it is an affront to her dignity. He hopes that she doesn't notice him.

He has always had a dread of fortune-tellers, and palm readers, and such. He has always imagined that they would tell him something he didn't want to know—that something terrible was going to happen, that he was going to die soon, that his life would be full of sadness. Maybe it wouldn't be something bad at all. But the idea of it scared him, nevertheless.

Perhaps the woman can sense this, because she calls out to him as he walks past. "Your future, your fortune!" she shrills, and he smiles, shaking his head briskly: "No thanks!"

"Only five dollars!" the woman says. "I have important information for you!"

F. D. has stopped, and is looking from the turbaned woman to Hollis, and back, hopefully.

"No, sorry," Hollis says to the woman. He smiles apologetically. "Sorry!"

She smiles broadly. "Your son thinks you should," she says, and addresses F. D. "Don't you think your father should know his fortune?"

Hollis laughs. "You're no psychic!" he says. "He's not my son!" And then he regrets saying this: The woman looks nonplussed, and F. D. seems to flinch a little. It would have been fun, Hollis thinks, to pretend that he was F. D.'s father. The woman looks at him stonily, then turns her attention to a group of teenage girls. "Your future!" she calls to them. "I have important information for you!" The girls hesitate, giggling, and Hollis and F. D. move on.

Here is the beautiful carousel. The horses are all brightly colored, posed in forms of agitation. They lift their red mouths as if calling out, their legs curved into gallops, their manes whipping in an imaginary wind. The calliope plays a tune he recognizes but cannot place, something like "A Bicycle Built for

Two," but not. The ride was built in the 1890s, according to the sign, and is the oldest carousel still in existence. As they get on, he sees the little girl from the Reptile Petting Zoo, her hand and forearm bandaged, sitting a few horses in front of them. A woman—her mother, probably—stands stoically beside the little girl's horse. He and F. D. are astride their steeds, side by side.

"There's the little girl who almost got eaten by the snake," Hollis says. He gestures with his chin, and F. D. looks over and nods contemplatively.

"The snake couldn't have actually ate her," F. D. explains. "She was way too big." He frowns, then smiles when he realizes that Hollis has been making a joke. "Oh," he says. "I get it." He beams at Hollis for a moment.

"Do you think it would hurt," Hollis says. "To be swallowed?"

"Oh, yeah," F. D. says. "Big time. The snake's muscles contract and it crushes and suffocates you with its coils. Every time you try to breathe, it tightens its coils, so finally your lungs can't expand."

"You know a lot about snakes," Hollis says, and F. D. gazes at him seriously.

"I know," F. D. says. He has told Hollis before that he wants to be a scientist when he grows up—a herpetologist, which is a word Hollis hadn't even heard of before, but which means a person who studies reptiles. Looking at F. D. now, Hollis can see the scientist in his face. There is a kind of dignified intensity that Hollis admires. "Uncle Hollis," F. D. says after a pause. "Can I ask you something?"

"Sure, kiddo. Anything."

"Is my dad really coming home?"

Hollis waits a moment. The boy's scrutiny is hard to lie to. "I don't really know, F. D.," Hollis says. He hesitates. The carousel has begun to move, and their horses dip and rise in time to the calliope music. He waits, feeling the steady, insistent velocity as they move in their circle. He thinks of Wayne—out there, somewhere, driving, sleeping in the passenger seat of his car at some rest stop along the interstate, a Wayne he knows and yet doesn't know. He's never coming back, Hollis thinks.

When they get off the carousel, F. D. is quiet, lost in thought, and Hollis thinks that it might be best to backtrack, to take back the doubt he has planted, to reassure the boy. But he's not sure of the right thing to say. After a moment, he reaches over and brushes his hand over the back of F. D.'s neck.

They sit there for a time, near the carousel, watching people pass, children awash in the urgency of having fun, parents following behind with indulgent, sleepwalking expressions. He knows that they cannot sense the dull panic that has begun to throb around him, beating time to the distant churn of the calliope. But it seems as if it must be visible, like a rash on his skin.

In his journal he would write: *Here is F. D. sitting in the grass. He is quiet, petting his stuffed snake. He won the snake at the carnival, by throwing a dart at the balloon. He looks at the snake as if he is going to talk to it, but he doesn't say a word.*

In high school he had a teacher who thought he was a good writer. "You have a good eye," the teacher said, "but you editorialize too much. Let the detail speak for itself." The teacher had given him a story by Hemingway to read, which he hadn't understood, but he thought he understood what the teacher was saying. It made sense.

Once, when he was in ninth grade and Wayne was a junior

in college, he had come into his room and found Wayne reading his journal. Wayne was home from college for Christmas, and Jill was already pregnant with F. D., though they didn't know it at the time. Wayne would soon drop out, though they didn't know that either. At that moment, they were just brothers, and Hollis stood there in the doorway, horribly embarrassed as Wayne looked up, smiling that knowing, half-adult smile, holding the journal loosely in his hand.

"Hey," Wayne said. "This is pretty good!"

"Yeah, well," Hollis said, and flushed a bit at the flattery, despite himself. "It's also kind of private."

"Why?" Wayne said. "You don't have anything to be shy about. This is really nice stuff. I'm impressed. I think it would be better if you tied things together more, though."

The thought of impressing Wayne so thrilled him that the sense of invasion and humiliation was quelled, momentarily. But he was cautious, thinking it might only be an elaborate mockery. Once, when Hollis was ten, Wayne had convinced him that he was adopted. And though Wayne had eventually been forced to recant, Hollis still had doubts. He has doubts, even now.

"It's just for me," Hollis said. "I don't want anyone else to read it. I don't want anyone else to know what I think."

Wayne had smiled. Wayne still thought, then, that he was going to become a famous lawyer, and he hadn't yet envisioned a life with Jill and F. D., working for the county as a clerk in the courthouse. Wayne couldn't imagine what it would be like to not want others to know what he thought. "Hollis," he said, combing his fingers through his bangs. "That's stupid. Why would you write stuff down if nobody's going to read it?"

"*I* read it," Hollis said. "That's all. Just me."

And Wayne shook his head. "That doesn't make any sense."

"I see what you mean," Hollis had said. But afterward, he started hiding the thing; he still hides it, at the bottom of his sock drawer, even though he lives alone. Years later, when they were sitting out in the garage, Wayne had asked him if he still wrote in a journal.

"No," Hollis said, though he seldom lied. "I just lost interest."

"Hollis used to be a really good writer," Wayne told Jill.

"I believe it," Jill said, and Hollis was sure then that they really loved him. It was one of those moments he would come back to—Wayne and Jill smiling at him kindly, their love for each other extending and encompassing him. Wayne rested a hand on one of Hollis's knees, and Jill rested her hand on the other, and they all leaned close. Now he wonders if this meant anything to them, if they even remembered it.

"F. D. ...." he says. He has been sitting there silent for a while, thinking, mulling things over, and he knows that F. D. wants him to explain things. "You know, the truth is," he says. "The truth is, I really don't know what's going on with your dad. Nobody has told me anything."

"Where is he?" F. D. says.

Hollis swallows, thinks. "I don't know," he says.

F. D. says nothing, and Hollis feels sorry. He would like to be a real uncle, someone who could explain the world to F. D., someone who could make sense of it.

"He ran away from home, didn't he?" F. D. says.

"Yes," Hollis says.

"I knew that," F. D. says. He sighs heavily, and Hollis puts his hand on F. D.'s neck, letting it rest there, warm and—he hopes—comforting.

"I'll always be here, though," Hollis says. "I won't leave you." He means it. But he is also nervous. What has he done? He hasn't thought out the consequences clearly, and now a gray uncertainty begins to glide through him. He thinks to say, "Don't tell your mom you know," but he knows that it would be wrong. Then he realizes what he should have said in the first place: *Ask your mother.*

"You should talk to your mom about it," he says. "If you . . . well, if you don't mention that I told you, that might be best. I mean, maybe she wouldn't have wanted me to be the first one to say something. . . ." He hesitates because he can't read what's behind F. D.'s heavy expression. "I'm not saying you should lie or anything. You shouldn't lie to your mom."

"Well," F. D. says, "she lied to me." He looked at Hollis sharply. "She lies all the time."

"No, she doesn't," Hollis says, but not insistently. He is trying to imagine how Jill will react. He is aware now that he has betrayed her, thoughtlessly, that he has trod into a place where he doesn't belong at all. He has always tried to think carefully about right and wrong, but often the gray areas other people see are invisible to him. He wonders if she will be angry. He imagines her saying, "How dare you tell F. D. such a thing. How dare you make me look like a liar! What makes you think you know anything about it!" He cringes. And then he thinks, What if Wayne really does come back? Then he will have done a truly awful thing. Then he will have damaged Wayne's relationship with F. D. No matter what happens, Hollis thinks, he has permanently altered things between them, and he feels a slow undertow of dread. Everyone is going to be disgusted with him, furious. He can imagine doors closing permanently, his excursions with F. D. ending, becoming unwelcome at Wayne and Jill's house. He and F. D. look at each other, and he sees that F. D. is quavering on the edge of tears.

"Oh, F. D.," he says. "Don't cry. Please don't cry."

And F. D. doesn't. They get up and begin to walk, and he feels humble and clumsy in the wake of F. D.'s churning thoughts. Terrible, terrible, terrible, he thinks. He wants to slap himself.

"F. D.," he says after a while. "I think I've made a terrible mistake. I'm thinking that I shouldn't have told you what I told you."

"I know," F. D. says. He is grim, though they are walking through a row of bright booths, through the hawkers' promises of prizes and fun. He shakes his head heavily.

"How do you know?"

F. D. shrugs. "I just do. Mom wouldn't have wanted you to tell me. She'll be mad, won't she?"

"She should be mad," Hollis said. "I did something that was really wrong."

"Oh," F. D. says. He seems to consider this for a moment. "Why were you wrong?"

"Because your mom trusted me not to say anything. And I let her down." He thinks for a moment, trying to explain it clearly. "It's like that little girl and the snake. She'll never trust that snake again. You see?"

"Oh," F. D. says. "Yeah." And Hollis realizes after a moment that the analogy is unclear; it doesn't make a lot of sense. He lapses again into thought, looking ahead to a group of people beginning to gather around where the motorcycle sits on a stage. The stage is festooned with scalloped ribbons and Chinese lanterns; tiny disco balls fracture the light into spangles that glimmer brilliantly on the motorcycle's chrome, and their faces.

"Uncle Hollis," F. D. says. "Who do you love more? My mom or me?"

"You," Hollis says. He doesn't even have to think. "I love you more than anyone else in the world. That's why I'm sorry that I did a wrong thing. I didn't want to make you sad."

"That's okay," F. D. says. And he reaches up and rubs against Hollis's arm, and Hollis can feel the eagerness of his affection. I have put him in a terrible position, Hollis thinks. But he doesn't know what he can do about it.

For the last month, Hollis has been trying to remember the last thing Wayne said to him. It was probably something mundane—"Good-bye," or "So long," or "See you around"—but of course, given that Wayne would disappear a few days later, even these pleasantries are potentially heavy with meaning. But he can't recall. It was an ordinary evening, like any other. He and Wayne had been drinking beer in the garage, and Jill had stayed in the house, watching TV. She often did this. "You need your 'boy time' together," she'd always said, ironically, though Hollis always liked it best when she sat with them and joined in the conversation.

But in any case, there was nothing to indicate that Wayne was planning to leave. What did they talk about? Movies, mostly, as Hollis remembered. They talked about a recent plane crash, in Scotland, that had been all over the news; the plane might have been downed by a terrorist bomb planted in the luggage. Hollis remembered this only now. The operator of the Hammerhead had brought it back to him, and he recalls Wayne mentioning it. "What do you think goes through your mind when you're going down like that? When you know you're going to die?"

"I don't know," Hollis said. "But you know what I'd be thinking? I'd be thinking, 'This is going to really, really hurt!' "

Wayne had laughed at that, and had told the old joke they both loved in childhood: "Q: What's the last thing that goes through a mosquito's mind when he hits your windshield? A: His butt." And they'd laughed some more, full of beer and dumb camaraderie.

And it strikes him suddenly, a heavy blow. Wayne *knew* he was leaving, even as they sat there laughing and telling stale jokes. But he would never have told Hollis. Hollis can see himself as they see him, even as they are making their secret plans and living their secret lives. He is a distraction to them, an amusement, and he understands Wayne's occasional flashes of anger, too—he can see himself as Wayne saw him, full of earnest, innocent stupidity, chattering vacantly about the "weird things he'd noticed," not someone who had ever really mattered. His cheeks grow warm, and he wishes that he'd responded to Wayne's question more seriously. *What goes through your mind when you know you're going to die?* He could have finally told Wayne about that kid, that kid whose corpse fell apart when he tried to pick it up. He could have said a lot of things. And maybe then Wayne would have respected him. Maybe Wayne would have told him the truth.

He is so lost in thought that when the man on the stage reads the winner's name, he begins to applaud with the rest of the crowd before he realizes that the man has just read his own name.

"Hollis Merchant!" the man says. "Is Hollis Merchant in the audience today? You are the winner!"

F. D. whoops. "That's us! That's us!" And Hollis is brought back abruptly from his reverie. The crowd has turned to look at him, their eyes wide and expectant. And miraculously, F. D. is healed, is made whole and happy again. He is jumping up and down. "We won!" he cries, his voice shrill with excitement, and hurls his body against Hollis's in a rough dance of joy. "You and me, Uncle Hollis! Remember? You and me!"

Hollis lifts F. D. onto his shoulders, and the weight of him settles easily into place. Despite everything, he can't help feeling proud and happy, just as F. D. does. The crowd applauds as they walk up to the stage, probably thinking that F. D. is his son, and Hollis is willing to borrow this for the time being. Once F. D. is on his shoulders, he can stride to the stage.

And he has a vision, what he should write in his journal: *What if you believed that everything in life was like a prize? What if you thought of the world as a big random drawing, and you were always winning things, the world offering them up with a big grin, like an emcee's: Here you go, Hollis. Here is a motorcycle. Here is a little boy who loves you. Here is a weird experience, here is something bad that you should mull over because it will make you a better person. What if you could think that life was this free vacation you'd won, and you won just because you happened to be alive?*

He is not deluded. He can see clearly that he is foolish, that his life is made up of a series of muddled interpretations and distractions, that he doesn't know anything about the world he's moving into. But he can also see the two of them on that motorcycle, in those golden helmets that F. D. dreamed up, going somewhere. "You and me," F. D. whispers, and the roads are clear, there are green fields and wildflowers on either side, and the motorcycle seems to be driving itself. He can even close his eyes for a moment, as the wind and velocity sweep over them. They fly down the highway, calmly, headed off to wherever it will take them.

THE ILLUSTRATED
ENCYCLOPEDIA OF THE
ANIMAL KINGDOM

On the second floor of an old Victorian house that has been converted into tiny apartments, Dennis dreams that he is holding a baby. The infant in the dream is wrapped in a gray-blue blanket, with only its round face peeking out. Dennis can feel its limbs squirming beneath the swaddling as he smooths his palm lightly over the infant's cheek. When his hand touches the baby's skin, he wakes up.

Above him, he hears the woman on the third floor, walking. Her floorboards—his ceiling—sigh as she goes, as if she's stepping over shifting ice. He is aware, even as he opens his eyes, that the dream is partially hers, a seed she has planted. He doesn't know her really, but he thinks about her often. She walks across his ceiling at all hours of the night. In certain rooms he will occasionally hear a radio playing above him, and on some evenings if he sits by the radiator in his bedroom he will hear her stumbling, sweetly awkward monotone as she reads her son a story. Dennis believes that her husband has left her. Perhaps he is dead. Perhaps there never was a husband to begin with.

It is the woman upstairs, or the dream, or maybe simply the fact that it is a new town and he knows no one and he is twenty-five years old and spends far too much time (he thinks) in his own head, too much time lying on his bed in his underwear with a beer growing warm on his chest as he listens. It is a combination of all these things, no doubt. Something makes him decide to call the hospital, which is located in the city that he lived in before he moved to this new one. He is aware that it is foolish to call the hospital. But he just wants to see what they will say.

So he calls one morning from work during his lunch when his coworkers are out, they all seem to have places to go, their days full of purpose, et cetera. He calls and is transferred several times. While he waits, classical music that seems somewhat familiar is played for him through the phone lines.

The lady who finally answers is very professional about the whole thing, very administrative. He has signed a contract that is legally binding, she says, and (hundreds of miles away) he nods earnestly into the receiver. I know that, he says. He explains that he doesn't want to cause trouble, he's just sort of curious, and she says, "That's sweet," in a condescending voice that suggests that she is probably pretty, probably used to turning men down quickly and cheerfully, a tight fake smile reducing them to a speck. Dennis feels himself shrinking. "You must get calls like this all the time," he says apologetically, and she says, "No, frankly, I don't."

Well, he thinks when she hangs up the phone. He can feel himself blushing, though of course no one knows whom he has called, and he certainly won't tell anyone. He feels stupid.

Maybe it is strange to wonder, he thinks: odd. It wasn't as if there were love involved, not even physical contact, just an easy fifty dollars he'd heard about through a friend who was in the first year of medical school. The friend had been doing it about once a week and he got Dennis in, though Dennis's vital statistics, his looks and IQ and extracurricular activities were probably not as impressive as those of the medical school boys. So maybe they didn't even use his. He'd only done it because he really had needed the cash at the time—it was his senior year in college.

When he went in he'd felt very embarrassed. The nurse was not much older than he—a short, stocky girl who wore her hair in a way that made him think maybe she'd had an unhappy childhood. She couldn't look at him. She just gave him some forms to fill out on one of those clipboards with a pen hanging on a beaded metal chain like the kind that is attached to bathtub drain plugs. He turned in the paperwork and the nurse led him down a hospital-smelling corridor, both of them shy, silence trailing down the long hallway until they came to a halt in front of a little bathroom. She gave him a kind of test tube with a screw-on lid and cleared her throat, shifting her weight in those chunky white shoes, and she opened a door and said that there were some magazines he could look at if he wished. She might have used the word "peruse."

He glanced in and there were some old *Playboy* and *Penthouse* magazines on the table next to the toilet. He nodded, not meeting her eyes. What was there to say? The nurse was trying to be professional about it, but he could see she was secretly mortified behind her nurse facade, and when he tried to smile ironically she just cleared her throat again and left in a hurry. Poor girl, he thought.

It was strange, because it was she, the nurse, whom he ended up thinking of rather than the centerfolds with their tawny unreal shapes and unmarked expressions. When he brought his test tube out and gave it to her he felt a sort of regret shudder through him. Her eyes were so sad that he was sure for a moment that she knew he'd been thinking of her. He sometimes thought that any baby that came out of it must be as much that nurse's as it was his own.

He finds it difficult to truly believe that there is a baby, but it's something he thinks about sometimes. It's interesting imagining someone—maybe an infertile couple or perhaps a single woman who has some money—someone going through pages of descriptions and deciding on him. Maybe he has the nationality they are looking for, the color of hair or eyes, or one of the accomplishments he's written down—his winning the state spelling bee in high school, his abilities in baseball, his college major— attracts them in some way, and they say, "This is the one." He wonders if that's how it works. He likes to imagine that there is the possibility of a person out there. The person might have a certain shape of face or fingers, or a certain way of smiling. He or she might even eventually have certain moods—a particularly vague and watery melancholy feeling sometimes—because of him. He doesn't know why he wants so badly for this to be true.

It's summer. Cicadas fill the air with an intermittent static, and in the weeks that follow he often sees them in the morning, in the tiny backyard out behind their apartment house, his upstairs neighbor and her son, who must be about four, a thin, deep-eyed kid with a head like a baby bird. Dennis gazes down at them, watching as the boy builds something with mud and sticks in the corner by the fence; watching as the boy reads his books: *The Illustrated Encyclopedia of the Animal Kingdom.* On the cover, there are drawings of a snake, a zebra, a parrot, a beetle, all the same size.

The woman sits quietly, smoking. She runs her fingers thoughtfully along the side of her bare foot, her curling-iron hair, crushed flat in the back where she's slept on it. When he thinks of her face in his mind, it looks hard and melancholy and almost cruel because of the traces of makeup that remain around her lips and eyes. She exhales smoke.

On the day he made his phone call to the hospital, he happened to be walking home from work and he found a box of books. The box had been put out by the curb for the trash man to pick up, right outside a big old house that looked something like his except it hadn't been split up into apartments. There was nothing wrong with the books that he could see—an old set of children's encyclopedias, not a complete set but nice nonetheless, with beautiful photographs. It didn't even look like they'd been read! He glanced around to see that no one was looking and then he lifted the box and carried it home.

After dinner that evening, he had gone up the stairs with the box and knocked on the woman's door.

"I found this," he said, showing her the books and smiling sheepishly. "I've heard you reading to your son and I thought it would be something he would enjoy."

He'd practiced this short speech several times, but after it left his mouth he realized that it was a mistake to say that he'd heard her reading. Her eyes narrowed a bit, suspiciously, and when she leaned down to look at the titles of the books, she wrinkled her nose. He was aware that they smelled a little like a basement.

"He's a little young for encyclopedias," she said, and Dennis shifted his weight. The books were heavy.

"Well," he said. "They've got nice pictures."

"Hmm," she said. She looked him over again, and he saw her eyes come to a decision. If they were to fall in love, Dennis thought, it would never work out. She saw something essential about him that she could never learn to like. He didn't know what it was, exactly, but he could feel it in the air around him, like a smell—a particular trigger which he lacked—a winking type of confidence, or body hair, or a temper. Whatever it was.

"If you want to leave them," she said, "that's okay. I mean, he'll probably just wreck them. Color in them and stuff. You could sell them," she said. She shrugged, and put a hand against her hair. "You don't have kids of your own," she said.

"No." He smiled, hesitating because she made no move to take the box. He braced it against his hip. "No, not really," he said thoughtfully. And then, after a second he realized that this was an odd thing to say. "I guess I might have kids," he said, "but none that I know of."

"Oh," she said, and then she laughed shortly. "You're one of those, huh?" She looked at him for a moment with something like, what? Flirtation? Sarcasm? Something familiar but not quite friendly. He couldn't tell, but it made him blush. He set the box down.

"No," he said. "No, it's . . ." and for a moment he actually considered telling her about the hospital and the rest, though he knew that would be worse, at that point, than just letting her think what she wanted.

"It's complicated," he said.

"Uh-huh," she said. She gave him that same look again, and he watched her thinking; a whole complex set of things were passing through her mind. She did not believe that he was the type, and she wondered, briefly, why he would say such a strange thing, what he really meant. She thought of her son's father, or maybe she didn't. She opened the door a little more, and Dennis could see the boy inside, sitting cross-legged in front of the television, his face lit unnaturally as he trotted a plastic elephant along the carpet. It would have been neat if the boy suddenly turned to look at him, but he did not.

"Well," the woman said. "Thanks."

When Dennis first moved into the apartment, the little boy upstairs was going through a period of having bad nightmares. The child would wake up screaming, and of course Dennis would awaken as well. "Help me!" Dennis thought he could hear the child crying. "Help me!" At last, Dennis would hear the woman's footsteps, and then her voice, gentle and tired. "Hush," she was probably saying. "It's okay. It's okay. Be still now." And then, after a time, she would begin to sing.

He doesn't know why this had affected him so, the sound of her singing, but he can remember shuddering. He had curled up a little more, thinking, "What is it? What's wrong with me?" and trying to decide that it was simple, that it was ordinary loneliness, being disoriented in a new place, boxes still not unpacked, his family far away, his own father, dead a few years now, buried in a cemetery some thousand miles distant.

But it had felt, at that moment, that there was something wrong with the world itself. He could have sworn he knew in his heart that something terrible had happened to the world, and that everyone knew it but him.

AMONG THE MISSING

My mother owned a lakefront cabin, not far from where the bodies were discovered. She watched from the back porch when the car was pulled out of the water. She could hear the steady clicking of the big tow chain echoing against the still surface of the lake. Brown-gray water gushed from the windows and trunk and hood as the car rose up. The windows were partway open, and my mother's first thought was that animals were probably in the car also: suckers and carp and catfish and crawdads—scavengers. The white body of the car was streaked with trailing wisps of algae. She turned away as the policemen gathered around.

There was a family in the car: the Morrisons. A mother and father, a seven-year-old girl, a five-year-old boy, and a baby, a little boy, thirteen months old. They had been missing since late May, over six weeks, and the mystery had been in the papers for a while. People around town reported having seen them, but no one had taken much notice. They were a typical family, apparently, no different from the hundreds that passed through during the summer months. Lake McConaughy was the largest lake in Nebraska, one of the largest man-made lakes in the entire Midwest, and it drew not only locals but also vacationers from Omaha and Denver and even farther. When the police came around with the pictures, people *thought* they had seen them, but they couldn't be sure. The investigation was bogged down by our town's uncertain memory. It didn't occur to anyone to drag the lake, especially since reported sightings continued to come in from as far away as Oklahoma and Canada. Most people believed that they would turn up, and that there would be some rational explanation—despite the claims of the grandmother, who lived in Loveland, Colorado, and who had first reported the family missing. She felt foul play was certainly involved. Why else hadn't they contacted her? Why else had the father, her son, not returned as scheduled to the real estate office where he'd worked for ten years?

Before the bodies were discovered, my father had a theory. He said that it would eventually come out that the father had embezzled a large sum from that real estate company. Sooner or later, he said, the authorities would catch up with them. They would find them living in a big house under an assumed name in some distant, sunny state. "Or maybe," said my father, "maybe they'll never catch them." He paused, a little taken with this romantic possibility. "Maybe they'll get away with it," he said.

When he heard they'd been found, he seemed almost bitter that the idea he had repeated and embellished turned out to be so far from the truth. "It just doesn't make any sense," he said, and glared darkly down at his hands.

The two of us were out at a local bar, a place called The Fishhead that he frequented, and he was already several beers ahead of me. He was slurring a little.

"I just can't fathom what could've happened. How do you drive your car into a God damn lake? And how do you get it out there as deep as they got it? Even if there was a drop-off?"

"It's freakish," I agreed. I sipped my beer. "A real tragedy," I said.

My father shook his head: I had failed to get his point. "Do you know," he said. "Every one of them was still buckled in. That's what Buddy Bartling told me, and he was there. The woman was driving, and she was strapped in behind the wheel. It just doesn't make sense. You know, if the water had been icy cold, it would've been just—*bam!*—hypothermia. But it wasn't that cold."

"Hmm," I said. It sounded like he was concocting a new theory, and I waited. The barmaid came over and asked how we were doing and my father tapped his empty glass.

"You know what gets me," my father said. He cocked his head at me, squinting one eye, and lowered his voice. "What gets me is your God damn mother. Here this happens not five hundred yards from her cabin. But she sees nothing, she hears nothing. That's just how she is. You know it. I mean, it's nothing against her really. That's not what I'm saying. She's your mother, and she's not a bad woman."

"No," I said. He was drunk, I thought. I felt the alcohol moving thickly through my own body, and I couldn't follow where he was going. I gave him the same one-eyed squint.

"You would think," my father said, "a person would think they would've hollered. Those kids. They had to have screamed, don't you think?"

"I don't know what you're saying," I said, and he hunched his shoulders.

"I'm not saying anything," he said, but his eyes had a strange intensity. "It's just a shame there wasn't someone else in that cabin other than your mom. That's all I'm saying. They would have found those folks a lot sooner."

My parents had been separated for almost three years by that time, though they'd never officially divorced. They had "parted ways" (as my mother said) sometime during my sophomore year in college, I wasn't even sure when. No one told me. My mother moved out to the cabin, and my father remained at the house in Ogallala.

I didn't quite understand the situation. My mother said that it had to do with his drinking—though, to me, he didn't seem to be an alcoholic, at least not in the way that you read about. He never did anything outrageous or abusive. He just drank beer or an occasional glass of whiskey, the same as he always had, and generally all that meant was that he was a little out-of-it after about nine o'clock at night.

My father felt that it had to do with the difference in their ages. My mother was ten years older than my father, and once I had left home, he said, the differences had become more difficult. It was hard to get a clear answer from him. He hinted that it had something to do with menopause (what he solemnly called "The Change O' Life"). She'd just—changed, he said.

Nevertheless, my father was out at the cabin regularly. All their finances were still intertwined, and whenever he got a check for work he did (he was a carpenter) he came out and gave it to her, rather than deposit it himself. It didn't make much sense to me.

The morning after our conversation at the bar, I awoke to the sound of them arguing. It was an almost comforting noise, familiar to me since childhood, and lying there in half-sleep I might have once again been thirteen years old, or ten, or seven.

"Damn it, Everett," I heard my mother say sharply, and I smiled because the phrase was so familiar, and because I knew it would make him blush and grow sullen. His real name *was* Everett, but everyone called him Shorty—he was five foot five, a compact, wiry little man—and some time in the distant past he'd come to see this nickname as a kind of badge of respect, and Everett as an insult, a sissified embarrassment. Even my mother used it only in anger.

I heard my father mumble back at her, a low stubborn sound. He was terrible at arguing, he always lost (even when he was right) and mostly he was reduced to petty, childish comebacks. He used to flip up his middle finger at her. "Sit and spin, darlin'," he would say. For a while, this was his favorite final word.

By the time I came into the kitchen, they had lapsed into silence. He was sitting at the table, moodily sipping his coffee, and she was at the stove, frying eggs, wielding her spatula with venomous precision. "Morning," I said, and my father raised his eyes and nodded. My mother said nothing. She flipped an egg and the grease crackled.

"I'll tell you something," she said after a moment, without turning from the frying pan. "If you're going to be drinking and carrying on until all hours of the night, you can stay with your father."

My father and I exchanged glances, and he rolled his eyes a little. The issue was sensitive, since the choice of whom I stayed with meant that one of them would feel slighted. The truth was that I had chosen my mother for selfish reasons—she cooked, and I had easy access to the lake. I kept my face neutral.

But no one said anything more. My mother set plates and silverware in front of us with an irritated snap of her wrist, and I saw plainly that their argument had been about me. It was an extension of earlier fights they'd had, when he'd taken me to bars before I was of legal age.

"Do you want toast?" my mother said, and I nodded.

"Yes, please," I said humbly. "With butter."

"There's oleo on the table," she said, and put two slices of bread in the toaster. "There's a knife by your plate to spread it with. There's no butter in the house. I don't buy it anymore."

This was her all-I-do-is-serve-people tone of voice. And it was true, we sat and she waited on us—"hand and foot," as she liked to say. On the other hand, if I were to attempt to fry my own egg, she would be right behind me, watching and making critical, disapproving faces. If I tried to get my own silverware she would say, "What are you digging for?"

In retrospect, I suppose that it was that morning when I first began to get a strange feeling about her. I realized that she must have an inner life—that she was a person who thought and felt and had memories and desires like the rest of us. But I sensed that there was something changed and hardened about that inner life. We had both become mysterious to one another, and I was aware that she wasn't particularly interested in my adulthood. I was still her son, naturally; but at some level, I was also something else—an invader, a grown-up mind that was beginning to commandeer the body of the child she had loved so much.

I don't know if I was an adult, really. That spring, for a variety of reasons, I had come close to failing my final semester of college, and, at the last minute, had managed to talk my adviser into helping me get an emergency withdrawal. I took incompletes in all my classes, and, two weeks before graduation, packed up my stuff and drove home. I left on the same weekend that the Morrisons disappeared.

I took a job at a video store in a little mini-mall near the lake, some five miles down the shore from my mother's cabin. When I was a child, it was simply a gas station and convenience store that sold canned goods and bait. But over the years, it had expanded; now, in addition to the video store, there was souvenir "Shoppe," a McDonald's, and a Domino's Pizza. It irritated me a little. "They" were taking over the lake, I thought, though I wasn't sure who "they" were—new people, I guess. I spent my days feeling scornful and superior to the movies most people rented.

Everyone was talking about the family who had died. My boss told me that there had been a number of reporters around, and even a TV news team from Denver. It was all a mystery. Had they simply run off the road, and perhaps been knocked unconscious before they hit the water? Had foul play been involved somehow? A pale fat man in cut-offs told me that he'd heard they'd been drugged, that it had been a mob hit—which, if true, never appeared in the papers.

What did appear that morning was an unnerving, posed studio portrait of the Morrisons, grainy and badly reproduced, on the front page of the *Star-Intelligencer*. They were all grinning for the camera, even the baby. The mother sat in front, holding the infant in her lap; the seven-year-old girl, plump and obviously proud of her waist-length hair, sat on the right; the five-year-old boy was on the left, his hair sticking up a bit, "a rooster's tail," my mother used to call it; the father was behind them, with one hand on each of the children's shoulders.

Looking at their photograph, you couldn't help imagining them all in that car, under the water. I saw it as a scene in a Bergman film—a kind of dreamy blur around the edges, the water a certain undersea color, like a reflection through green glass. Their bodies would be lifted a bit, floating a few centimeters above the upholstery, bobbing a little with the currents but held fast by the seat belts. Silver minnows would flit past the pale hands that still gripped the steering wheel, and hide in the seaweed of the little girl's long, drifting hair; a plastic ball might be floating near the ceiling. Their eyes would be wide, and their mouths slightly open; their skin would be pale and shimmery as the inside of a clamshell; but there would be no real expression on their faces. They would just stare, perhaps with faint surprise.

I thought of all the times I'd been swimming in the past month, and I felt a vague need to scrub myself again, as if that vision of them had seeped into the water, as if the existence of those unknown bodies had left a film on my skin. My mother had gone through the freezer and thrown out all the fish she'd caught that summer for the same reason: It seemed contaminated. I was sickened to remember the catfish—a scavenger—that she'd caught a few weeks ago, and that we'd eaten, breaded and deep fried, one Saturday evening.

People who knew where my mother lived would ask about it. I said that she didn't hear anything. I wasn't back from school at the time, I said. I would talk about how strange it was. It didn't seem logical; maybe the police would be able to figure out what happened. I honed small speeches for reporters, or news cameras, but I was never interviewed.

The police had stopped by to talk to my mother the day they'd found the car. She said they'd asked a lot of questions but wouldn't go into specifics. All she could tell them was that she hadn't heard anything. I could picture her sitting there on our old cabin sofa, the policemen across from her. I could see the stiff, official way she held herself, her careful monotone when she spoke. She felt as if she were being judged—like she was one of those Kitty Genovese people, who sat in their apartments and ignored the cries for help while a woman was murdered in the courtyard below.

She really was that type of person. It wasn't that she didn't care; it was simply that it was hard for her to take the initiative in a situation that wasn't her business. She would have assumed that someone else had already done what needed to be done.

When I came home from work, I only briefly mentioned the things I'd learned: the photo in the paper, the TV news team, the speculation I'd heard. She rested her hand against her forehead. "Oh, oh," she said softly. She shook her head, sadly, and was silent. Then she asked me if hamburgers were all right for dinner.

At the time, this weird juxtaposition, her insistence on switching to the mundane, seemed like pure irony. Sometimes I thought that she was so repressed she was more or less blank on the inside—or at very best, one dimensional, her consciousness a space where simple commands were given and executed: "Eat. Sleep. Make food for offspring. Sleep again." Perhaps an occasional emotion or idea would flutter through, briefly, and then disintegrate. If anyone could fail to be curious about this horrific event, it was my mother.

This was our life together: dinner, dishes, perhaps a video I'd brought home from work, which she usually fell asleep in front of. When I asked her what kinds of movies she liked, she shrugged. "Oh, I don't care, really," she said. "They're all about the same to me. Half of them don't make any sense, anyway." When I pressed her to name a film she'd liked, she at last came up with *Wait Until Dark*, about a blind lady being menaced by criminals. I brought home some thrillers after that, which she watched dispassionately but with interest—sudden deaths, killers hidden behind doorways, screaming women pursued down endless halls. When it was over, she always claimed that she knew how it was going to end.

Looking back, I realize that this was my last chance to get to know her. I would never again live at home—apart from occasional visits at Christmas or Independence Day. Sometimes I think that if I'd only been paying more attention, I might have been prepared for what happened to her later. It might not have happened at all, had I been watching for the signs that I can now only search for in my memory.

•   •   •

But back then, whatever puzzles my mother's inner life presented were not nearly as interesting as the mystery of the Morrison family. I called my college friends and talked to them about it, feeling a little indignant that it hadn't been picked up by the national news. "It's pretty amazing," I told my friends. "It's almost like there's no rational explanation, you know?"

I walked down to the site of the accident and examined it for myself. Here was the place where the car had inexplicably gone off the road. They must have been going *fast* down that curving dirt road—in the dark, one would assume, though no one knew. They had to have been going so fast that the young, man-high saplings didn't slow them down. They flew over an embankment—since surely, if the tires had hit the strip of sand between the low cliff and the water, they would have stopped, merely bogged down in an unpleasant but eventually hilarious situation. Somehow, the car sailed over the sand. It hit the water and sank. The lake was shallow for several yards before it dropped off swiftly. Somehow, the car got past that, too.

"But don't cars float for a while before they sink?" one of my friends asked. He was sure they did. And even then, there would have surely been time to roll down the windows, even while they were submerged, there would have been time for at least some of them to escape.

When I walked along the edge of the road, there were no signs of any accident—no tire marks at the edge of the ditch, not even a broken sapling. Of course, almost two months had passed; the elastic trees had straightened, summer plants had grown wild, rain had smoothed the ground.

As I came back to the cabin that day, walking along the line of shore, I saw that my father's work van was parked in the driveway. He had probably stopped in for lunch. I came up the beachside steps—which my father had built many years before—padding barefoot, quiet though I didn't necessarily intend to be. I could hear them talking in the kitchen. The sliding glass door that led from the kitchen to the deck was open, and their voices floated out, clear and disembodied as I approached.

"Call her up," my mother was saying. "Tell her that if she doesn't pay you this week you're going to take her to court."

"I have half a mind to go out there and take down the whole damn addition, two-by-fours and all."

"You should."

He laughed. "Can you see the look on her face?" he said, and my mother chuckled deeply.

"I'd like to be there to see it," she said.

I sat down at the top of the steps to listen. They were always at their best when they were talking business, making plans and strategies. I couldn't help feeling sad, hearing them. It could be like this, I thought foolishly, we could all be friends, sitting around, joking, talking easily. That's what it could be like.

"She probably thinks I owe her something," my father said.

"Do you?" my mother said coldly.

"No," my father said. "Not really." He cleared his throat.

"Well, then," my mother said.

Then they were quiet. I heard a plate being set down on the table. I got up and went inside.

They both looked up, startled. "Hey, bud," my father said. "What have you been up to?"

"Nothing," I said. I watched as their expressions tightened, as whatever they were talking about was buried away, out of sight. I was coming to realize that I didn't really know them very well. Somehow, twenty-two-year-old Shorty had fallen in love with my mother, a sharp-tongued, thirty-two-year-old telephone operator. Somehow, they'd stayed married for twenty years, and then, abruptly, somehow they'd decided to give up. It didn't quite make sense, and I looked at them, for a minute aware of the other mystery in my life.

"Do you want some soup?" my mother asked, as if I were a customer.

Looking back, I wish that I'd gone about finding answers in a more systematic way. I don't even know if "answers" were what I was looking for at the time. Mostly, I was thinking of myself—where would I be at thirty-two, forty-five, fifty-five? How did people go about falling in love, getting married, having jobs, families, living their lives? I wanted to frame my parents' lives like scripts—plot, conflict, motivation, theme—anything that could be easily analyzed, anything that might give me a clue about how to proceed, or how not to.

Perhaps this was what I thought of as my mother and I sat on the deck, as we often did on hot nights. We sat, smoking cigarettes, staring out at the dark shape of the lake—at the lights of houses on the other side, at the soft brightening and dimming of fireflies in the air, which reminded me of the way the lit end of her cigarette would glow more intensely when she breathed in, and fade when she exhaled.

I can't remember that we talked, though we must have. Perhaps we spoke of the weather, or whatever mundane daily activities we'd gone about; maybe we joked about the "news" in those supermarket tabloids she liked to read. I believe that was the year Princess Grace of Monaco died, in her own mysterious car accident. We might have discussed that.

But it was the things that we didn't talk about that seemed most present. I wanted to know what she *really* thought of me; what had *really* happened between her and my father; what she was going to do with her life now. But it was as if we were deep underwater—those conversations drifted over the surface, far above us, like the rippling shadows of rafts and swimmers that fish might notice, and startle at.

I said, "So . . . what are your plans for the year?"

"Oh," she said, and sighed. "I don't have any idea. I'll probably just do the same old thing. Live here in the house, take care of your dad's books, and try to get by."

She was silent, as if the process of "getting by" were fraught with secret perils. A couple of kids came running along her stretch of beach, laughing and calling out, their flashlights bobbing like will-o'-the-wisps. We watched as they ran off toward the spot where the bodies were discovered. The lights dipped and swayed as the kids ran past, growing smaller in the distance.

"That part of the beach is going to be haunted," I said. "Don't you think?"

"What do you mean?" she said sharply.

"Oh, you know," I said. "The way people make things up. When something like that happens."

"Hmm," she said suspiciously. "Well, that's the way people

are," she said. "Full of stupidity." She looked at me as if I might be one of them, a spy from the world of the ignorant. She tilted her head back and breathed out a long trail of smoke. "I don't think about it," she told me, firmly, and frowned. I thought, as she gazed out toward the water, she looked troubled. The tall cottonwoods alongside the house trembled a bit in the breeze. She stubbed out a cigarette and lit another one.

This was the way my mother had always been, as far as I could remember, though you don't notice it as a child—or at least, I didn't. It seemed the natural course of things. I can't really guess what her life was like, from day to day. I recall only little things, mostly. I remember how, when she took out her curlers, she would let me put my fingers through the holes in those tight, tubelike curls. I would stretch her hair out to its full length and then watch it bounce back, perfectly, into its hollow shape against her skull. Then she would brush her hair until the curls turned into a kind of bubble around her head, perfectly round, like a helmet. She would hair-spray it until it was stiff. This was her late-morning ritual. She would drink coffee and watch TV, or do crossword puzzles. When I wanted a hug or kiss, she would give it to me.

I don't think she was ever vivacious. Her laughter, if it came, had a grudge underneath it. I have seen early pictures of her and my father where she appears to be laughing, yet still she seems self-conscious about it, glancing a little off to the side, uncomfortable. She is never especially pretty in these younger pictures—there is too much hardness and cautious ambivalence in the set of her features. It is my father who seems to have a glow about him.

You can tell in his face, in the way he looks at her, that he is in love. He is a little in awe of her, it seems—as if she is an older sibling who will always, always outdo him, but he doesn't mind.

In the middle years of my growing up—between, say, nine and thirteen—she was depressed a lot. I knew why. I was told why. It was because of my sister, Teresa Joy, who died.

Teresa Joy wasn't actually a real sister, though that was what my parents always called her. "Your sister," they said. She was a stillborn baby, whom I never saw. My parents had a grave for her, though, with a little headstone that they decorated with flowers on Memorial Day. There were, I learned later, a number of miscarriages between me and Teresa Joy, though none of them got very far along. Teresa Joy, on the other hand, was one of those flukes. She strangled on the umbilical cord, and there was nothing, apparently, the doctors could do.

I remember the time my mother tried to kill herself. No one ever spoke of it as such, but at that age I was old enough to put it together. I recall the ambulance coming to our house, the men trying to put her on a stretcher and her just aware enough to struggle with them—flailing her arms when they lifted her, her mumbled protests through lips that seemed claylike and un-natural, moving like a badly dubbed Japanese film. "No, no, no," she said. "No, no." I think now that she must have taken an overdose of pills.

My father and I were at The Fishhead one night, talking. He wanted me to play pool, and though I'd never been any good at any sort of game, I agreed. I figured it was something I owed him, something a father and son should do together.

"That's all right," he said as the cue ball I'd hit drifted in between the colored balls it was meant to strike. "Good try," he said as he squeaked blue chalk onto the end of his stick.

I don't know why this should have called up an image of my mother in extremis, but it did. Perhaps it was the way he glanced over his shoulder, edgily, worrying that someone might laugh at my ineptitude. Perhaps it was simply that we had been talking about her.

"You remember what she was like when you were a kid," he said. "She was something else, then, boy! You might not have known it. She was intense."

"Intense?" I said. An image sparked in my mind—her, struggling with the ambulance drivers. Where was my father at that moment? Standing aside? Watching? I couldn't remember. He leaned over the pool table and ran the stick between his fingers.

"I don't know," he said. "She keeps a lot of things bottled up inside her." He struck, sending a striped ball into a pocket. He stared as it vanished. "Ah, Sean," he said. "You know I tried to be a good husband to her. You know that I tried to be good to you both. I was a good dad to you, wasn't I?"

"Sure," I said. "Of course."

He was a little more drunk than usual, I thought. He was looking at me in that crafty, sidelong way of his, as if he had a secret and was trying to decide whether or not he could trust me with it. He'd squint one eye and fix on me with the other, sizing me up. He might say something interesting if he had a few more.

"You feel like having a shot?" I said slyly.

He shrugged. "I wouldn't mind," he said.

I went back to the bar and brought back two glasses of bourbon, neat. He was in the process of finishing off our second game. He named the pocket for the eight ball, defeated me again, and then took his glass of whiskey, clicking the glass against mine with a muted pride in his victory.

"You need some more practice, my son," he murmured teasingly.

Little did he know that I had scored a small victory of my own—for as soon as we sat back down at the bar, he began to rub his chin ruefully, studying his own reflection in the mirror behind the rows of liquor bottles. "I've been thinking," he said. "You know what I think? I think she did it on purpose, that woman."

"What?" I said. I was still thinking of my mother.

"That woman that drove into the lake," my father said. "I think she did it on purpose. She had it planned out, you see? That's what they're not getting. She had it planned out. Maybe the husband was in on it, too, I don't know about him. But she definitely knew what she was doing."

"Dad," I said. "Why would someone do that?"

There must have been something snotty in my tone of voice, because he snorted as if I'd offended him. "Why do people do anything, Sean?" he said. He looked at me, a slow, drunken film over his eyes, a sad and scornful look. "Do you think you can say why people do what they do? They teach you that in college?" He stared at me thoughtfully, and later, when I was older, it was something I recalled, that expression. It was the stare of a man who has realized that he doesn't know his son and his son doesn't know him. He shrugged. "Ah, well," he said.

"I just asked," I said. "I'm not doubting you."

He put his hand to his forehead, soddenly. "I'll tell you a story," he said. "You probably don't remember this, you were just a kid at the time. You remember when Teresa Joy was born?"

"Yes," I said.

"You know, your mom—she was real upset. She was having a rough time of it. Women go through a lot of bodily changes when they give birth, hormones and that. You've been to college, you probably know more about it than I do." He paused for a moment, and I shifted self-consciously.

"No, not really," I said. "I didn't take that kind of course."

"Mm," my father said. He gazed down, running his thumb over a wet circle on the bar's varnished surface. "Well, anyways," he said. "She was depressed. You know that. We struggled with it, I felt like . . . I had to watch her. You didn't know what she might do. She . . . well, she was at a point where she was a danger to herself. You remember. But it was hard. She had never been a weak person, you know, and . . . I wasn't . . . I can't say I was doing so well that I could be the person for her to lean on. I never thought I'd have to, you know? I thought she'd always be herself—like she was.

"I'll tell you," he said. "I think about this one night. She wasn't sleeping much then, you know, and I don't know what woke me up, but I suppose I heard her out there in the kitchen moving around. Those days you had to sleep like you were half-awake, in case something happened. She'd tried stuff.

"So I got out of bed, you know? Maybe I was still part in a

dream . . . it must have been sometime after midnight, which was not all that unusual for her back then, she'd wander around at all hours. But I had a funny feeling. And so I got up and I sort of—called to her, but she didn't answer. So I went out to the kitchen and then I could smell the gas from the stove.

"She wasn't herself then, Sean," he said apologetically, though I was just sitting there, my face neutral and attentive. "She wasn't even there, not really. I could see that. She was just standing, looking at the burners of the stove. I guess she'd blown out the pilot light. I could smell it pretty strong. And then I saw that she had a cigarette—it wasn't lit—she had a cigarette in her mouth, and she was fingering her lighter in her hand, waiting. Thinking about it. I don't know what I said. I think I said something like, 'Honey, don't.'

"I don't know what I was thinking. I don't think I panicked at all. I guess—I don't know, when she finally looked up at me, there was part of me that wanted to let her go ahead and do it. I loved your mom a lot, and she had those eyes. Those eyes, boy—I could do a lot of things when she looked at me a certain way. I just thought—a part of me thought—well, why not? Everything has gone to shit. Do you see what I'm saying? It's just a matter of a second. Like that family. The *Morrisons*," he said cynically. "The big God damn mystery people. That's what we would have been. They would have writ it up in the papers, like 'Family of Three Dies in Mystery Blaze,' or some crap, and they would have yammered and gossiped and wondered . . ."

"But," I said. "She didn't do it. She decided not to do it."

He gave me a tight smile. "I reckon she didn't," he said. "We're still here, aren't we?"

I felt my skin prickle. Would I have awakened when the air

caught fire? I wondered. I saw myself, myself at nine, sitting up in bed as a red-orange cloud rushed into me, the flash of a single synapse. Would it have hurt? What would it be like, to suddenly cease to exist? I felt my back tense at the image of that bright red burst, that blotting out. What about me? Weren't they thinking about me at all? But I didn't say this.

"What stopped her?" I said at last. "Why didn't she—?"

My father shrugged. "That's all I'm saying. It's a second. I don't know. We might have looked at each other for a minute or five minutes—who knows? But then she just—turned off the stove. Walked over and opened a window. There wasn't any . . . big scene. I don't think we ever talked about it again."

"Why not?" I said, and my voice felt hushed and ragged. I stared at the neon letters above the bar, which spelled out BEER.

"What was there to say?" my father said. "What do you say about something like that?"

Years later, I would try to replay this conversation in my mind, thinking it might hold some clue. I can only make up his exact words, though they sound honest in my imagination. I can picture my drive home that night—I parted ways with my father, awkwardly on the sidewalk outside the bar, standing near our cars, and there was a moment when we might have hugged but didn't. "Good-bye, see you tomorrow!" "Good-bye, sleep well!" I must have gotten in my car and put the key into the ignition and my hand on the wheel. The night must have been dark, maybe with a little rain, and the thick trees along the roadside were heavy with foggy moisture, and the yellow lines in the middle of the slick highway kept dividing, pulling apart like blurry amoebas beneath my beery gaze.

All of this must have happened, but what I really remember is the image of my mother with her lighter and the room full of gas. I remember a particular faux-velvet red nightgown she would have been wearing, I can see her naked, bony feet against the black-and-white kitchen tile. I can see my room, when I was nine years old, the taped posters and drawings of robots on the walls, the microscope, the rock polisher, all of that *stuff* is vividly imprinted. I remember television shows I watched more clearly than I recall what was going on between my parents.

My mother was asleep when I got home, and would have been angry to find me stumbling in drunk at all hours, as I'd promised not to. But she didn't wake. I distinctly recall standing over her bed, watching her. The quilt was pulled up to her neck. She was breathing deeply, loosely, her mouth slack and vulnerable and innocent. Her knees were pulled up near her belly. Rain made a sound like sleep outside the window. She didn't appear to be dreaming. It was quiet.

I want to tell you that something else important happened that summer, that the mystery of the Morrisons was solved, that I finally understood my parents' relationship, that my mother herself became suddenly clear to me. I want to say that I finally confronted my mother, shortly after the conversation with my father in the bar, that we had an in-depth conversation. I wanted to—I meant to talk to her.

But I was very busy at the video store. I was going back to

college in the fall, and I had to decide what I was going to do. I had this enormous, virgin expanse of time in front of me that needed to be claimed, and colonized, and strip-mined: *My future.*

And there was a girl, too, someone I met. She was staying with her parents in a cabin not far from my mother's—a recent high school graduate in the midst of her summer-before-college, eighteen years old. I think her name was Michelle. We made love on the beach, on the edge of the Morrisons' watery grave. It was her first time, she said, and afterward I made a hole in the sand with my bare foot and buried my used condom— my seed, my potential sons and daughters sealed in their plastic coffin, earth tapped down gently over them with the palm of my hand. Michelle sat close by, shawled in a beach towel, silent and full of regret.

My mother, in her cabin bedroom, was asleep. She appeared in my mind, but I thrust her away. She was the one thing I didn't want to think about.

To tell the truth, that last summer I spent with my parents was soon forgotten—just as the Morrisons were, moving from the front page of the paper to the back sections, and, finally, drifting out of the range and interest of journalists forever. I went on: I finished school, I took various jobs, I moved into different cities and apartments and shuffled through girlfriends. All through my twenties I kept thinking, *My life would make a great movie!* It wasn't until I sat down to write it that I realized that it didn't amount to much of anything. It was just a series of disconnected incidents.

Then, almost ten years after the Morrisons, my mother herself disappeared.

My mother vanished sometime in August. I had been trying to telephone her for a few weeks, and then I finally called the police—thinking, naturally, that she would be dead, rotting alone in the hallway between the kitchen and the bedroom, or sitting on the toilet like Elvis, frozen in a heart attack.

But this wasn't the case. The cabin, they said, appeared to be abandoned, and when I drove out a week later this seemed to be true. Most of the furniture was there, but the closets were nothing but bare hangers, and the refrigerator was empty and unplugged. The front door had been left wide open.

In some ways, I suppose I wasn't surprised. My father had died three years earlier of a sudden stroke, fifty-two years old, buried beside Teresa Joy's tiny grave. Since then, I hadn't been able to get any perspective on things she told me. She had been saying strange things lately—the cabin spooked her, she said, she felt like someone was watching her, and then she was sure of it, and finally she began to think that someone was trying to break in. Outside, she claimed to have found thin scrapes around the lock on the door—the new lock she'd put in—and on the windows, scuff marks on the wood, as if someone were trying to jimmy them open. "I get afraid," she said. "Sometimes, I get really scared." That was the last time I remember talking to her.

Her fears had not sounded that serious, I have to admit. They were buried in a long list of complaints and worries—from her health to the new people who had moved next door—which had become the main topic of conversation when I called. I would tell her what I was doing, but I could sense her impatience.

Yet she didn't seem crazy. That's what I told the police when they asked. "Did she seem disoriented in any way?" one officer asked me, and I had to simply shrug my shoulders. "Not really," I said. "Maybe a little." I told them that last Christmas, when I visited, she had given me a bunch of old photo albums and memorabilia. "You might as well have this junk now, as soon as later," she'd said. "Keep what you want and throw the rest away." It was mostly pictures of us when we were a family—me, my father, and her—and old relatives I didn't recognize, and gifts of jewelry and knickknacks my father had given her, and some of my old report cards and childhood drawings that she'd saved.

There was nothing of that sort left in the cabin: The closets, the drawers, the storage spaces were spotlessly empty and smelled of disinfectant. I found a nickel in one of the bottom drawers of her dresser. In another, I found an ant trap. The kitchen floor had been waxed. I opened the cabinet under the sink and found that she'd put a fresh garbage bag in the trash can.

I don't know why, but it was at that moment that I was certain that she was dead. A sort of terror slid over me like a cloud's shadow, and suddenly I was aware that it was night, and I was alone in the silent cabin. Outside the kitchen window, a certain tree looked like a human figure, standing there. The tree was at the very edge of the light from the kitchen, and for a moment it appeared to be a woman in a long robe—a nightgown, maybe. I let out a small sound and fled the house as quickly as I could.

• • •

There are times, lots of times, when I think that maybe she is still alive. They never found her car, or her clothes, and her bank account was nearly empty. I can picture her, driving through various landscapes, her eyes straight ahead, her driving sunglasses reflecting the road. I see her living under an assumed name, in New Orleans, in Fargo, on a beach in Florida. Sometimes, when the phone rings at an odd time, I have the quavering sense that it might be her. When there is silence at the other end of the line, I can't keep from whispering, ". . . Mom?" And yet, I don't think she would call me, even if she were alive.

There are times when I would like to tell this story to my father. What would he make of it, I wonder? Is it the story of a woman who fell out of love with her son? Is it the story of a woman who realized that love wasn't that important, after all? Or is it the story of my failure—my failure to figure things out, my failure to interpret, my failure to need her?

What can you do with a woman like that, my father would say, and I would recall her wading in the lake one day, about a week before the Morrisons were discovered, knee deep in the calm gray water, running the tips of her fingers across the surface of the lake, wearing that blue one-piece bathing suit she had. "Water's warm!" she called to me on the shore. And if I would have lifted my head from the book I was reading I would have seen her expression, I would have seen what she thought as she looked at her son—a grown-up man, now— I would have watched more carefully as she walked into the lake, deeper and deeper, until just her head was showing. I know the lake was glowing with the reflection of the sundown. I know she was looking back at me. I know she was thinking something.

"Why do people do anything?" my father would ask, and he would dismiss every moment I thought important. He would ask me if they'd dragged the lake for her body. And I would tell him, yes—of course. They trawled all along the line of beach, but as far as they could tell, she wasn't there, either.

PROSTHESIS

There was a man Suzanne met at the library. He spoke to her back as she was standing in an aisle of shelves, staring at a book. She was lost in thought. "Excuse me . . . ma'am?" he said.

His voice was gentle and plaintive, almost on the verge of cringing. She turned, and he was standing a short distance behind her—a young man with shaggy dark hair, somewhat shoddy in his dress. He had a prosthetic arm, a hook instead of a hand. She registered this immediately but composed herself almost at once. She looked at his face, as if she hadn't noticed his arm. Polite. Quizzical.

"Ma'am?" he said. "Could you help me, please?" And she noticed that he adopted a loping, submissive posture.

He held up a few napkins in his real hand. "I'm trying to . . . get a grip on these," he said, and slipped them in between the two prongs of his hook, which he could pinch open and closed, like mandibles. "I think I need to put a rubber band around them," he said apologetically.

"Oh," she said. He was younger than she, with a brown-eyed, scruffy handsomeness. "Of course," she said. She took a step toward him, and he held up his arm. The prosthesis extended from the sleeve of a T-shirt. The upper and lower arm was made of plastic, like a mannequin, pinkish, in an approximation of the color of Caucasian skin. The hook emerged from the wrist and was silver and steely. She smiled as she guided the napkins into the pinchers, but her hands trembled. The smooth, cool metal sent a thrum through her fingertips. She dropped the napkins and had to pick them up.

"Sorry—sorry," she said, and their eyes met.

It was said that her former lover had been badly disfigured in a fire. Suzanne's mother had called to report the news, as she often did when something horrible happened in the small Iowa town where Suzanne had grown up, and this was how her mother said it: "... disfigured ..." with a small pause before and after.

"You were friends with him, weren't you?" Suzanne's mother said, either oblivious or deliberately cruel. "He was in your class in high school."

"Yes," Suzanne said. She was at work, very busy. She had asked her mother before not to call her at the office unless it was important. Several times, Suzanne had been forced to speak sharply to her mother, and had hurt her mother's feelings. Now, Suzanne's mother would condense everything she said into mysterious, gnomic phrases. Then, claiming she had to go, her mother would hang up.

• • •

After work, because she could not stop thinking about it, she stopped at the library. In a medical book were photographs of people who had been severely burned. Horrible—yet she sat there staring for a long time, at the end of a long tunnel of bookshelves. A person coughed from some other aisle, a sound like a dog barking far off in the distance at night. She hadn't known what fire could do to flesh; the things people survived.

When she got home, she found that her husband had cooked a special dinner for them—steaks, naturally, so that the house was full of the smell of it—and he had the children in bed and wineglasses and place settings on the table. He stood smiling as she disengaged her key from the door, hopeful and helpless in the stream of whatever had been happening to them lately. He did want to change things, or at least to slow what had begun to seem inevitable.

"Hey, sweetheart," he said, and then, after a moment: "What? Is something wrong?"

"No, no," she said. "I'm just tired, I guess."

The burned man had not been her first. Really, he was not even one that she had been particularly attached to. Both she and her husband had had many relationships before they married. Her husband would probably recognize the burned man's name, since they had gone through a period of intense self-disclosure and examination when they first married. But her husband would not recall him as a person she had dwelled upon. Which was true, she had not. Sometimes, during the act of love, she would close her eyes and the image of that particular boy would occupy her for a moment. There was a certain way that her husband would touch his mouth against her ear that would particularly remind her.

The man who had been disfigured in a fire might have once made her pregnant. There was a time, during their senior year in high school, when her menstrual period was almost three weeks late. She had been regular for some years by that time, so it frightened her badly. She spoke to him, in a rush, after band practice. He held his glittering trombone loosely at his side. She almost started crying, but didn't.

That night, on the pretext of going out to a movie, she had driven out to the farmhouse where he lived with his parents. He was waiting at the edge of the long dirt-road driveway that led to his house. He spoke hurriedly, distractedly. "If it's in there, it's in there loose," he said. "It doesn't have to stick if we don't want it to."

He led her out to a field where bales of hay were stacked up like blocks, almost as high as houses. He showed her a stairlike passage that led her to the top of the haystack and they stood there at the top. A half-moon glowed over them. The ground was about ten or twelve feet below.

"If I held your hand," the boy said. "If we jump together," the boy said. He looked at her and his eyes were bright with assurance. "Okay?" he said.

They leapt together. She felt his hand hardening against her own, and then they were in the air, plunging, limbs flailing, a blur of stars and fields rushing past them. She landed hard on the soles of her feet and fell forward on her hands, crouched like an animal.

"Okay," he whispered, as he pulled her up. "Again . . ."

The next morning, in her own bed, she woke up and she was bleeding. A cramp clenched just above her groin. The sheets were already dirty.

Her husband was concerned as he poured the wine. He could sense troubled thoughts in her expression and assumed that it must have something to do with him. She saw how his eyes attempted to find something underneath the vague, hedging conversation. He wanted the wine, the steaks with their crisscrossed grill lines, the delicate potatoes in their skins, to mean more than they did. Sometimes it seemed that he suspected life of holding some mysterious significance that he could not quite figure out. This bothered him more than it did her. He said her name, hesitantly, and when she lifted out of her thoughts to look at him, he wasn't sure what to say.

"It's good," he said. "The food?"

"Yes," she said. "Delicious." He watched her put a piece of steak to her mouth.

What she ought to tell him she cannot tell him. It makes no sense. Or else it makes sense in the wrong way. She has just turned forty, and there is a growing unease that they could name and analyze and discuss.

There is a picture on her desk at work. It is of her father holding her first child, who, in the photograph, is a drooly infant of six months. The child, Michael, leans against his grandfather's thick shoulder, his mouth open in a one-toothed, loose smile of sleepy comfort. He clutches his grandpa's finger in one absent fist.

The grandfather, five years dead, no longer exists, and the child, Michael, a fourth grader whose face is only vaguely recognizable in the soft, plump cheeks of the infant, has already long disappeared into his own thoughts and feelings: He likes shells and stamps, he is affectionate, not much trouble, but of course she will never really know what he is thinking. The current Michael has very little to do with the photograph she has on her desk. She often folds her hands in front of the photograph and observes it, aware of a sort of emptiness opening around her, spreading like ripples around a stone tossed into a still pool.

For several weeks, perhaps almost a month, she was in love with the man with the prosthetic arm. That is to say, she began to think of him regularly, a slow romantic ache opening up inside her. She saw his brown, deerlike eyes, his mouth, surrounded by dark stubble. She felt the cold smoothness of that hook against her hand. At night, her husband asleep beside her, she shuddered, imagining the curved metal brushing down the hollow at her throat, between her breasts, down her stomach. She traced the path with her finger. She was at a loss to explain it, the power of this image.

Eventually, she knew, it would pass. She would never see the man again, though for a while she even went to the library regularly and walked through the aisles. She found herself replaying the small scene in her head. She held the napkins in her hand,

and hooks clamped over them. She looped the rubber bands over the hook. Their eyes met. Something might have happened, then.

After a while, she knew that this would fade. Her life would change again. Even now, there was an infinity of paths she could take.

Her husband was feeling blue. He came up behind her and put his arm around her waist while she was standing in the kitchen. "I love you so much," he said. "I don't know what I would do without you."

"I know," she said, as he pressed his lips against her ear. "Ditto." She closed her eyes, enjoying his touch.

What if they'd never met? It made her stiffen a bit, because it seemed so governed by chance, so improbable. How many small, offhand choices had led her to the college where they met, had led her to the room where they first looked at one another, had led her to be sad and in need of someone who thought she was beautiful? She thought, if they had not jumped off that haystack, would there have been a fire? Would there, instead, be a grown-up child, another husband, another life? How many people were forever different, how many people ceased to exist every time she turned one way rather than another? Surely, if it were so random, she could not be held accountable?

But she couldn't be certain. As her husband held her close, she could feel the pulse of other choices, other lives, opening up beneath her. Her past crackled behind her like a terrible lightning, branches and branches, endless, and then nothing.

HERE'S A LITTLE SOMETHING
TO REMEMBER ME BY

I was grown up now, married, with a family of my own, but still the Ormsons wanted to see me, just like always. "Sharon Ormson called," my mother said the morning after we arrived. We had flown into Colorado from Fort Lauderdale the night before, the children bickering through the entire flight, and all I really wanted at that moment was a cup of coffee and a television to vegetate in front of. I rubbed a finger over my eyes, which still felt sticky from sleep.

"Geez," I said. "Does she have radar or what?"

My mother gave me a heavy look. "Well," she said. "What could I say? They called me, and they were asking about you. They wanted to know if you were going to be home for Christmas. Should I have lied to them?"

"No, Mother," I said. I had noticed that since my father's death she had taken to using on me the same stern, combative tone that she had once reserved for him. Deep down maybe she associated the two of us in her mind. "It doesn't matter that much," I said.

"I can't help it," my mother said. "I'm sorry, but I feel bad for them."

"Of course," I said. "So do I."

I had just turned thirty years old. Once upon a time I had been best friends with the Ormsons' son, Ricky. But over fifteen years had passed, which seemed like a very long time.

As far as anyone knew I was the last person to ever see Ricky Ormson. This might have made me famous, at least according to the Ormsons, who said that after the long article, "The Strange Case of Ricky Ormson," appeared in the *Rocky Mountain News*, some producers who were interested in making a television movie had called. If that had happened I suppose that they would have had to hire an actor to portray me. But nothing ever came of it. It was a story with no hero and no obvious conclusion and I assumed (rightly, it turned out) that they would finally give up on it.

I had given up on it a long time before that. Thinking back, I guess that I had accepted the fact that Ricky was dead a few days after he had failed to return home, though of course hope continued for weeks and months, and, in the Ormsons' case, years. There were searches and police inquiries and news articles. The Ormsons appeared on television, appealing for information about their son's whereabouts. I myself was interviewed on several occasions—by the police, by reporters, by the Ormsons themselves, who wanted to hear the story over and over.

They wanted to see it as I did: their son vanishing around the edge of a lilac bush in the park, the shadows of leaves passing across his figure, the call of small children on the slides and swings echoing in the distance. They wanted to hear, again and again, Ricky's last words as he turned to wave to me. "See you tomorrow, I guess," Ricky had said.

Even then I might have known at some level that I would never see Ricky again. His words had that feeling about them, like they were a part of the shade he was moving into. I knew even then that there were ways to hide things. It did not seem so unusual that a body might not be recovered, that it might remain secreted, rotting, turning back to earth in some undisclosed spot. Really the only surprise was the Ormsons' insistence, year after year, that there was still the possibility of Ricky's return. I often thought that if there was a ghost haunting me, it wasn't Ricky. It was them—Mr. and Mrs. Ormson.

They continued to trail me through my entire life. When I graduated from high school, nearly three years after Ricky's disappearance, there they were in the audience, applauding with their sad, hollow clapping. As it turned out, I was the first recipient of the Richard Ormson Foundation Scholarship—not because I was Ricky's friend necessarily, but because I had the highest grades and had shown "the citizen and leadership qualities that Richard Ormson embodied." I had been in Band and Math Club, and was president of both Drama Club and the local chapter of the National Honor Society. I was also active in cross-country and track.

But it didn't end with high school graduation. When I became treasurer of my college fraternity, the Ormsons sent me flowers. They came, as guests of my mother and father, to my college commencement. They were present at my wedding and sent elaborate gifts after the births of my two sons. It seemed clear that, in addition to living my own life, I was also living the hypothetical life of Ricky Ormson.

"I really don't understand why they bother you so much," my wife, Patricia, had said on any number of occasions. She had always felt sorry for them. She listened respectfully, even at the wedding banquet, as Mrs. Ormson described what Ricky might feel about the occasion. "They are such nice people!" Patricia said when I would groan about the Ormsons' inevitable appearance. "And so sad! Such a tragic thing!"

"I'm sorry," I said. "I can't explain it. I mean I really do feel bad for them and everything, but they just drive me crazy. It's like, every happy thing in my life I know they're going to be there—infecting it. I know that's wrong to say, but I can't help it."

"No," Patricia said. "I understand what you're saying." But her eyes were puzzled. "We don't have to talk about it if you don't want to."

But we did talk about it—much more frequently than I'd expected. After our first son was born, she'd had a long period of postpartum depression during which she spoke of them obsessively: "I know how they feel, the Ormsons. Oh, God, it must be so horrible for them. I'm just so scared for us. I mean, you can't protect your children from the world forever. There is so much danger," she said. "It's terrifying."

"Yes," I said. But I didn't say any more. I couldn't explain it, but something in her attitude was infuriating—her depression, her terror, seemed willfully childish, like someone who flirted by using baby talk. I could feel an angry scoff rising in my chest, a shameful sarcasm twisting its way through my thoughts. When I went outside, I threw down the cup I was holding and it bounced once against the cement before it shattered against the edge of the sidewalk. That calmed me, and I bent, reasonably, and began to pick up the shards.

The sound of Sharon Ormson's voice always had the same effect on me. It was a round voice, round as her dumpling-cheeked, high-colored face, echoing with sorrowful vowels. "Hello, Tom?" she said, and the os had a sad well underneath them. "How are you?" and I could picture her immediately, her golden hair permed into some kind of glowing shape, the careful, neat suburban woman's suit, the sensibly short high heels. She was a realtor, and there was always the sense that she wanted to quietly sell you something. In my case, she wanted to sell her earnest, endless grief. She walked me through its many rooms with an air of eager respect, but at the same time it was clear that she felt that the house was probably beyond my means.

"It's good to hear your voice," she said. "How long are you in town for?"

"A while," I said vaguely. "I don't know for sure how long we'll be able to stay."

"Well, I sure do hope that we'll have time to get together. It's been quite a while!"

"Yes, it certainly has!" I said.

"How are the children?"

"Oh, fine."

"Growing every day, I'll bet!"

"Yes, indeed."

"And Patty?"

"She's fine, too."

"That's good."

"Yes."

In the deadly pause, I looked across at my mother, who sat at the kitchen table peeling potatoes for supper. She stared back at me grimly.

"Well, anyway," Sharon Ormson said. "I certainly hope we'll get the chance to visit with you while you're home!"

"Yes," I said, and watched as my mother stripped an excruciatingly long piece of skin from a potato with her peeler. She was pretending not to listen. "Let's plan on it," I said, and my mother plunked another naked potato into the colander.

This was the second Christmas after my father's death, and, if anything, the place seemed even sadder and more foreign than it had last year. The last traces of my father had vanished: The mail had stopped coming in his name and there were no more stacks of unread *Outdoor Life* and *National Geographic* sitting next to his chair; his ashtrays were gone, too, since my mother had quit smoking; the little shelf of the refrigerator that once held his brand of beer was now simply another storage place for leftovers.

I experienced all of this as an almost visible absence. It was as if I could feel the things that weren't there when I walked into a room. I had a similar feeling when I drove through town. Every new building, every changed storefront, every repainted house seemed like a blot, an attack on the town I held in my memory.

I had been away for over ten years by that point. My two younger brothers had somehow escaped the teenage selves I most associated them with. Matt was twenty-seven, a truck driver with the thick torso of a regular beer drinker; Bryce, a sullen outlaw when I left home, was a twenty-four-year-old policeman and had managed to marry and divorce a pale blond woman whom I'd met only once, whose face I couldn't remember. Even my mother didn't much resemble the mother I had in my mind. She was an aged and hardened version of the person I'd known—an understudy who would be portraying my mother for the duration of my stay.

It was strange, because only the Ormsons remained as I remembered them. They had grown older, of course, but they still looked like themselves. Mrs. Ormson retained the smooth, heavily made-up expression of a person who has undergone several face-lifts (though I don't think she *had*, really); Mr. Ormson, though grayer, remained permanently boyish and dazed, still stumbling around in the tweed jackets that Ricky and I used to mock. Ricky used to call him "the Nutty Professor," though actually he was, and continued to be, the county judge.

The park had changed quite a bit. It was a few blocks from my house, but I don't think I'd been there in years—maybe not since Ricky had disappeared. I suppose that I'd unconsciously avoided the place.

We'd decided to walk down there at Patricia's urging. My sons had been bored at my mother's house, and Patricia didn't feel like it was good for them to just sit around watching TV.

It was an unusually warm afternoon in mid-December. There was no snow, and it wasn't even below freezing. It felt like late autumn weather, like the October day Ricky had disappeared. There was the same chill, muddy feel to the world, the same taunting sunshine that never managed to feel warm. The boys scampered ahead of us as we walked, picking up stones that interested them. Patricia called out, unusually tense: "Don't go too far!"

I expected some kind of shock of recognition, the stunning blow of a landscape that you dream about, but what presented itself to us as we rounded the third block had little resemblance to the park Ricky and I had crossed on our way home from school. Ricky and I had entered from the far end, near the pond, passing the proplike smattering of ducks and swans, then crossed the bridge to the playground. We were fourteen, ninth graders, and when we walked across the playground the little kids watched us with a sort of eager awe: Big kids! Teenagers! They pushed themselves in circles on the merry-go-round, took flying leaps from swings, cast themselves belly down, headfirst, into the tornado slide, as in a kind of basic training for the lives we were leading, full of (they imagined) secrets and adventures.

That old playground had been replaced, naturally. It was now a framed area, and cushioning wood chips had been brought in to cover the hard, bare earth. A complex wooden and plastic jungle gym, a sort of maze, had replaced the merry-go-rounds and the metal, coil-spring horsies. The tornado slide was still there, but it was haggard looking, set apart and incongruous, like the old outhouses that still sat behind some of the country houses.

Sharon Ormson had been behind the changes in the playground, as she was often, in the years after Ricky's disappearance, behind community projects. The Park Beautification

Committee was one that she had chaired, and I assume that people must have been creeped out by her solemn cheerful determination to raze the old park, the one into which her son vanished. She went door to door, collecting for the beautification project, and people gave and gave.

"You seem tense," Patricia said. We were sitting in the park, on one of the new memorial benches. "You get so stiff whenever you come back here."

"It's just the usual," I said. I watched as our younger son disappeared into a plastic tube-tunnel and then emerged on the other side. "I don't know," I said. "It seems like every time I'm home, I have to go through this. It drives me crazy."

"You don't seem like yourself."

"I'm not myself," I said. "That's the thing. You know, I get back here and then first it's my mother and then it's the Ormsons. It's like . . . I don't know—like they want me to be the person I would have been if I'd just stayed around here and never left. It gets uncomfortable."

"Yes, well," Patricia said. "But there's more to it than that, isn't there?" She paused for a moment, craning her neck until both the boys were clearly in her sight.

I shrugged. I felt awkward and uncertain. I was usually pretty happy, pretty stable in my moods—a good husband, a good father, a man of steady routine. Most of the time I was, or tried to be, kind. "I don't know," I said at last. "Do you ever get the feeling that there's more than one of you? That's what I feel like when I'm here." I looked at her. "I'm not making any sense."

"No, no," my wife said, and gave me a sympathetic look, but one that was still creased with bewilderment. "I think I see what you're saying. I just don't know what caused it."

"Yes," I said. "I guess I don't really know what caused it, either. It's just a mood."

I shrugged again, smiling a little. I was looking out toward where the old creek used to be. Some years ago, the Corps of Engineers had decided that there needed to be a floodplain around it, so now this little trickle of a brook was in the center of a wide ditch with high sloped walls on either side. They had tried to decorate it with grass and flower beds and small shrubs, but it was still a ditch. I could remember how it used to look when I was a kid. The banks, as they ran into and out of the pond, were lined with foliage—thick bunches of willow saplings, cattails, high water weeds. There was a jungle to get through before you could reach the water, where children sometimes caught minnows and crawdads and leeches. Wading down the creek was like following a secret, hidden path. The echoes of voices on the playground, of cars on the streets, seemed to come from far away.

And so, naturally, I had to think of it, to recall the day Ricky had disappeared. We had walked, Ricky and I, along the edge of the creek, toward a copse of lilac bushes, where the man parked his car.

I don't know where Ricky heard about the man by the creek. Maybe he'd heard rumors through other boys at school. Probably he'd somehow encountered the man in the park one day. I never did find out the exact facts of the matter.

What I did know was that, during second-period study hall, Ricky Ormson had opened his math book and displayed a fifty-dollar bill tucked in between the pages.

"Hey," I said, admiringly. "Where'd you get that?"

Ricky just shrugged. He had this sleepy way of smiling, which suggested that he knew a lot more than you did, but he didn't hold it against you. That was one of the things that made him popular. "Actually, I know a lot of guys who have come by fifty lately," he said, in his slow, relaxed voice. "It's kind of sick, if you want to know the truth."

He gave me that half-smile again, as if to say, "You don't want to know." I realized later that we had a strange friendship. He thought that he was better than me, and so did I. We had been grade school buddies—we lived near one another. But the fact that we'd played cops and robbers and sat together in a tree house, watching people with his dad's binoculars, that fact was holding us together less and less as we moved toward high school. It was funny that later I was always portrayed as "the best friend," because I always knew, deep down, that in a few years I wouldn't have been as cool as Ricky was and we'd have ceased to be close. If he had lived, we'd have long forgotten all about one another.

But right then, we were still friends, still "best friends," in a way. We walked home from school together every day, probably more because of our old connections than what we had in common. And, probably, it was because of our old connections that he felt compelled to let me in on his big secret. A lot of guys, he said—people I'd be surprised to hear about—had been making money in the park. Fifty bucks here and there, he said. It was sort of *sick*, he said again, with emphasis, and with the same sly, knowing, condescending smile. "Do you know what I mean?"

I guess I did. That is to say, by the time we walked along the edge of the park to the place where the man was sitting, I had a pretty good idea of what we were going to do.

The man did not look like the typical pervert. He wasn't nervous and sweaty, or overweight, or pocked with pimples, or arch and effeminate. He seemed like our dads, though he was probably a little younger—there was something youthful and hearty about his features. He had a look of a friendly adult, one who might casually talk to you like a grown-up.

Looking back, I can say to myself that it really wasn't that big a deal. I've heard other stories, other such men, and it's probably not that out of the ordinary. It's certainly much tamer than most of the stuff we read about now in the paper. And perhaps, growing up in a small Midwestern town, I was much more inno-cent than might seem normal these days.

All of which is to explain that I thought I was doing some-thing really shocking. I was stunned, and also—I have to admit—honored that Ricky believed I was sophisticated enough for him to confide in me. I didn't want to let him down. And wasn't it true that lots of guys—"guys I would be surprised to hear about"—had done it?

Later, I would realize that my big secret, the thing I couldn't bring myself to tell anyone, was actually rather mundane: I sat in the bucket seat of the man's car with my pants down. The man crouched between my spread legs and gave me a blow job.

Afterward, the man pressed a crisp, folded fifty-dollar bill into my hand. Our eyes met for a minute, and he ran a finger across his lips. "Here's a little something to remember me by," he said softly.

There was something in his eyes that must have scared me. Or I was scared by what had happened, and embarrassed. Ricky was standing at the edge of the lilac bushes, and I must have looked pale and frightened, because his face grew cautious. We stared at each other, and his eyes said, "You aren't going to *tell,* are you?" He looked at me hard for what seemed like a long time. Then he waved his hand at me. "See you tomorrow, I guess," he said.

When Patricia and I got back to the house, I saw my brother's policeman's uniform before I saw his face, and my adrenaline leapt. But then he turned and it was just Bryce. Just Bryce. "Hey, Tommy," he said, and he came over and gave me a hug. "Rrrr," he said, squeezing. "You get shorter every time I see you, big brother."

"Yeah, yeah," I said. "But at least I've got a tan. You're as pale as fish, kiddo."

We bantered like this for a while, insulting each other, and my wife stood back and watched until Bryce noticed her, and whirled her around in an exaggerated display of affection. The kids watched, wide eyed, until Bryce called them over to see his badge and handcuffs. He had already put his gun away.

We used to be close, Bryce and I. He was six years younger than I, and had gone in for a fairly pure version of hero worship where I was concerned. We used to go fishing together on Saturday afternoons after the television cartoons were over. We would ride our bikes down to the park and sit on the banks of the pond, occasionally reeling in a bluegill or a small catfish. And he would listen to whatever I told him.

There was a time—a moment, maybe—when I almost told him about what had happened to Ricky and me in the park. I could feel it creeping into my mind as we sat there at the pond, watching our bobbers floating on the still surface of the water. We had been talking about Ricky. "Do you think he ran away?" Bryce had asked. "Or do you think some bad guy snatched him?"

"I think it was a bad guy," I said. "I think Ricky's probably dead." I hesitated, and for a moment I almost—almost—said more.

But then again—what would I have said? Imagine telling this to an eight-year-old kid. Or telling it to two policemen, men your father's age, who sat on folding chairs while you faced them. Imagine your parents hearing about it, having to tell them about the way you'd willingly sat there as the man ran his mouth over your privates. Imagine the look on your father's face: his shame and disgust. "You let this man touch you like that?" his eyes would say. "What kind of a person are you?" And what if it got into the newspapers, what if the other kids in school heard about it? It would be easy to concoct a story, to say that Ricky had moved into that huddled cave of lilacs without you, and that you'd wandered around for a time before going home. And then, later, could you change your story? After days, weeks, months, could you change your story? After you'd lied and the trail of the murderer or kidnapper had grown cold, what would it be like to admit that you hadn't told the full truth?

What would they think of you then? Or what if years passed? What good would it do, at that point, to admit your cowardice, your steadfast willingness to lie for well over a decade? Imagine the look on your wife's face, your mother, the Ormsons staring at you. How could you withhold such important information, they'd wonder, stunned with horror and hatred. "Maybe our son could have been saved, if you'd only spoken up!" they'd cry. "Maybe his killer could have been brought to justice!" Under such circumstances, would it ever be possible to confess? Under such circumstances, didn't it seem reasonable to continue to say nothing?

I was thinking of this as Bryce and I walked into the living room, my own self-justification blooming again in my head. Then I saw the Ormsons sitting there and my heart went blank.

There was a time in college when I used to think about committing suicide. I would plan it pretty carefully in my mind, but I was always too afraid to carry it out. Once, I even took a handful of over-the-counter sleeping pills. But by the time I got up enough nerve to put a razor blade to my wrists, I was so sleepy and clumsy I wasn't able to follow through. I ended up nodding off instead. When I woke up, almost twenty-four hours later, I was so grateful to be alive that I thought I was cured.

Nevertheless, as Mrs. Ormson rose from the couch to give me a hug, the old feeling roosted heavily onto my shoulders. I wished I were dead. She kissed my cheek.

"It's so good to see you," she whispered against my bare ear. I felt her cool hands against my neck as she pulled me closer, tighter against herself. "It's been a long time," she said. And when she released me, Mr. Ormson was standing there with his hand extended.

"It's good to see you, son," he said, and clenched my palm in his fist. He had been calling me "son" since before Ricky disappeared, but given the circumstances it seemed uncomfortable. I closed my eyes and let him pull my body toward his, a quick, uncertain, masculine hug.

Just as Mr. Ormson enclosed me in his arms, Mrs. Ormson let out a cry—somewhere between a coo and a shriek—and I knew that Patricia and the children had entered.

"Oh. My. God!" Mrs. Ormson exclaimed. "I can't believe it! Oh, Patty, they're so big!" Mrs. Ormson swept toward my sons, who stood rooted, hypnotized by her enthusiasm.

By the time she reached them, Mrs. Ormson had begun to weep. Her shoulders quivered as she bent down to kiss each of the boys on the forehead. "Sweet, sweet," she was murmuring.

For years, I had been trying to get over the feeling that people saw through me. They never did. Slowly, I came to realize that I was a good actor, a good liar. No one knew what I was thinking. Not the Ormsons, though sometimes their eyes seemed to judge me, to wait for a confession; not my mother, though her mouth sometimes pursed with disappointment; not Bryce, who often seemed puzzled during conversation, as if he thought I would say something entirely different; not Patricia, even when she asked me, point-blank, once, "What's really going on with you and the Ormsons? Why do you get so upset?" She looked at me, hard, and it came to me that, even after years of marriage, she didn't know either. The truth was, only I knew what I was thinking, and I sometimes wondered whether that fact was more a torture than a comfort.

I thought of this when my mother came in bearing a plate of cheese and crackers, traitorously smiling and behaving as if I'd expected the Ormsons to be there when I got back from the park, pretending that it wasn't an ambush. Then she looked at me. I didn't know what expression was on my face, but my mask was clearly not perfect. She frowned, and gave me a flicker of her eyes—two parts accusation, one part apology—before settling down next to Sharon.

"Tom was just telling us about his new job down in Florida," Sharon Ormson said to her. "It sounds wonderful!"

It wasn't. I worked as a consultant for a software company, and I was constantly bored and irritated by the meaningless work I did. I had made no real friends since we'd moved to Florida, and I hated the humidity and the fetid sense of constant growth: bugs, mold, weeds, everything slathered with atrocious animation. "Yeah, I'm really enjoying it," I said. "It's very different from here, as you can imagine." My mother gave me a look, and I realized that this comment had come out wrong. "Of course," I said, "I enjoy it here, too."

"I'd love to live near the ocean," Sharon Ormson said. "I'd go there every day!"

"Well, maybe someday," Mr. Ormson said. "We've been thinking of moving to Florida when we retire," he confided.

"Take me with you," my mother said.

The thought of the Ormsons and my mother living in Florida, perhaps nearby, silenced me. I had an image of two little bungalows, one on either side of my home. The Ormsons looked at me, blinking, and I gazed back, wondering what they wanted from me. When I was with the Ormsons, there was something about their eyes, their attentiveness, that always made me feel as though they'd just asked a question but I hadn't heard it. "Excuse me?" I said.

Bryce leaned back into the sofa. "I was just asking if you ever get alligators in your yard," he said. "I heard they're a real problem down there. Like, they come out of the swamp and eat people's dogs and stuff. I was reading where one got a little kid."

"I've never heard of that," Patricia said. "It was probably in some backwoods area. Not Fort Lauderdale."

"No, all the alligators in Fort Lauderdale are human," I said humorously. The Ormsons laughed politely, but maintained their soft, magnetic gaze.

"The last time we were in Florida," Mrs. Ormson said, "Ricky was ten years old." She zeroed in on me, and I had the image of myself being vacuumed into a narrow drain. "We drove down to Disney World. Oh, my goodness, Ricky thought he was in heaven!"

"We enjoyed it, too," Mr. Ormson interjected. "It's very beautiful down there, isn't it?"

"Yes, indeed," I said.

It was always like this. I don't think we'd ever had a real conversation, even when we talked about Ricky. Their sorrow, their rage, their anguish, all of it glided by murkily, like a shadow of something underneath the water. What I heard was that Bob was Sharon's "Gibraltar"; that Bob didn't "know what he'd do without" Sharon; that Ricky was "always with them, like a guardian angel"; that "cherishing his memory" gave them strength. Everything they said had the gloss of an elegy, which made the truth even more impossible.

Of course, I didn't really *know* the truth. I didn't know that much more than they did. For all I knew, Ricky might not be dead at all. I had realized this, eventually, after years of thinking otherwise. Perhaps he'd simply run away, for reasons of his own. Didn't that make more sense, really? Maybe he was alive and happy, living under some assumed name in some tropical resort, and "Ricky Ormson" would barely bring a shudder to him, so thoroughly had he forgotten it. If it *was* that man in the park that day, if that man did kidnap Ricky and perhaps—probably—kill him, then why didn't anyone else see him? Why wasn't his car reported by some nosy little old lady, why didn't anyone else come forward, one of the other guys that Ricky had said was "doing it"? Why was I the only witness, the only possible witness in a mystery that, as the *Rocky Mountain News* said, "seems so complete as to suggest the supernatural."

Once, my first week in Fort Lauderdale, I thought I saw Ricky walking along the street. It was a man who looked to be about my age, who could have been Ricky's twin. I forgot about the store I was walking to, and followed him through a web of people along this narrow row of shops, my heart racing, until quite suddenly he vanished down a side alley near the mall. "Ricky!" I called, but this person didn't turn.

We sat down to dinner and I sifted through all of this in my mind, as I always did, eventually, when I was at home. My brother Matt had arrived, shortly before mealtime, and even as I chatted with him, these thoughts were going around in my brain. It was as though I went under anesthesia for a while, and though I could hear the voices of my family and the Ormsons, it was as if they were sounds floating far off in the distance, neighbors chattering through thin walls. I was so lost that for a moment, lifting my head, I was surprised to see Patricia sitting next to me, in the chair my father should have occupied.

"Tom?" Patricia said. She was looking at me, puzzled. "Are you there?"

"What?" I said.

My brother Matt snickered. " 'Ground control to Major Tom,' " he said, quoting an old David Bowie song he used to torment me with. "He's always been like that, Patricia," Matt said. "Does he still walk into *walls* like they're doors?" He turned to Bryce. "Do you remember the time that Tom locked himself out of his car with the motor still running?" My two brothers exchanged glances, grinning conspiratorially, in a way that reminded me of my high school years.

But Patricia didn't join them. She looked at me seriously. "Your mother just asked you a question," she said, and I looked down to the end of the table to see that my mother was staring at me. She had that stiff, offended look on her face, and my heart sank.

"Never mind," my mother said. "It wasn't important." She looked silently down at her plate for a moment and I knew— and my brothers knew as well—what that meant. "I think we bore him, Patricia," my mother said to my wife, as if confiding. I saw Matt widen his eyes comically, as if to say, "You're in for it now!" The Ormsons sat quiet as mushrooms.

"I think Tom has always been a little bored by his family," my mother said. "I don't suppose I am very interesting, I guess."

"Mom," I said. "Come on, let's not . . ."

"Even if I do only see you once a year, I suppose it's pretty hard for you. I'm sure you'll be glad to get away from us again."

"Mom," I said. "I just spaced out for a minute, that's all." I smiled for her, a shrugging, self-deprecating grin that sometimes worked. But not now. Her mouth pinched further.

"I'm serious, Thomas," she said. "I can be honest around Sharon and Bob because they are my friends." She looked over at them fiercely. "We've talked about this before," she said.

"Well," I said, "I'm sorry. What can I say?" I made a small gesture, including everyone around the table in my apology.

"Sorry," my mother said. "You only come here because you feel guilty, and I don't even want you here if that's the only reason! I have better conversations with you on the phone than I do when you're here!"

"That's not true," I said. "You're exaggerating."

But of course it was true. Now that she'd said it, it became a reality. I could feel something emanating from me—the unwholesome aura of an actor who is noticeably *acting*. My mother stared at me, and I looked down at my plate.

After a moment, Matt came to my rescue. "Mom," he said quietly. "Will you pass the potatoes?" And then Bryce, kind Bryce, changed the subject.

After this, I kept waiting for the evening to come to a climax. But it didn't. If anything, things became calmer after my mother's outburst, embarrassed and scrupulous. Bryce spoke for a while on the subject of "kids these days," which he had been analyzing since he became a police officer. They were sneakier, they knew more about the dark side of life than they should, they lacked the morals and respect that he'd personally had when he was a teenager. Mr. Ormson added some thoughts on this, drawing on his experience as a judge, and even Patricia spoke up at one point. I was attentive, trying not to let my mind wander, nodding in the right places and making listening sounds. At one point I glanced over at my mother and she gazed back sternly.

In the midst of this, the Ormsons seemed almost harmless. But of course they weren't. They appeared to sit passively and sympathetically through the family tensions and awkwardness, but they were merely biding their time, waiting patiently for their chance to ambush me. And at last, just as I was beginning to relax, they saw their chance. I saw Mrs. Ormson give Mr. Ormson a look, and then they both turned to me, smiling.

"Tom," Mrs. Ormson said. "I'm so glad that we got a chance to see you while you were back. I don't know whether I've told you how important you are to us." I smiled and nodded, trying to seem modest and appreciative.

"Thanks," I said.

"It's true, Tom," Mr. Ormson said earnestly. "You're really important to us. Honestly."

"Well," I said, opting for a forthright sincerity. "You're really important to me, too."

"We've been talking about this for a while," Mrs. Ormson said. "And I have some things of Ricky's that I'd really like you to have. We've been saving and saving these things, and we've finally decided that we just need to . . ." She cleared her throat. "We just need to pass them on to people who they'll mean something to."

"It's been really important that we get a chance to give you this in person," Mr. Ormson said. "For a while I thought that we'd never give away anything. But it seems like it's time."

"Yes," I said. I put my hand over my mouth. "Well, thank you," I said.

Mrs. Ormson caught me in a hug. "We love you, Tom. Like you were our own son."

Some of Ricky's things: a drawing of me and him as jungle explorers, from around third grade; a watch he used to wear; a few photos of the two of us, aged five, ten, twelve, grinning for the camera; his magnifying glass, which we used to fry ants with; one of his baseball shirts, from a team we'd played on together.

I admired each item, studying it carefully. Then I excused myself, went to the bathroom, and vomited into the toilet.

Bryce said, "Don't bother about Mom." We were at his place, late at night, drinking beer, and a beery feeling of camaraderie had permeated our usually limited conversation. He said, "Don't worry about Mom. She's been like that more and more, ever since Dad died."

"Yeah," I said. "I don't know. I suppose I deserved it."

"Nah," he said. He waved his hand dismissively. We had gone back to his place, late, after Matt and the Ormsons had left and Patricia and my mother had gone off to bed. We were sitting in his garage, feeding pieces of lumber into his woodstove. "She goes off on everybody like that," Bryce said. "Everybody gets their turn. It's too hard on her, being without Dad. She doesn't know how to handle it." He took a swig from his beer, thoughtfully. "She lets herself get worked up over nothing."

"Yeah," I said. We sat smiling at one another. Every time I came home there would be a night like this—when we pretended that no matter how much time and distance separated us, no matter how different our lives were, we were still brothers. We laughed and told stories of what had happened to us in the past year, rehashed old times, and we would always end the evening swearing that we would keep in better touch.

He said, "That was weird tonight, with the Ormsons. Didn't that freak you out, with that box of his stuff?"

"Not really," I said. He spit against the side of the stove, and I watched as it hissed and evaporated. "I mean, I appreciated it and everything, but to tell the truth, I'm getting a little sick of hearing about Rick Ormson. I suppose that's terrible to say."

"No, no," he said. "I understand where you're coming from." He took me in thoughtfully. "I always thought that it was too bad that there was never any body. I always thought that would make a big difference."

I was quiet for a moment. "What do you mean?"

"Oh, I don't know," he said hesitantly. "I just think it's a shame that they spent so much time hoping that he was still alive. And maybe, partly, they still aren't sure. If there was a body, then there'd be ... I don't know, closure or something. Isn't that what they call it? Closure?"

I took this in, nodding my head slowly. I was more than a little drunk, I realized.

"So you don't think there's any chance that he's alive," I said at last.

"Nah," he said. Then he raised his eyebrows. "You don't, do you?"

"I don't know. Not really. But . . . I had this weird experience when I was down in Florida. The first week there, I thought I saw him. I was down in this mall area, right? And I could have sworn that this guy I saw looked exactly like Ricky."

"Whoa," Bryce said. He was thoughtful, picking at the tab of his beer. He, too, was drunk. "That's freaky," he said at last. "But, you know, that whole thing, it must have, like . . . affected you. I mean, we never talk about that stuff, but it must have been hard for you."

I shrugged. "Not so much," I said. "I mean, it was bad and everything, but it's not like . . ."

What? *It's not like it ruined my life,* I was going to say, but then I didn't. Because it occurred to me that maybe it *had* ruined my life, in a kind of quiet way—a little lie, probably not so vital, insidiously separating me from everyone I loved. The idea scared me, because of course there was no turning back now. To turn back now would be infinitely worse, I thought, infinitely more damaging. At least I could pretend, most of the time, to lead a normal life.

"Tom, man," Bryce said, after my silence had extended into several minutes. "Look, I didn't mean to get you upset or anything. I shouldn't have brought it up."

"No, no," I said. "No problem. I was just thinking."

"Yeah."

"Hey, Bryce," I said. I felt the beer eddying through my head, stirring things up, muddying them. "Hey . . . you love me, don't you? You love me no matter what."

"Of course I do, bro," he said sheepishly. "I'm your brother—of course I love you."

For the second time in my life, I almost told him. I could feel the whole story lining up in my head, ready to spill out.

But Bryce cleared his throat. "I'm going to walk you home, bro," he said. "I think we're both getting kind of tired, you know?"

"I can walk myself," I said. "No problem."

"Are you sure?" Bryce asked. "I mean, it's only a few blocks. I could walk with you."

"That's all right," I said. "I want to clear my head."

It was late, maybe three in the morning, and as I walked home from Bryce's place, I passed again along the edge of the park. The air had turned cold now, and the bare trees rattled, the wind pulled through the playground, back toward the creek, toward that hedge of lilacs. I hunched my shoulders, tucking the collar of my coat up, quickening my pace. I made myself think of Ricky alive, of Ricky grown up and in some sunny place, the tanned, breezy version of Ricky I'd seen vanishing into the crowd of an outdoor mall in Boca Raton. He had forgotten us entirely, had freed himself long ago, for reasons of his own.

I tried to build the story in my mind, but I ran the last few yards past the park, nevertheless, a terror quickening in me. By the time I crept into my old room, where Patricia was sleeping, curled softly in my old bed, all I could think of was a corpse under the leaves or the muddy bank of the creek, the skeleton of a teenaged boy.

I took off my clothes, letting them drop heavily to the floor, and when Patricia stirred, half awakened by my climbing into bed, I whispered, "Shhh." She moaned gently, and I murmured, "It's me." I huddled against her, shuddering a little as her mouth traced sleepily against my neck. "Mmm," she murmured, as if the physical touch told her what "It's me," meant. Me, I thought. Me. Me. Her hand moved up the inside of my thigh, slowly, steadily, and I tried to hold myself very still as her fingers traced lightly over my skin. I could feel the box of Ricky's stuff staring down at me from the top of the dresser, the T-shirt, the pictures, the drawings. "It's you," my wife whispered, and the December wind exhaled a long, raspy breath, rolling down through the park, into the yard, against the window.

LATE FOR THE WEDDING

Trent was having an affair with an older woman. Fifteen years older. People who knew about it were titillated. They asked prying questions, and Trent would have to admit that yes, Dorrie was a teacher at the small college where he had been a student. And yes, he had been in a class of hers, though he'd dropped out before they ever got involved. What did people want? Yes, Dorrie had been married before; yes, she had a son, who was only five years younger than Trent himself; yes, it was kind of weird. He didn't know what else to say. People would compare the situation to various movies they'd seen. Was it like *The Graduate?* they wondered. Was it like that one movie with Susan Sarandon and the young guy? No, it wasn't. If it was like a movie, it was one that he didn't belong in, one he'd stumbled into by mistake, an awkward and unprepared understudy. He spent a lot of time alarmed with love, a nervous, uncomfortable feeling, as if a warm piece of smoky glass were lodged in his chest. His mind frequently produced such poetic images, and they humiliated him with their dorkiness.

Which is why, after a time, he didn't really talk about Dorrie with people he knew. Things kept happening—they got into fights, they made up, they moved in together—but he kept that part of his life pretty separate from his friends and coworkers. He didn't tell anyone, for example, when Dorrie's son decided to come out for a visit. He didn't want to hear what they would have to say—he didn't want to imagine them gleefully discussing it behind his back—and so he kept quiet, even though he was in a terrible state of anxiety. Whose advice could he ask? He thought about telling it to Courtney, the young woman who bartended with him, but then thought better of it. He thought that she had her own agenda.

He had decided that he wouldn't go with Dorrie to the airport. This was the first time she'd seen her son in many years, and Trent would have felt intrusive. So he told Dorrie that he couldn't get out of work, and he told Courtney nothing, though she raised an eyebrow when he began to obsessively wash the used beer mugs that were submerged in a bus tub full of gray, soapy water. She watched as he moved a rag in and out of the opening of a glass.

"How are things going?" she said as she scooped a few quarters' worth of tips into her palm. "You look depressed lately," Courtney said.

"I do?" Trent said. He looked over his shoulder at the large mirror on the wall behind the liquor bottles. His face did look a little pinched, he thought, and he frowned. "No," he said, and shrugged, smiling up at a fraternity guy who was standing at the bar, expectantly gripping a twenty. "I'm fine," he told her, and she waved her hand.

By the time he got home that night, Dorrie and her son were already asleep. It was just as well, Trent thought. This way, they'd had a chance to reacquaint themselves again, without him hovering around. Still, as he walked into the darkened house, he felt uncomfortable. He didn't even turn on the television. He just sat on the sofa, drinking a beer to unwind, feeling like a person in a waiting room.

This wasn't an unusual feeling for him, actually. Though he'd been living with her for almost six months, it was still Dorrie's house. The house hadn't absorbed much of him yet. It was still her furniture, her dishes, her wall hangings and bric-a-brac. He sat staring at a small sculpture that had been given to her by a friend from New York who was now almost famous: an abstract piece of polished marble, which looked vaguely like a naked body.

Earlier, before the son had arrived, Trent had said: "I shouldn't be living here when he comes, do you think?"

"Don't worry about it," Dorrie said. "Where would you go, at this short notice?"

"I could probably find some place."

"It's all right," she said. But, remembering her tone of voice, he didn't go into their bedroom to sleep beside her. Instead, he fell asleep on the couch.

• • •

In the morning, he woke to the smell of coffee. Opening his eyes, he was disoriented to find himself sprawled on Dorrie's sofa. Trent had been dreaming of his mother and, for a moment, he expected to be fifteen years old, living in the back room of his mother's trailer house, staring up at the stains on the corkboard ceiling. In the dream, his mother was getting ready to pour cold water on him.

So he sat up abruptly, and the image of his mother vanished. He could hear coffee perking, and he rubbed his palm against his hair. Then he padded barefoot into the kitchen.

Dorrie's son, David Bender, was standing at the counter in a velour bathrobe, and he turned expectantly as Trent came to the door of the kitchen. He looked a little like Dorrie in the face—something about the slant of the mouth. Their eyes were similar. But he was also different from what Trent had imagined. He was taller than Trent, for one thing, and his hair was thinning, so that for a moment Trent thought the boy was thirty years old or more. They were not that far apart in age—Trent was twenty-five; David Bender was twenty. But for some reason, Trent had been expecting a kid.

"Hullo," David Bender said, and Trent felt conscious of standing there in his boxer shorts. "You must be Trent. I'm David."

Trent stepped up, awkwardly, and shook David's hand. "How do you do?" Trent said.

"I do fine," David Bender said. "Want some coffee?"

"That sounds good," Trent said, and wished that he'd pulled on his jeans before he'd come in. David Bender handed him a cup of coffee, and Trent nodded thank you, shifting from foot to foot. He couldn't think of anything to say.

"Well, this is an uncomfortably Freudian moment," David Bender said. "Maybe we should both take off all our clothes and brandish our dicks at one another."

Trent wasn't sure what to make of this remark, and so he just stood there. "Ha!" he said.

"I'm sorry," David Bender said. "That was assholish of me, wasn't it? I don't mean to be passive-aggressive."

Trent put down his coffee cup. "No, no," he said. "I'm thinking about maybe getting showered and dressed, though."

"That might be a good idea," David Bender said thoughtfully. "Maybe I'll think of some conversation."

"Me, too," Trent said.

By the time he got out of the shower, Dorrie was awake. She and David were sitting at the kitchen table, and they looked up as Trent entered. It was another moment when Trent wished himself somewhere else, and they all froze, as if in some terrible, stagy tableau.

"Trent," Dorrie said. "I think you've met David?"

Dorrie was nervous, and had been nervous for weeks. She did not see David Bender often, and he had not been to visit her since she'd taken her assistant professor position at Western Nebraska State, three years ago. Apparently, there had been tension between Dorrie, David, and David's father, Robert, for some years by that point. She was vague when she told him about it, but Trent had gathered enough facts that he could put together a skeleton of a history. He knew, for example, that Dorrie had dropped out of college to marry Robert Bender, whom she called a "financier," some twelve years her senior; that, shortly after David was born, they'd separated; that a lawyer friend of her ex-husband had Dorrie declared an unfit mother some time later and that her visiting rights had been circumscribed; that David called his stepmother, Robert's third wife, "Mom," even though the stepmother was also divorced from Robert Bender; that Dorrie and David had a stormy relationship when he was in junior high and high school; that an ongoing e-mail exchange had led to a kind of reconciliation, which eventually culminated in David's visit.

These were the facts, as Trent knew them. He hadn't asked her more than she offered, respecting her silence, knowing that the subject put her on edge. It made her snappish, he thought, such as the day before David arrived, when she came home from the grocery store in a foul mood because of the lack of fresh produce. David was a vegetarian, and she hadn't been able to find ingredients for a number of dishes she planned to prepare.

"Well," Trent had said. "Is he the kind of vegetarian who won't eat meat at all?"

"Yes, Trent," she said. "I believe that's the definition of the term."

"Okay," Trent said, and held up his palms in a gesture that men used to use to show that they were unarmed. He had noticed before that Dorrie's anxiousness came out in the form of a kind of distracted disdain for people, a sharpness that, Trent had realized, was why she always did so poorly in job interviews. That was why she had ended up at a Nebraska state college, in the middle of the sandhills. Trent understood this about her, and even felt strangely tender toward her moody skittishness. It was something other people didn't know about her. But he did.

Now, sitting in the kitchen, he could sense the effort she was putting into containing herself. She chatted affably, she smiled, she touched her hand to Trent's arm, she put her palm on the back of David's neck. But when she put her fingers on the handle of her coffee cup, he could see her grip tighten, until the pads of her fingertips blanched.

Trent could not contribute much to the conversation. Mostly, they were talking about New York City, where both David and Dorrie grew up, and where David now attended college, at Columbia. Trent had never been there; had never, in fact, been east of Omaha. Dorrie had once said that she found this "refreshing," though she also tended to become barbed at his ignorance, as when he called Staten Island, "Satin Island."

"Oh, yes," Dorrie said. "That's where the old lingerie goes when it dies."

Such gibes bothered him more than he cared to admit, and so he found himself remaining thoughtfully silent as they talked. He wondered if he was coming across as oafish and dull. He kept waiting for a moment when he could chime in with something clever, but the opportunity didn't come. From time to time, he started as if to speak, but he was not quick enough. The conversation was already off in another direction.

He had been considering asking Dorrie to marry him, probably sometime after David Bender left. He didn't know whether he would really go through with it, and even if he did, he wasn't sure how Dorrie would react to such a proposal. Nevertheless, it occupied him as he listened to them banter. They were not talking about anything important and yet he recognized that something significant was happening. This was the way that Dorrie talked to him in the first few months that he'd lived with her. It was the way she established love: She paid attention, and Dorrie's attention was wonderful.

When he first moved in, Dorrie and Trent would walk in the morning down the narrow old wagon trail that traced the alfalfa fields behind her house. The wheel ruts had become deep and bumpy with disuse, eroded by wind and rain into valleys that were miniatures of the low, hill-lined valley where they lived, and in which the town rested. Between the wheel ruts, the sod had grown dense and weedy, and though they walked side by side, it was always as if there were a low hedge between them. They joined hands over it despite the fact that it hindered their steps somewhat and slowed them. But it was all right. He liked that feeling.

Dorrie did most of the talking. She spoke of her life, of growing up in Manhattan. She told long stories about her former lovers and commented on film, on books and politics, and works of art. Trent felt like he was always learning.

This was one of the first things that he noticed about her, even before he was really attracted to her physically—that she could hold forth on any subject. When he was in her class, he'd found himself listening despite the fact that he didn't really want to be there, fascinated by the way she could stretch a train of thought between some personal experience she'd had and an abstract idea they were studying, until there was a kind of cat's cradle between the two.

Dorrie didn't suffer fools gladly. That was what she said on the first day of her class, and he remembered folding his hands over the syllabus grimly. It was another class he'd have to struggle to earn a C in, he thought, though he never did find out because he'd dropped out of school about halfway through the semester.

That was how they'd met. A few months later, he happened to be sitting in a café near campus, waiting for his shift to begin at the bar when Dorrie passed him, carrying a cup of coffee. He'd nodded at her when she looked at him, the way you do with people you vaguely know, but instead of merely nodding back, she paused.

"Isn't your name Trent?" she said, and he'd been taken aback that she remembered him.

"Yeah," he said. She gave him a funny look.

"So what happened to you?" she said. "You disappeared out of class, and I never heard from you again. You just a fly-by-nighter, or what?"

"I don't know," Trent said. He knew she was from New York, with that pushy way of talking. "Actually, I kind of dropped out of school."

"That's terrible!" she said, and her face grew serious and concerned. "What happened?"

"Just money, I guess," he said, and shrugged. "I don't think I'm much of a student."

A person was behind Dorrie, waiting impatiently to get past her in the narrow aisle, and she glanced behind her; then, as if making a decision, she sat down in the chair across from him.

This was how it started, according to Trent's version of the story. He didn't know where her version would begin. He didn't even know if she thought of it as a story. What would they say, if things continued on? People would ask, and he'd have to say, "Well, actually, I was Dorrie's student. . . ." And they'd raise their eyebrows.

David Bender didn't raise his eyebrows. He was as confident as Dorrie, though less serious. Trent couldn't get a fix on him. At first, he had a clear impression that David Bender disliked him. But then, when Trent went outside to have a cigarette, David Bender followed him.

"Hey, man," David said. "Do you have a cigarette?"

Trent handed him his pack, and David Bender took it with a small, secretive smile. "Wow," he said. "Cowboy smokes." But he put the cigarette into his mouth, nevertheless, and lit it, gazing at the horizon. "What a place," he said. "Spooky."

"Really?" Trent said. He looked out, trying to see what David might be seeing. There were times when he didn't realize that the place he lived in might be considered strange. It was just prairie—you couldn't see a tree from Dorrie's backyard, or another house. A barbed-wire fence separated Dorrie's property from the cow pastures and fields that surrounded her. It was a place that pioneers had passed through, a hundred years before, not stopping.

"So," David Bender said. "Tell me about yourself."

Trent cleared his throat. "What do you want to know?" he said. "I'm a bartender. College dropout. Maybe I'll finish if I can get the money together. And if I can decide what to study. Dorrie's probably told you most of the basics."

"A little," David said, and he bent down on his haunches to examine a large grasshopper. He picked it up, and it spit a brown substance, what kids in Trent's grade school used to call "tobacco juice," from its mandibles. He dropped it.

"Dorrie tells me that you grew up in a trailer house," David said. "That must have been interesting."

Trent stiffened a bit. "Not really," he said.

"I don't mean to sound snotty," David said, and he straightened up. "It's just not something I've ever had experience with, except, you know, via clichéd movies and so on. It's just, in terms of Dorrie, it's interesting. Your backgrounds are so different."

"I suppose," Trent said, and David Bender gave him a disarmingly friendly smile.

"It's a good thing, I think," David Bender said. "Dorrie's been having affairs with her students for as long as I can remember, but you're the first one that she's actually introduced me to. So that must mean something, don't you think?"

"I don't know," Trent said. He crushed his cigarette under his shoe, thoughtfully. He didn't know that Dorrie had had other affairs with former students. "What do you think it means?"

"Well," David Bender said, "it seems that she's more serious about you. Don't be threatened. She's told me a lot about you, that's all."

Early on, when David Bender was just a figment of Trent's imagination, he had built up a whole scenario. He had imagined confiding in David Bender, telling him confidentially that he'd planned to propose to Dorrie. He had the idea that it would be a kind of bonding moment. The David Bender of his imagination was a lanky, friendly, streetwise kid with a thick New York accent and an angular grin, someone who might have been portrayed by a younger, nonviolent Robert De Niro, someone who would clap him on the shoulder heartily and grin. "Mazel tov," his imaginary David Bender said. "Dorrie, she needs a guy like you!"

He realized that this was ridiculous. But he was still a bit surprised by the actual David Bender. It wasn't supposed to be this way, he thought.

Dorrie had spent weeks trying to think of ways to keep David Bender entertained while he visited. There were no restaurants of note and only one movie theater, which consistently played films that Dorrie scorned. "My God," Dorrie said. "This town is full of twenty-year-olds! What do they do with themselves?"

"Well," Trent said. "I guess that mostly they drink. That's why I'm making a living."

And so it fell to him. As afternoon approached, Dorrie said, "So, what do you want to do today?" And David Bender said, "I don't know. What is there to do?" And Dorrie looked at Trent helplessly.

He had talked to Courtney about it, but she had been very little help, though she'd offered to sell him some marijuana. "Get him stoned," she said. "He's from New York, and he's going to be expecting a hick town. So what can you do? I'd say, get him good and stoned and then take him out to the bars. Not the college bars, either—the cowboy bars: Green Lantern,

Dude's, that kind of place. At least it will be something he'll re-member!" Courtney looked at him and smiled in a kind of sleepy, suggestive way—she was attracted to him, he guessed; she wondered what he thought he was doing with a person like Dorrie, expected, perhaps, that it wouldn't last long.

"If he's cute," Courtney said, "bring him in here." She tilted her head a little, looking at something other than Trent, then bent to fill a bucket full of ice. "Maybe I'll hit it off with him and end up as your daughter-in-law."

2

Trent had been married before, briefly, when he was eighteen. His wife's name was Brooke, and she was a girl he dated in high school. She had gotten pregnant, of course, and in the begin-ning there had been all sorts of tortuous debates—abortion or no abortion, adoption or no adoption, staying together or not staying together. It had been harder on Brooke than on him, he thought. She had been the bright one, the one with the aca-demic scholarships, the one who actually had a future to lose, and he felt bad for her.

She was four months pregnant when they finally got married in a little courthouse ceremony. He wore a white shirt and black jeans and a tie he'd borrowed from a friend of his from the track and field team; she wore a modest, oversize blue dress, which came down past her knees. It was the only time in their whole married life that he saw her more or less dressed up—after that, up until the baby was born, she wore sweatsuits, day and night. Her face grew puffy and tired, and she began to suffer from acne, which she'd never had to worry about before. He remembered the look on her face when the judge had told them they could kiss—a kind of slack, distant stare. Then she recovered herself, and gave him a big smile. They pressed their lips together.

He loved her, he thought. They had been dating since the beginning of junior year, and had done everything together—studying and going to movies and eating their lunches across from one another in the cafeteria—and though nothing spectacular had happened, no skinny-dipping or running hand in hand through the rain or licking food off one another, he thought that they fit together. She had been the first girl he'd had sex with, and, in his mind, everything about her was entwined with the stunning pleasures of the body: her lips, the pink palms of her hands, the hollow of her throat, the line of her pubic hair. He didn't think he'd ever be drawn to other women, since each part seemed endlessly interesting. A few times, they had watched pornography together, but it hadn't aroused him. It wasn't something general that he wanted—a breast, a buttock, a daintily pointed toe—but something specific. *Her,* he thought—Brooke. Her skin, her face, her smell.

There was more to it than that, he knew. You had to live a life beyond fucking, but at the time it didn't seem all that important. He had never been particularly ambitious, even before Brooke got pregnant, so it wasn't that hard to adjust his expectations. In his mind he began to build a sort of life—looking at houses, buying baby stuff, finding some sort of trade, like carpentry or plumbing, and it didn't seem so bad, though he knew that Brooke was scared and depressed by such prospects. Probably, both of them would have ended up unhappy eventually, restless and dissatisfied like the statistics said. There were plenty of bad examples wandering around town—guys who got their high school girlfriends knocked up and ended up in this dusty speck of a Nebraska town. All you had to do was look at them to see how trapped they were.

In any case, it didn't turn out that way. As it happened, the baby died. She was born with a severely malformed heart and only lasted a little over a day. Sitting in the hospital, he'd known that the future he imagined was over with. Brooke hardly looked at him. The doctors had drugged her into a kind of calm, and they'd gone together to see the baby.

It was a little girl. They had named her Carol Lynn, for the purposes of the funeral and the headstone, but really she didn't look human. She was a mammal of some unknown species, attached to a myriad of machines, her mouth full of a plastic tube, surrounded by frowning, bustling nurses. How incredibly tiny she was, his daughter—her skin red and blotchy beneath the lights, a downy, peachlike fuzz on her skin. He found himself staring at the perfectly formed little ear, which was shaped, he thought, a bit like his. He wanted to touch it, but he was afraid he wouldn't be allowed, was afraid that such a request would seem trivial, childish. Beside him, Brooke swayed a little, making a thick, low-voiced sound. Her female chemistry was in a state of anarchy, preparing for a life that wasn't going to happen; her breasts leaked milk onto her hospital gown, and her nerve network was full of instincts—he thought—instincts carrying mother-messages through her body, despite the sedation. She breathed from her mouth in long, deliberate inhalations, as if she were tasting air for the last time, and when he touched her, put his arm around her, she flinched, and her muscles tightened. For a moment, he thought she might slap him, but she didn't. She was contracting, he thought, as if she might fold herself up into an infinitely small point, and when she looked at him, it was as if he were shrinking, too—she just wanted him to go away, that was all; she never wanted to see him again. She had loved him, or thought she loved him, up to that moment. Then she didn't.

That was the end of their marriage, more or less. After the little funeral, Brooke moved back home, to her old room. Arrangements were made—there were a few phone calls, and meetings with lawyers, and papers to be signed—but all in all he was surprised at how quickly and efficiently a divorce could be managed. They'd been married a little over six months, and by the end it hardly seemed real. It was more like the ghost of a marriage—a future that had never happened, in which their daughter grew up and they grew old: Trent, an aging plumber with a gut and a way of looking off into the distance; Brooke, throwing herself into the usual frustrated things—community theater or a local writer's group or starting her own business; Carol Lynn emerging into a sweet, hopeful, vaguely ambitious teenager, such as they themselves had been. It would have never been anything spectacular, but it didn't seem, to Trent, to be a bad life. At the funeral, he had the notion that everyone probably thought it was for the best. There was not much crying, and looking out at the bowed heads, the congregants with their hands clasped solemnly in front of them, he felt certain that they all thought that things were returning to their normal state. Now Brooke could go to college as she'd planned before she got pregnant, and Trent could do whatever it was that he thought he was doing. That was it. "The Lord is my shepherd," every-

one mumbled, "I shall not want." It was hard not to imagine a
guilty sense of relief rippling across their faces, and he turned
his head away, looking at the waves of July heat flickering like
holograms over the alfalfa fields beyond the cemetery.

Afterward, he didn't talk to people about it. He moved away
from town, traveled around for a while, and finally ended up
back in Nebraska, where he thought he might try college to see
if it suited him. By that time, he had been silent for so long that
it almost seemed like something he was protecting—something
unsavory, private, which he would sometimes stir around in his
mind when he was deep into a conversation, nudging at it like a
sore tooth. There. *There.* Almost glad of the way this unspoken
history kept him separate from people.

He knew that if he asked Dorrie to marry him, he would
have to tell her. He would have to tell her *before* he asked her to
marry him, he thought, everything would have to come out in
the open. He thought of this when she had told him the story
of her marriage to Robert Bender, when she'd talked about
David. She was not a very forthcoming person—which was one
of the things he liked about her—and he realized that when she
gave him this bit of her history, offered it up to him, it was his
duty to reciprocate.

But he didn't. It seemed too complicated, he thought, and
his pathways through his own memory seemed as complex and
delicate as the holes earthworms and other small insects dug
through the soil of a garden. When you put a shovel to the skin
of the ground and turned over the dirt, all those tunnels fell

apart. The worms and bugs crashed into the sunlight, dazed and wriggling, and the winding ways of their secret cities were lost forever.

It was a corny metaphor, he knew, but it came to him nevertheless as he made a garden for her out behind her house. He turned over the earth, spading up a weedy patch behind her house and mixing it with manure, planting tomatoes and basil and sunflowers and squash and hollyhocks, while she sat on the back porch in shorts and sunglasses, reading and occasionally looking up to watch him. She loved him at such times, he thought, when he was simple with physical work, she loved him more than she did when he talked and offered opinions.

"I don't feel a bit sorry for Virginia Woolf," he had told her, once. "I mean, don't you think that most men are just like 'Shakespeare's Sister,' too? You know? Do you think guys out here get the privilege of education more than girls do? Not really. Look at Woolf—she was rich, wasn't she? And a huge snob, too. I'd rather be her than some butler on her estate. Do you think her male servants had any better chance than she did?"

Dorrie hadn't been very patient with this argument—"provincial," she'd called it—and had pointed out various working-class men who *had* overcome their situations, while there were almost no examples of working-class women who had gone on to achieve literary fame. "I don't think you have a broad enough view to make a legitimate case," she had said. She had given him some books to read—but she hadn't looked at him in the way she did when he was planting the garden, when she had run her smooth hands over the blisters on his palms, when she had softly put her tongue to his fingers, her nose drawing in breath as it passed across his skin. They'd taken off their clothes in the patch of lawn just beyond the garden he'd dug, and she'd pressed her breasts against his chest as he lay beneath her, her lips on his, her hand finding the zipper of his pants, his thoughts falling apart like a shovelful of dirt.

Later, when the tomatoes and squash were beginning to flower, they were side by side in bed, and she asked him about his mother.

"You don't ever talk to her?" Dorrie said.

"Not really," he said. "I sent her a card on Mother's Day."

"But why?" Dorrie said. She reclined back in the darkness, her soft thigh moving away from his, the musky, powdery smell of her still in his nostrils. "Do you have a problem with your mother?" She was silent for a moment, then said, as if joking: "Is that what this is all about?"

"No," he said, and shifted awkwardly in the bed, passing his hand over his quieting penis, pushing it down. He thought then to tell Dorrie about his first marriage, about the baby. He couldn't tell her about his mother's blankness—about the way he'd come into the house, drunk, on the night of the funeral, to find his mother sitting on the couch, watching television and smoking pot. She was watching an old horror movie in which Charlton Heston ran through the future, screaming. "Soylent Green is people!" he cried, and Trent's mother looked up, glazed, when Trent walked in. She stared at him for a long time. They had nothing to say to one another.

"What are you watching?" Trent said, quietly, and his mother shrugged.

"Nothing interesting," she said, and they both grew awkwardly silent. He pressed his palm against the wall to steady himself. He thought that she might be comforting to him, but even now, she wasn't. She didn't think that he felt anything, or at least that's how she acted. He thought of things that she'd said about him—that he liked to manipulate people, that he was sneaky, cold-blooded. "As long as you get what you want, you're happy," she'd said to him once. "No matter about anyone else." She didn't say that after the baby died, but he felt that she thought it, and he put his hand over his mouth.

"Mom," he said. "I'm sorry."

But she didn't look at him. She kept her eyes on the television, even though it was now just a commercial for used cars.

"What do you have to be sorry about?" she said. "Nobody's blaming you for anything." And then she was quiet, closing her eyes, clasping her bare feet in her hands. She watched as he tottered along the edge of the living room, sipping from a bottle of schnapps. "Go to bed," she said. There was a poster of a wolf behind the couch she was sitting on, a wolf with its muzzle upraised howling at a big blue rising moon, and Trent stared at the poster stupidly as his mother's eyes examined him. She lifted a bong from the coffee table and drew smoke from it.

She didn't want him there anymore, he thought, hadn't wanted him around for a long time—they had been living for a long time like roommates or cousins, sharing the same space but not really thinking much of it, beyond day-to-day bickering or watching television together. They were mother and son, but they didn't love each other, really—not nearly as much as he'd loved Brooke, or his baby, or later Dorrie herself, who slept, breathing thickly into the dark. The steady, solid shadow of her body was nearby and warm when he pressed his hand against it.

"I'll have to meet her someday, your mother," Dorrie had

said, after his vague answers had bored her into sleepiness. "You don't have anything to hide, do you?" Dorrie murmured.

"Yes," Trent whispered. But Dorrie didn't answer. She lolled against him, and if his answer registered at all, she didn't want to know the rest.

"I was married before, you know," Trent said softly.

"Oh, please," Dorrie mumbled. "When was that? When you were ten?"

And he was silent. He waited for her to ask again, but she was already asleep.

3

He thought of all this again as Dorrie came out onto the back porch, into the crisp September evening, to find him passing a marijuana cigarette to David Bender. The garden he had planted was going to seed, dying: A few old cherry tomatoes hung on the vine, and the hollyhock flowers had closed into hard seed-pods, and the weeds near the fence had begun to grow stiff and yellow.

"Oh," she said, her face tightening as David Bender tried to hide the joint in his cupped hands. She gazed at them both for a moment, and Trent wished he had told her. He wished that she knew that he'd gotten the marijuana, was getting her son stoned, for her sake.

"Hey," she said, and smiled as if she were just another girl at a party. "Hey," she said. "Are you guys getting high?"

David Bender was the first to break the tableau. He giggled a little, nervously, then brought out the marijuana cigarette that

Trent had given him. The cherry of the joint had gone out, and he dipped his head as he offered it to Dorrie.

"You want some?" he said, and they paused nervously as she took it from him, flicking the lighter David Bender offered. They watched as she drew deeply, holding her breath for a long time before exhaling. David and Trent exchanged glances, feeling embarrassed for their various reasons, and Dorrie coughed delicately, putting a fist to her throat.

"Dorrie," Trent said, and she raised her hand to silence him.

"What?" she said, and looked at David Bender, who shrugged his shoulders, still grinning uncertainly. "You're really easily shocked," she said, turning to Trent. "Marijuana has been popular for several generations now, you know."

"I know," Trent said. Her eyes held him, but he didn't know what she was thinking—whether she was hurt or amused or angry or merely challenging, and he wished there were some word he could say, some button he could push, that would make her expression solidify into something he could understand. "I didn't mean to exclude you or anything," he said, and tried to smile at her. "I was just—getting to know David, you know? And I thought . . ."

"No problem," she said, and took another drag from the joint. "There's no problem," she said, and Trent was so flustered that he got down on his hands and knees and kissed her toes, which were sticking out of a pair of sandals. Then he stood up again, embarrassed; he didn't smoke pot very often, because it made him prone to do ridiculous things—jokes, he guessed, by which he meant to disarm people. It seemed to work with Dorrie, who stared at him for a long moment with a look somewhere between laughter and bewilderment.

"Wow," David Bender said, with stoned dispassion. "No one ever kisses *my* feet!"

The bar that Courtney had suggested, The Green Lantern, was on the outskirts of town, and when they walked in, patrons turned to look at them, but they didn't draw any real attention to themselves. Most of the clientele were what Trent and other bartenders called townies, locals not associated with the college, and Dorrie hesitated for a beat, taking it all in. "I wondered where the Old West was hiding itself," she said wryly, and Trent felt, for the first time that day, somewhat pleased with himself. Dorrie seemed mellowed, and David Bender seemed to be having a good time, drifting with a kind of hazy merriment toward a booth. He was glad that he'd taken Courtney's advice and purchased a small bag of marijuana from her. He felt as if he had gotten a grip on what could have been a bad situation.

"This is *wonderful*," David Bender said, and surreptitiously eyed a man with a cowboy hat and a handlebar mustache, and an older countrified couple who were dancing, the stuffed heads of elk and antelope and antlered deer that hung on the walls. Various cattle brands had been burned into the pine wood of the wall by their booth, different simple symbols and combined letters, like rows of hieroglyphs, and Dorrie studied them thoughtfully—as if, Trent imagined, she could see something there that no one else could. He felt a teeming of irrational love wash over him— a series of goofy similes for Dorrie, who was as dreamy and mysterious as an anemone in the eddies of cigarette smoke, who was like a picture of the mythological goddess Diana, which he'd seen on the cover of one of Dorrie's books, Diana turning a hunter into a stag, or like—but he was already embarrassed by his own brain.

"Do you want to dance?" Trent said at last, because a slow song was playing, and Dorrie looked up from whatever she had been thinking, seeming to register this idea from far away.

"No," Dorrie said. "I don't believe I do."

"That's a great idea," David Bender said. "Come on, Dorrie. I'd love to see you boogie down. Or honky-tonk. Whatever."

"I don't like to dance," Dorrie said, and lowered her eyelids in a way that made Trent realize that she was, in fact, very stoned. The notion struck him as deeply erotic.

"That's okay," he said. He smiled at David Bender and held up his palm in some vague signal. "It's okay," he said to David Bender, to whom he felt a new and friendly affection. "I'm going to get us a pitcher of beer. We don't have to dance. We can just talk."

"That sounds good, too," David Bender said. "If Dorrie is willing to drink a beer."

"I think I can manage that," she said.

Standing at the bar with his money held out, it occurred to Trent to think of something David Bender had said earlier. *Dorrie's been having affairs with her students for as long as I can remember.* It came back to Trent in little shards of words, and he mulled each one over as he leaned on the bar. It was probably true. Of course it was true, but it didn't necessarily mean anything. Hadn't David Bender said that Trent had lasted longer than any of the others, that there seemed to be something special about Dorrie's relationship with him? Trent wielded his twenty-dollar bill at a passing, hurried bartender, and thoughts turned around inside him. "Affairs," he thought. "For as long as I can remember," he thought. He looked over his shoulder, toward where Dorrie and David Bender were talking avidly. Maybe they were talking about him, Trent thought as he snagged the bartender and ordered a pitcher and three glasses. It occurred to him that he could do something outrageous; he could climb up on top of the bar and propose to her, right here, in front of all these people. "Dorrie," he could exclaim. "I love you! Will you marry me?" He thought of this as the bartender sloshed the pitcher onto the surface in front of him; he thought of this as he picked up the pitcher and glasses and headed back to their booth. "Dorrie!" he called, and she looked up, searching through the milling people to find him, lifting her hand, puzzled.

She was sitting alone. David Bender had gone off to find the rest room, and when he set down the pitcher she was gazing vaguely at something in the air beyond, like a cat observing a bee. He had begun to pour the beer, carefully, into the glasses when she finally seemed to notice him.

"I can't believe that you got him stoned," she said. "I didn't even know you smoked pot."

"I don't," he said. He scooted into the booth beside her, sliding his arm over the back of the booth, around her shoulder. "I mean, I'm not a regular pot smoker, if that's what you mean. I hope you're not mad."

She shrugged. "To tell you the truth, I'm not sure what to think right now. This whole thing is very strange. I think it's a big mistake."

"I'm sorry," he said. "Maybe this was really an uncool thing to do."

"Probably," she said, and she mused a little, privately. He was aware that she was drifting beyond his reach, and he pressed closer to her. "I'm an idiot," she said.

"No, you're not," Trent said. "It's really okay. We'll have a good time. That's all. Everything will be fine!" He watched as she nodded, as she looked off again, toward something abstract she saw in the distance. He leaned over and pressed his lips against her mouth. "Mmm," she said, half protesting, and it was a moment before she began to kiss him back, letting her tongue slip between his teeth, along the inside of his cheek. She caught his hand as he pressed it against her breast, his fingers tracing along the edge of her bra.

"Oh, my God," he heard David Bender say, and Trent glanced up to see him sliding into his seat across from them. "Stop it, you two. I'm experiencing the primal scene." And Dorrie struggled for a moment when she heard David's voice, stiffening and edging out of Trent's embrace. He drew back.

"I'll just avert my eyes for a moment," David Bender said. "Maybe I'll be able to forget, though of course maybe I'll also go blind with the shock of your scandalous behavior."

"Don't," Trent said. He wanted to say, "Don't be an asshole," but he cut himself off before the words emerged, and instead he merely settled back in his seat, feeling awkward as David Bender took a drink of beer. Dorrie straightened herself in her corner of the booth, giving Trent a steady look as she ran a hand over her hair. She wasn't mellow, as he'd thought before; she was sad.

But David Bender didn't seem to notice. He smiled at the two of them, leaning forward confidentially. "You guys," he said. "I have to say that this is probably the scariest bar in America. Do you know that? I just saw a woman in sequined jeans. My God! And she's dancing. She's honky-tonking before my eyes." Trent shifted uncomfortably, but didn't look over his shoulder to observe the woman that David Bender had noticed. He looked over at Dorrie, hoping that she might ask David Bender to lower his voice, but she seemed to be thinking of something else entirely.

"David," Trent said after a moment, trying to sound gentle. "Don't stare."

"Sorry," David Bender said, and made a show of feigning sheepishness. But he held his eyes on Trent for a long moment. Then he took another deliberate sip of beer. "Dorrie," he said. "Baby? Are you awake?"

Her eyelashes fluttered. "What?" she said, and David Bender looked at Trent conspiratorially, as if the two of them were playing a joke on her.

"You know, Dorrie, it's going to be time pretty soon for you to start going native. I mean, you're going to have to get yourself a new hairdo, and some dainty little cowgirl boots, and maybe some tight, cattle-rasslin' jeans." He grinned at both of them, but it made Trent cringe. He watched as Dorrie glanced around, observing, soaking up information, and her expression grew heavy as David began to giggle into his hand. "I'm just picturing it," he said. "I mean, tenure track is wonderful, but *Dorrie*. What's a girl like you doing in a place like this?"

"I don't know," she said, and didn't look at Trent. "I have to be somewhere, I suppose."

"Good point," said David Bender. He let his eyelids lower

with catlike awareness as he looked at Trent. "And what about you?" David Bender said. "I suppose you have to be somewhere as well."

"Yes," Trent said.

"And that would be——?" David Bender said. "Where? In my mom's panties, maybe?"

There was a moment, right before Trent hit David Bender, that the whole thing seemed more or less logical. They were mother and son, he thought—and there was no way of knowing what had gone on between them in the past—the sets of emotions that drew them together, the hopeless ache that opened up as she widened her eyes in that long moment.

Trent didn't know why, but later he'd thought of the day of his wedding, of the way he'd sat in his car, waiting for his mother to come out of the trailer so they could drive to the courthouse where Brooke—his bride—was waiting. He was afraid that they'd be late, that this was another small moment of potential happiness that would be spoiled by petty details, that once again he would feel cloddish and inept and somehow re-sponsible. *Late for his own wedding,* Trent thought, and he honked the horn.

Then, when his mother came out, he was sorry. "Don't you honk that horn at me!" she yelled. "I'm not some little slut you're taking out on a date!" She was surprisingly furious, and he stiffened silently, staring at the dashboard as her high heels clicked down the steps and across the gravel driveway, as she flung open the passenger door of the car. She glared at him as he climbed in, and he saw with regret that she had been trying, as he waited, to make herself look nice. She was a little stoned, it was true, but she'd put on makeup, and her long hair was pinned back, and she had on a new blouse, silky red, to which she'd pinned a white lily. The lily hung crookedly, listing, and he watched as she poked at it with her fingers. There was no changing her mood now, he thought, and he looked away, back to the trailer where he'd grown up.

"You left the door open," he said softly, but she only shrugged.

"Forget it," she said, and pulled the unsteady corsage off her chest, tossing it onto the dashboard. "Forget it," she said. "There's nothing in there anybody would want to steal."

And he nodded, feeling the atmosphere of her sadness, her rage, her hopeless, bitter love close over him as he put the car in gear. In the rearview mirror, the screen door swung weakly in the wind.

This was the memory that came to him, even as he took to David Bender with his fists, even as Dorrie cried out and the beer spilled on the table and the other bar patrons murmured and craned to stare; even as Dorrie's expression seemed to contract, as if she'd never seen him before. He could see Dorrie's stricken, frightened face as she flailed between them, but he couldn't hear what she was saying. Inside his head, everything was silent and sealed tight, just as it had been on that day in the car with his mother, on his way to his wedding.

FALLING BACKWARDS

AGE 49

This is a braid of human hair. The braid is about two feet long and almost two inches wide at the base. It seems heavy, like old rope, but is not brittle or rough. Someone has secured each end with a rubber band, so the braid itself is still tight—the simplest braid, which any child can do, three individual strands twined together, A over B, C over A, et cetera. It smells of powder. There is a certain violety scent, which over the years has begun to reek more and more of dust. The color of the hair is like dry corn husks. At first, Colleen thought it was gray.

But it must have been blond, she now thinks. There was a newspaper clipping among the effects in her father's strongbox, concerning the death of a girl who would have been Colleen's aunt: her father's older sister, though he'd never mentioned her, that she could remember. The clipping, which is dated October 9, 1918, is a little less than an eighth of a column. "Death came to the home of Julius Carroll and wife Sunday evening and claimed their daughter, Sadie, aged eleven years, who had been ill with typhoid fever for two weeks. All that loving and willing hands could do did not save the child." The article goes on to describe the funeral and to offer condolences. Perhaps erroneously, Colleen has come to believe that the braid belonged to that long-ago girl. There is no one to ask, no one alive who can confirm anything. She found it, curled in the bottom of a trunk along with some of Colleen's grandfather's papers. The braid wasn't labeled. It seems to have been removed rather abruptly, or at least uncarefully. The edges at the thickest end of the braid are ragged and uneven, as if it has been sawed off by a dull blade.

It reminds her of a conversation she'd had with her father years ago. She'd been very interested in genealogy at the time and had sent him a number of charts, which he'd dutifully filled out to the best of his ability, but he'd really wanted no part of it. When she'd asked to interview him about his memories of their family, he'd balked. "I don't remember anything," he'd said. "Why do you want to know about this garbage, anyway? Let the dead rot in peace," he said. "They can't help you." She'd made some comment then, quoting something she'd read: Genetics is destiny, she told him. Don't you ever wonder where the cells of your body came from? she asked.

"Genetics!" her father said. "What's the point of it? All that DNA stuff is just chemicals! It doesn't have anything to do with what's real about a person." Anyway, he said, a cell is nothing.

Cells trickle off our body all the time, and every seven years we've grown a new skin altogether. The whole thing, he said, was overrated.

Nevertheless, for years now she has carried the braid with her. She keeps it in an airtight plastic bag, in a zippered compartment of her suitcase. No one else knows that she carries it with her, and most of the time she herself forgets that it is there. She cannot recall when, exactly, the braid began to travel with her, but it has become a kind of talisman, not necessarily good luck, but comforting. Occasionally, she will take it out of its bag and run it through her hands like a rosary. The braid has traveled all over the world, from Washington, D.C., to the great capitals of Europe, from Mali to Peru. She supposes that this is ironic.

For the last ten years, she has worked for an international charitable organization that gives grants to individuals who, in the words of the foundation's mission statement, "have devoted themselves selflessly to the betterment of the human race." For years, she has anonymously observed candidates for the grants and written reports on them. Her reports are passed on to a committee that divides its endowed monies among the deserving. It is a great job, but it leaves her lonely. She is divorced, and she rarely speaks to her grown son. Most of the relatives whom she remembers from her youth died a long time ago. There are a number of regrets.

AGE 42

She is in a motel room in Mexico City when her son, Luke, calls. "Mommy?" he says, in a voice that is drunk or drugged.

He is twenty years old, telephoning from San Diego, where he had been a student before he dropped out. The last that Colleen had heard, he was working as a gardener for a lady gynecologist from Israel and living in a converted greenhouse out behind the woman's house.

"She's really weird," her son says now, trying to carry on a normal conversation through his haze. "Like, when I'm clipping the hedges or something, sometimes she lies out on a lawn chair, totally naked. I mean, I'm no prude, but you'd think she could wait until I was done. It's not a pretty sight, either. I mean, my God, Mom, she's older than you. I'm starting to wonder if she's trying to come on to me."

He *is* drunk, Colleen thinks. What sober person would talk about this kind of thing with his mother? But the comment about her age sinks in, and she hears her voice grow stiff: "It must be really grotesque, if she's older than me," Colleen says.

"Oh, Mom!" Luke says. Yes: there is the petulant slur in his voice, a wetness, as if his mouth is pressed too close to the phone. "You know what I mean." And then, as is Luke's habit when he is intoxicated, his voice strains with sentiment. "Momma, when I was little, I thought you were the most beautiful woman in the world. I just idolized you. You remember that blue dress you had? With the gold threads woven in? And those blue high heels? I thought that you looked like a movie star." Any minute now, Colleen thinks, he will start bawling, and it disturbs her that she can't muster much compassion. He has used it up, expended it on the histrionics of his teenage years, on the many, many ways he has found to need "help" since going off to college. He has already been treated once for chemical dependency.

"Oh, Mommy," Luke says. "I'm so screwed up. I'm so lost." He takes in a thick breath. "I really am."

"No you're not, honey," Colleen says. She clears her throat. He is still a kid, she thinks, a child yearning for his mother, who has been cold. But what else can she say? They have had these conversations before, and Colleen has learned that it is best to simply pacify him. "You'll find your way," Colleen says soothingly. "You've got to just keep plugging away at it. Don't give in." Of course, Colleen thinks, the truth is that Luke is clearly wasting his life. But he'd never listened to any advice when he was sober, and to say anything when he was drunk would only lead to an argument. She considers asking Luke if he is on anything. But she knows that he will deny it—deny it until he is desperate. What could Colleen do for him at such a distance, anyway? "Are you all right, baby?" Colleen whispers. "Is everything okay?"

Luke is silent for a long time, trying to regain his composure. "Oh," he says. And his voice quavers. "Yes—I'm fine, I'm fine. I'm not doing drugs, if that's what you're thinking."

"I'm not thinking anything. You just sound—"

"What?"

"Sad."

"Oh." He thinks about this. Then, as if to contradict Colleen, his voice brightens. "Well," he says. "How are things going for you? Anything exciting happening?"

"No," Colleen says. "The usual." He is her son, and she has failed him.

"How's Grandpa?" Luke says. "Is he still holding up?"

"He's okay," Colleen says. She pulls the shade, shutting out the lights of Mexico City. There is nothing special about this place, nothing particularly outstanding about the candidate she is observing, a man who runs a free AIDS clinic for street people but who is not nearly selfless enough to be awarded money by her firm. Does Luke realize how endless the world's supply of sorrow and hard luck stories is? Does he ever think that even if he were a saint, he might not be worthy of notice upon a planet of billions? She is so tired. She can't believe how far away she is, how distant from the people that she should love.

AGE 35

"Why does everyone have to be so smart-alecky," her father says, and throws his tennis shoe at her TV screen. "That was a steaming pile of crap."

He has been drinking a lot since he came to her house, sitting alone in her guest room—the only place he is allowed to smoke—sipping at a never-empty tumbler of Jack Daniel's. She has seen him drunk before, but he has never been this belligerent, this temper-prone.

"That didn't even make any sense," he says. He is referring to the video they just watched together, which she'd loved, and which she'd thought he would like, too. "Why can't they just tell a good story anymore?" he says sullenly. She can't believe that he actually threw his shoe at her television.

"Dad," she says. "You can't just throw things! This is my home!"

"Jesus H. Christ," he says, and stalks out of the room.

He has been staying with her for almost a month. She hadn't known he was coming: He just pulled into the driveway one morning. He'd been trying to get ahold of her for over a week, he said, and Colleen had frowned. How did you try to get ahold of me? she wondered. Smoke signals? Telepathy?

"Well," her father said. "Your damn phone's always busy. How many boyfriends do you have, babygirl?" He tried to smile, tried to ease things a bit by evoking this old pet name from her childhood. But he knew that things were not as simple as that. The last time he'd stayed with her, they'd fought constantly; he'd left one night after an argument and hadn't called her for almost two months.

The argument had been about her son, Luke. Her father thought she was spoiling him; she said that she didn't dare to leave Luke alone with him because he drank so much. Each had hurt the other's feelings, which was how it often was. Neither one could bear the other's disapproval.

After a time, she goes to his room. He is sitting on the bed, smoking, and he looks at her balefully as he lifts his tumbler to his mouth. He has taken off his toupee and it lies beside him on the bed, like a fur cap. She could never have imagined him wearing a hairpiece; he has always been embarrassed and scornful of male vanity, but she sees that he is right to wear it. He is completely bald, except for a few fine tufts wisping here and there over his pinkish scalp, like the head of a four-month-old baby. Without the toupee, he looks awful—frightening, even.

He is going to live a while longer. The cancer, much to the doctors' surprise, is gone. It is not merely in remission; as far as they can tell, it has completely left his body. Sometimes, he seems aware that something miraculous, or at least vaguely supernatural, has happened to him. But not often—more frequently, he seems frazzled, even haunted by his good fortune, and he turns even more fiercely toward his old habits.

"I brought your shoe," she says. He looks at her, then down.

"I'm sorry I didn't like your program," he says. "I guess I didn't understand it."

"Well," she says. "You've never been one for ambiguity."

He frowns. He knows these "two-dollar words," as he calls them—he has done crossword puzzles all his life—but he disapproves of people actually using them. He thinks it's showing off.

"Ambiguity," he says. "Is that what you call it?"

"Dad," she says, quietly. "What's wrong with you? You never used to . . . go off on little things like that. It's not good."

He shrugs. "I guess I'm just getting old. Old and cranky." His hands shake as he puts the nub of a Raleigh cigarette to his lips, and she thinks of how badly she needs him to be normal and happy, to be an ordinary father. *Don't be this,* she thinks urgently. She is a divorced woman with a thirteen-year-old son, and she works forty hours a week as an administrator at a charity organization, where all she thinks about is helping people, helping, helping, helping. She does not want him to need her, not right now. But she can see that he does. His eyes rest on her, gauging, hopeful.

"I don't have anywhere to go, Colleen," he says. "I don't know what to do with myself. I'm sixty-two years old, and I'm damn tired of working construction."

"Well," she says. "You know that you can stay here. . . ." But she hesitates, because she knows it's not true. He can't stay here if he's going to drink and smoke like this. He knows this, and his eyes deepen as he looks at her. She doesn't love him as much as he'd hoped—she sees this in his eyes, sees him think it, struggling for a moment. Then he lifts his tumbler and tastes his drink again.

"That's all right," he says.

AGE 28

From time to time, she loses her temper. Like this one time, he pushed her, for no reason, teeth gritted: "Leave me alone!" he said, and that got to her. Oh, I'll leave you alone, she thought. See what it's like, see how you like to be alone.

She knows it is wrong, even as she presses her back to the bark of the tree that conceals her. It is a bad thing, but her anger buoys her, makes her breathing tight and slow. She isn't hurting him, she thinks. She is teaching him a lesson.

It takes him a while to realize that she is gone. It is a warm day in early summer, a little breezy. From her hiding place, she can see the wobbly reflection of the sun and clouds floating in Luke's inflatable swimming pool. Luke plays without noticing for some time. Then, as if he's heard a sound, he stands straight and alert. "Mom," he says. He scopes the yard and the roads and the pasture beyond. They live a few miles outside the small college town where she is studying for her master's degree; the nearest neighbor is a mile away. "Mom?" he says again, but she doesn't move. An army man drops from his hand into the grass, near where the hose makes a sinewy, snakelike curve through the lawn. "Mommy?" he says, more anxiously. Her heart beats, quick and light, as she presses herself into the shadows. She has the distinct, constricting pleasure of having disappeared—a pleasure that, since her divorce, has occupied her fantasies with odd frequency: to leave this life! To vanish and be free!

And, more than that, as he begins to panic—there is a kind of tingly relief. For what if he hadn't noticed that she was gone? What then?

She lets it go on too long, she knows. He is almost hysterical, and it takes a long time to get him calmed down—rocking him, his face hot against her shoulder, whispering: "What's wrong? It's okay. Don't cry!" A kind of warm glow spreads through her. "I thought you wanted Mommy to go away," she whispers—Horrible! Horrible!—she can sense that it is wrong, but she keeps on, running her hand through his hair, long-nailed, thin fingers: vampire fingers. "I thought you wanted Mommy to go away," she murmurs. "Isn't that what you said?" And then she begins to weep herself, with shame and fear.

AGE 21

She is just out of college, staying at her father's house for a week or so, when the tornado hits. It is the most extraordinary thing that has ever happened to her. Parts of the roof are whisked away. The windows implode, scattering shards of glass across the carpets, the beds, into the bathtub. Apparently, there had been a beehive in the upper rafters, because dark lines of honey have run down the kitchen walls.

Colleen and her father have been hidden in the cellar, among rows and rows of dusty jars: beets and green beans and applesauce that Colleen's mother had canned, or that her grandmother had canned when her father was a boy. Some of the jars go as far back as 1940, their labels written in a faded, arthritic cursive. Her father has been planning to get rid of this stuff for as long as Colleen has been alive. She had been warned, as a child, never to open anything from the cellar. Her mother had heard of poisonous gas coming out of ancient, sealed containers.

She recalls this, sitting on the cool earthen floor that reminds her of childhood. As the storm roars overhead, she and her father huddle close together.

When they come up to see the world, after the howling has stopped, it is raining. There are no trees standing as far as they can see, only the flat prairie and branches and stumps everywhere, as if each tree had burst apart—as if, Colleen thinks poetically, there were some terrible force inside them that they finally could not contain.

"Jesus H. Christ," her father keeps saying. He goes to the door of the house, and Colleen follows after him. The rain is falling into the kitchen, dripping off scraps of insulation that hang down like kudzu. Her father touches the kitchen wall and puts his finger to his mouth. "Honey!" he says, and laughs. The room is full of the smell of honey and the sound of water. She doesn't know what to say. It is the house that both she and her father grew up in, and it is destroyed.

Her father finds his bottle of Jack Daniel's under the kitchen sink; he finds ice, still hard, in the refrigerator's freezer; and he pours them each a drink.

"At least the liquor's okay," Colleen's father says. "There's one blessing we can count."

Colleen smiles nervously, but accepts the drink that's offered to her. She had thought that this would be a rest period in her life—that it would be the last time she really lived at home, and that there would be a number of conversations with her father that would bring closure to this stage of her life. She had been a psychology major and was very fond of closure. She likes to think of her life in segments, each one organized, analyzed, labeled, stowed away for later reflection: another stage along her personal journey. Nevertheless, a tornado seems a melodramatic way to end things. She would have preferred some small, epiphanic moment.

Her father settles into the kitchen chair beside her, leaning back. The sky is beginning to clear; cicadas buzz from the dark boughs strewn about the lawn. Through the hole in the roof, they can see a piece of the evening sky. The constellations are beginning to fade into view.

"Well," her father says. He puts his palm on top of her hand, then removes it. He sighs. "Now what?"

AGE 14

"Here's babygirl, with her nose in a book!" Colleen's father crows. "As usual!"

She is stretched out on her bed and looks up sternly, closing the book quickly over her index finger, hoping maybe that he will let her alone. But it is not likely. He is standing in the doorway, in a clownish, eager mood. He does a weird little dance, hoping to amuse her, and she is terribly embarrassed of him. Still, kindly, she smiles.

"What good is sitting alone in your room," he sings, and capers around. She leans her cheek against her hand, watching him.

"Dad," she says. "Settle down." She takes a tone with him

as if he is a little boy, which has become their mode, the roles they act out for one another. Her mother has been dead for a little over a year, and this is how things go. They have accepted that she is smarter than he, more capable. They have accepted that things must somehow continue on, and that she will leave him soon. He says that she is destined for great things. She will go on to college, and become educated; she will travel all over the world, as he himself wanted to; she will follow her dreams. They don't talk about it, but she can see it—in the morning, as he sits hunched over his crossword puzzle, sipping coffee; after dinner, as he sits, watching the news, rubbing salve onto his feet, which are pale and delicate, the toes beginning to curve into the shape of his workboot. She can feel the weight of it as he stands in her doorway, looking in, trying to get her attention. He dances for a moment, and then he stands there, arms loose at his sides, waiting.

"Do you want to go out to Dairy Queen and get a sundae?" he says, and she looks regretfully down at her book, where the hobbit Frodo is perhaps dead, in the tower of Cirith Ungol.

"Okay," she says.

She is a pretty girl. Older boys have asked her out on dates, juniors and seniors, though she is just a freshman, and she is flattered, she takes note, though she always turns them down. Her hair is long, the color of wheat, and her father likes to touch it, to run the tips of his fingers over it, very lightly. These days, he only touches her hair very rarely, such as when she's sitting beside him in the pickup and he stretches his arm across the length of the seat. His hand brushes the back of her head, as if casually. He believes that she is too old to have her father touch her hair. He will kiss her only on her cheek.

Their little house is just beyond the outskirts of town, and as they drive through the dark toward Dairy Queen, she wonders if she will ever not be lonely. Perhaps, she thinks, being lonely is a part of her, like the color of her eyes and skin, something in her genes.

Her father begins humming as he drives. The dashboard light makes his face eerie and craggy with shadows, and his humming seems to come from nowhere: some old, terribly sad song—Hank Williams, Jim Reeves, something that almost scares her.

AGE 7

On Saturday after supper, Colleen's father asks her if she'd like to go on over and see his place of employment. He tilts his head back, draining his beer. He smiles as he does this, and it makes him look sly and proud. "It's a nice night," he says. "What do you say, babygirl?" He seems not to notice as Colleen's mother reaches between his forearms to take his plate. He is not inviting *her*.

Colleen is not sure what is going on between them. It is an old story, though, extending back in time to things that happened before Colleen was born—things Colleen's mother should have gotten, things she is still owed. Every once in a while, it begins to build up. Colleen can feel the heat in her mother's silences.

But her father doesn't appear to notice. He gives Colleen's hair a playful tug and makes a face at her. "I'm only taking you, babygirl, because you're my favorite daughter."

Colleen, who is sensitive about being teased, says: "I'm your only daughter."

"You're right," her father says. "But you know what? Even if I had a hundred daughters, you'd still be my favorite."

Colleen's mother looks at him grimly. "Don't keep her up too late," she says.

Colleen's father works for the Department of Roads, and he drives her out to a place where a new highway is being built. The road is lined with stacks of materials, some of them almost as tall as houses, and with heavy machinery, which looks sinister and hulking in the dusk. Her father stops his pickup near one of these machines, a steamroller, which she has seen before only in cartoons. He wants to show her something, he says.

Just at the edge of the place where the road stops, they are building a bridge. The bridge will span a creek, a tiny trickle of water where she and her father occasionally come to fish. Every few years or so, the creek has been known to flood, and so it has been decided that the bridge will be built high above it. The bridge, her father says, will be sixty feet off the ground.

The skeleton of the bridge is already in place. She can see it as they walk toward the slope that leads down to the creek. Girders and support beams of steel and cement stretch over the valley that her father tells her was made by the creek—over hundreds of years, the flowing water had worn this big groove into the earth. They have cleared earth where buffalo and Indians used to roam, he says, and then he sings: "Home, home on the range."

She is only vaguely interested in this until they come to the edge of the bridge. It *is* high in the air, and she balks when her father begins to walk across one of the girders. He stretches his arms out for balance, putting his one foot carefully in front of the other, heel to toe, like a tightrope walker. He turns to look over his shoulder at her, grinning. He points down. "There's a net!" he calls. "Just like at the circus!"

And then, without warning, he spreads his arms wide and falls. She does not scream, but something like air, only harder, rises in her throat for a moment. Her father's body tilts through the air, pitching heavily, though his arms are spread out like wings. When he hits the net, he bounces, like someone on a trampoline. "Boing!" he cries, and then he sits up.

"Damn!" he calls up to her. "I've always wanted to do that! That was fun!" She watches as he crawls, spiderlike, across the thick ropes of net, up toward where she is standing, waiting for him. The moon is bright enough that she can see.

"Do you want to try it?" her father says, and she hangs back until he puts his hand to her cheek. He strokes her hair, and their eyes meet. "Don't be afraid, babygirl," he says. "I won't let anything bad happen to you. You know that. Nothing bad will ever happen to babygirl."

"I know," she says. And after a moment, she follows him out onto the beam above the net, cautiously at first, then more firmly. For she does want to try it. She wants to fly like that, her long hair floating in the air like a mermaid's. She wants to hit the net and bounce up, her stomach full of butterflies.

"You're not afraid, are you?" her father says. "Because if you're afraid, you don't have to do it."

"No," she says. "I want to."

Her father smiles at her. She does not understand the look in his eyes when he clasps her hand. She doesn't think she will ever understand it, though for years and years she will dream of it, though it might be the last thing she sees before she dies.

"This is something you're never going to forget, babygirl," he says. And then they plunge backwards into the air.

BURN WITH ME

After my Uncle Stu killed himself, my father started to go downhill again. He gave up on his vows about not smoking in the house, and then he started to drink late into the night. He was writing poetry, he said, though I thought he'd gotten past that phase years ago. He had a filmy gleam in his eyes when he talked about it, and that worried me. But I didn't know what to say. It wasn't as if I could sit down for a heart-to-heart and ask him: "Dad, now tell me honestly. You're not thinking of harming yourself, are you?" It wasn't as if I could just drop it into conversation: "Oh, by the way, please don't commit suicide while I'm out. That would upset me."

Instead, I had the idea that we should take a trip together. "Why don't we drive out to Nebraska before I leave," I said, and he got enthusiastic for the first time in a while. Nebraska was the place of his birth, and his remaining relatives still lived there. He had the kind of sentimental attachment to Nebraska that some immigrants have to their mother country, and I think he was touched that I had thought of it. "It's a nice gesture," he said.

He knew that I wouldn't be living at home for much longer. I played bass in a band—The Flagrants, we called ourselves—and in a few months we would be leaving for a tour of Japan and the Far East, after which we were scheduled to go into the studio to cut a full-length CD. I didn't know where I'd end up after that, but it was pretty clear that I wouldn't be living with my father again.

It was a three-day drive from New York to Nebraska, and I sat there as we hurtled down the interstate in the gray Volvo, trying to think of the sort of conversations fathers and sons might have at such a point in their lives. But I couldn't think of anything—silence spreading through Pennsylvania and Ohio, sleeping through Indiana, listening to demo tapes on headphones through Illinois, since our lead singer, Zed, had yelled about my missing two weeks of sessions, fingering along to the various songs as my father watched me surreptitiously with those tired, blank eyes. I gave him a smile and pretended to jam on my imaginary guitar.

He wasn't having a very good life. He was forty-two years old, and recently, his second marriage had fallen apart. His wife, Josie, had left him in January, taking their three-year-old daughter, my half sister Meredith, with her to Guam, where Josie had a new boyfriend. My own mother had run off at a similar juncture, when I was four, though she'd left me with my dad. Eventually, she'd pulled herself together, ending up in California where she married a balding, overly sincere guy who had something to do with movies. She had two young children (more half siblings) but I didn't have any feelings for them. Mostly, I saw them in pictures, where they looked like props—posing in front of Christmas trees and national monuments, always smiling confidently. We would get these photographs from time to time, and my father would study them as if he had just failed an important test. Where had he gone wrong? he wondered. What had happened to his nice life?

He always got a certain bright look in his eyes when he was punishing himself. He was energized with it, you could see that. The last time we'd been out to Nebraska, he'd gone through a big transformation, some kind of epiphany. That was five years ago, at his mother's funeral, which was the cap to a long line of deaths—some uncles and aunts, a car-wrecked cousin, his father. There had been a traffic jam of them during my childhood, it seemed like two or three a year, every year—one of those inexplicable things.

But it did something to him. I was fourteen when his mom died, still half a kid, still goofy and out of it, but he gripped my arm. "I have to do something, Harry," he said. "I've got to get in control of my life." And he drank up a storm. Less than a year later, he was married to Josie, and she was pregnant.

We talked about it a little, as we drove through Iowa. He told me that he'd thought he was starting anew, and I had to admit that I'd known from the beginning that things wouldn't work out with Josie.

"You never liked Josie, did you?" he said, and lowered his eyelids thoughtfully.

"I liked her," I said. "It was just sort of obvious that she was really insecure and unstable. I thought so, anyway."

"I see," he said. And for the next four hundred miles, we were quiet.

And so we arrived. Here were the dirt roads that led to the small village where he'd once lived. Here was his grandparents' house, the one by the railroad tracks, now inhabited by violent-looking roughnecks. Here were the stubble fields, the ditches full of pigweed and sunflowers, here was the old home place where he'd grown up, the house his mother had died in and where his brother Stu had been living before he killed himself. We drove past silently, and then here was Great Aunt Lois's house, at the end of a row of empty buildings. The entire town took up no more than two blocks, and she was at the edge, living in the most recently built home, a ranch house that looked like it was waiting to become part of a suburb.

As we drove up, the dogs converged on the car, barking fiercely, baring their teeth. They were two plump Brittany spaniel bitches, Flossie and Maple, who had once been my dead uncle's hunting dogs, and who, after my uncle's death, had passed on to my aunt Lois. The dogs raised their muzzles, baying in alarm at our arrival, bringing Lois out of the screen door of the porch, clacking lightly in her thongs, to greet us.

"Howdy, howdy!" she called as we emerged from the car, gingerly, amid the barking of the dogs. Her smile stayed fixed, but I saw her eyebrows lift as she took us in. My dad was much balder since she'd last seen him, and he'd gained about forty pounds, but of course it was me she was looking at. Sometimes I forgot how I looked. I wasn't prepared for people's reactions, though I should have been by then. I tried to gauge what she was registering: the tattoos on my forearms, the piercings in my ears, my nose, my eyebrows; my shaved head, the tattoo on the front of my scalp—a bar code, which even my father thought was funny, though he wished it weren't on my body. There was also the fact that I'd been lifting weights for several years and had bulked up considerably. I could see in her eyes, the way they took all this in, that my father hadn't warned her. The last time she saw me, I was still skinny and small for my age, lost in those oversize comic book T-shirts and my slope-shouldered posture, still flaccid and mopey.

"Oh, my God!" Lois said brightly. "Harry, you're a punk rocker!"

"I guess so," I said, trying to smile as a growling dog pressed her nose to my crotch.

"Flossie!" Lois called. "Quit that!" Then she yelled over her shoulder. "Dick! Get out here! You have to see this kid!"

These were the people my father had grown up with, or what was left of them. Lois and Dick, his favorite aunt and uncle from the days past. Oh, the happy days of extended family! Uncles, aunts, cousins, second cousins. Great aunts. Great-great grandpas, even. They began to talk about it almost as soon as we got in the house. Beers were offered and cigarettes were lit, and here they were, the missing and the dead, the scattered and the lost. I just stood back. There had once been a different world: I knew only through stories that there was a time when all of them were within miles of each other, these huge holiday gatherings at the old home place, and no one ever went away. My father had a great aunt who had never seen a city, except on TV.

I remembered some of this, vaguely—playing Ghost in the Graveyard with cousins in the summer, the adults playing cards; Christmas shut-in snowstorms at my grandma's, the smell of cooking and stranger-relatives drifting through her house. But it didn't seem real to me. Let's think about the Family as a concept, I wanted to say to them. Let's think about it as a *construct*. It's a dying institution. It doesn't even make sense in the modern world—it's like having a village blacksmith, or a milkman, or passing the farm on to the firstborn son. A kind of storybook idea.

But my dad's face looked saner as he fell into this conversation, so I kept my mouth shut. They passed through a catalog of relatives, most of whom I didn't know. I picked at a bowl of mixed nuts. Oh, the happy days! They passed, and then it was the story of my uncle, which I had heard before. It was already hardening into a story for my father, and I guessed that was a good thing, that he was getting a little distance on it.

"He called me the night before, you know," my father said. "I should have known something was wrong," he said. "I thought about it."

Dick and Lois were silent and respectful, but I had already heard the story several times, how Stu called in the middle of the night, very drunk, how my father had awakened groggily. It was a few days after my father turned forty-two, and at first he imagined that Stu was calling to wish him a belated happy birthday. But that wasn't the case. Instead, he wanted to tell my father about his new idea. "Listen, Carl," Stu said. "I have this great idea. I know exactly what I want to do for my funeral. I've got it all planned out."

"Stuart," my father said. "Stu, it's two-thirty in the morning!"

"Just hear me out before you start talking," Stu said snappishly. "Listen, because this is important. When I'm dead, I don't want to be embalmed or put in a coffin or *nothing*, okay? I just want you to take my body out to the edge of a clearing or out to the hills and leave it there, all right? Just leave it for the wolves."

"Stu," my father said. "There aren't any wolves anywhere near you."

"Screw that!" Stu said. "I don't care what it is. Wolves, coyotes, badgers, wild dogs. I don't care. I just think it's a cool idea. All I'm saying is that I want to be part of the food chain. Promise me that you'll do this. No phony crap."

"I don't even think it's legal," my father said. "Besides which, you just woke me from a sound sleep."

"I don't care," Stu said belligerently. "I just want you to remember what I'm telling you." Now he was mad. Drunkenly offended.

"Okay," my father said. "Don't get bent out of shape." But Stu hung up on him.

I don't know whether my father had a photographic memory, but he told this story word for word the same, every time. It's like that with a lot of his stories. It's as if he has a book of them in his head that he recites, verbatim. After a while you begin to feel the shape of his stories the way a blind person knows the layout of his house. You don't even have to listen.

So I knew, for example, that the next part of the story would involve him sitting up after the phone call, unable to sleep. After a time, he'd try to call Stu back, but the line would be busy.

And I knew that there would be the part where he talked to me, as I stood at the refrigerator in the darkened three A.M. apartment, eating carrot sticks.

"Listen," he said. "Doesn't that sound like something someone who was suicidal would say? It's just—too classic, don't you think?"

"I don't know," I said. "Maybe you should call the police."

"Oh, man," my father said. "He'd never forgive me if I called the cops."

"That's true," I said thoughtfully. "Well ... maybe you shouldn't?"

"I don't know, Harry," my father said solemnly. "I don't know what to do."

But the truth was, despite my father's story, Stu didn't kill himself the next day. I remember the incident, and I know that it was months before Stu died. The two of them had a number of conversations after the "eaten by wolves" call, talks full of trivia and inconsequence, and the truth is that on the night Stu killed himself my father went to bed early, after watching *The X-Files* and the news, with not a glimmer of anxiety or presentiment.

But he liked to make his story dramatic and tragic, and in that way he was not unlike his brother, who sat naked on a craggy rock in the hills and put a shotgun in his mouth. My uncle lay there dead for a few days before they found him, but as far as anyone knew not a single animal touched him. That's the way my father liked to end his tale. No wolves. No coyotes. Not even a mouse.

The next day, my father thought it might be fun to go driving around. There weren't many people to visit anymore, but there were various graves and monuments. I put on a cap and a long-sleeved shirt to protect us both from the stares of people who might be alarmed by tattoos or piercings, and my father put his arm around my shoulder cheerfully, despite the fact that he looked terribly hungover.

"You're a good kid, Harry," he said. "Do you know that?"

"Yeah," I said. "Sure."

"I'm sorry I've been such a mess," he said. "I'm going to try to be happier, okay? I want us to have a good time." I just nodded.

"I guess your Aunt Lois is going to get some people out to the house later this week. Some of the cousins and such," he told me as we drove. "I don't know how long it's been since you've seen them—" He listed a few names that had only blurry associations for me. Most of them I remembered only as children; a couple I couldn't picture at all. He told me that my cousin Monte was already married and had a daughter, though he was only two years older than I.

"Wow," I said. "I can't even imagine."

"Oh, no?" he said. He wiggled his eyebrows.

"Not for a long time, Dad," I said. We were joking, but sort of not joking, too—he got oddly quiet for a moment, and I watched as he lit a cigarette.

"Well," he said. "I hope you have a kid before I die. I think it would be really interesting to have a grandchild."

"So don't die for a while, okay?" I said. I reached over and took the cigarette from between his fingers. "Give me a few years to work on it." He didn't say anything as I poked the cigarette out in the ashtray. "Cut back on the smoking, for example," I said.

What a weird little exchange that was, I thought. We lapsed into silence again, and I stared out at what I used to think would make a good set for a science fiction movie—those enormous metal skeletons of electrical towers lined up along the gray-green rocky hills, the grasshopper oil wells like robot insects, and no houses anywhere to be seen. I didn't know how to even begin to understand what was in his mind, what we were supposed to be talking about.

As we'd driven west from New York, he'd spoken sketchily about wanting, someday, to move back here—after he retired, he said. Back home, he said, though he hadn't lived here in twenty-five years, and most of the people he'd once known were dead or gone or radically changed.

I thought I understood this, I really did. But I didn't *understand* it, if you know what I mean. It just wasn't part of my concept of life. Not to say that I didn't appreciate my family—my dad in particular—but it wasn't as if I felt some empty hole because I didn't know or like my mother very much; it wasn't like I had some burning urge to connect with her little mannequin children, any more than I felt some warm sense of belonging here with Lois and Dick and their stories of dead old relatives

I'd never met. It wasn't the key to my existence, and I didn't quite see why it should be for my father, either. After all, he chose his life: He was the one who moved away and hardly ever visited, he was the one who picked a career—first as a tech writer, then in PR—that would keep him in cities, far away from all of them. He'd done the right thing, I thought, getting away from these dysfunctional people and this empty place, making a new life for himself. He'd done an honorable job, I thought. He was a good dad and a lot of the time he was happy. All this obsessing about his old home and the people he grew up with didn't make a whole lot of sense, if you thought about it, and I'd imagine, sometimes, that I could just grab him by the collar and shake him out of it. He was a smart person, after all.

Nevertheless, he could do very dumb things. He could find intellectual reasons for his behavior, of course—soul-searching, he would call it, and point out some philosophy book he'd read. He could manage to cogitate himself into stupidity.

For example, here we were, pulling down the narrow dirt wheel-tracks that led to the hill where Stu had killed himself. What could the point be? Maybe Heidegger could tell you, but I couldn't. I sat in the car when he got out, watching him tottering through waves of wind, walking along the jagged, rocky bluffs, his hair blown up and awry like a scared cartoon character. After a moment, he bent down, examining one of the pocked boulders; then he kneeled beside it. I figured that he'd found the bloodstain he was looking for. I watched as he ran his fingers over the surface of the rock, and then, finally, I got out of the car.

"Dad?" I said, and he looked up. For a second, I could see the addled old man he might become—a puzzled, delicate senility that was waiting for him down the road. Then he was forty-two again, and he rose to his feet, sheepishly, the tail of his shirt flapping in another gust of wind.

"Well," he said, and gestured halfheartedly. "This is the place."

"Yeah," I said. I scoped through my mind for something to say, something like, "He's in a better place now," only not so corny. Despite myself, I glanced down at the rock my father had been examining, and it made me shudder. "Wow," I said glumly. Nothing else came to me.

"You know why he did it here, don't you?" my father said at last, softly. He gave me a strange kind of smile, and I shrugged. "You probably don't remember," he said. He pointed down into the valley below us—a barbed-wire fence, a length of wheat field, a patch of high weeds and the tilted, crumbling frame of an old shed. "That's the old Leatherwood place," my father said. "I guess Stu thought it would be a good joke."

"Ha, ha," I said. "I guess I don't get it."

"Yeah, well, that's Stu's sense of humor for you." He cocked his head, giving me another impossible smile. "Don't you remember me telling you about the ghost lights?"

"Oh," I said, because then I knew what he was talking about, though I hadn't thought about the old story in many years. It was a local legend. There was a certain patch of highway where mysterious lights were occasionally noted, flickering off to the left of the road, usually along the ridge of hills—the hills we were standing atop, I assumed. My father claimed to have seen them once when he was a teenager. As he was driving, several clear, bluish, glowing bubbles rolled across the road like tumbleweeds. He almost drove off the road to avoid hitting them. They bobbed over the barbed-wire fence and vanished.

When I was a kid, I'd written a little paper about the lights. One explanation for them, I remember, was ball lightning. Ball lightning was associated with thunderstorm activity but didn't behave in ways that current physics could understand. Other explanations included phosphorescent reflections, gas emissions, and Saint Elmo's Fire.

I remembered telling all this to Stu once, when I was about eight or nine, still scrawny and probably a little officious, still kind of spoiled by my father's doting—that's the way Stu must have seen me at least, because his eyes narrowed as I held forth. I watched as he flicked his cigarette, leveling a dark look on me.

"Your dad never told you about Old Man Leatherwood, did he?" Stu said, lowering his voice. "I'll tell you the *real* story about those lights," he said. "There's an old farmhouse near there, and that was where Leatherwood lived with his seven sons." It was late at night, I remember, when Stu told me this story—we might have been camping or sitting out in the yard—but I knew he was trying to scare me. He told me that old Leatherwood had gone crazy after his wife had left him and had lit his own house on fire, splashing the floor and the clothes and the bed with kerosene. All the sons were burned to death, Stu told me, but Leatherwood himself had survived—his face and hands burned and twisted, the skin melted like an old candle. The ghost lights were the souls of the boys who'd died in the fire, Stu told me, and he said that if you followed them they would lead you to their father, who still wandered through the hills, staring, always staring, since his eyelids were burned away.

245

He would reach out his hands to grab hold of you. "Burn with me," he would whisper.

Then Stu shot out his hands and caught me by the neck, and I let out a little scream. Which tickled him. He bent over laughing. "Gotcha," he said, and kept snuffling into his hand, his eyes bright and jokey. "I did get you, you have to admit." He mussed my hair affectionately—in his own mind, perhaps, just a teasing, playful uncle—and I smiled at him wryly, not wanting to seem like a bad sport, not wanting to admit that the story had hit close to home, that I'd have nightmares later, as the son of a man whose wife had left him, a man whose weird moods often scared me—"Burn with me," I'd think, and I could see my father's face, his hands reaching out for me.

All this came back to me as we stood on the hill where Stu had killed himself, and I remembered once again the relish he took in the story, his good-natured pleasure in scaring me. His choice of this hill was a joke on me, too, I realized, though I didn't find it particularly funny.

"Well," said my father, and laid a gentle hand on my back. "I guess it's what he wanted. I don't know what else to say." He hugged me, briefly, one-armed, welling with tears for his brother and then shaking them off. "I miss him," he said, and the wind lifted the hat off my head. We watched silently as it flew over the cliff edge of the hill, rising like a balloon for a moment and then swinging down to earth, tumbling out of sight, into the brush and boulders below us.

Sometimes, my father would ask me what I remembered. He had great hopes for my memory, I think—as if someday, I'd be able to re-create a sort of virtual reality of his past life. As if, someday, I'd want to.

But I hated to disappoint him. I would never admit, for example, that I had hardly any image of my grandmother at all. I remembered her hearing aid, a small pink mechanism that made me think, when I was little, that she was partially a robot. I could picture the way she would stand with her back to the stove, smoking cigarettes. But I don't know whether I ever had an actual conversation with her. I didn't recall her voice, or anything much that she did.

But I knew he would hate to hear that. He'd argue with me about it, probably, try to convince me that I really *did* remember, if only I'd try harder. Every day we would get up in the morning and go out for drives, and he would look at me expectantly as we pulled up to one place or another—in town, to park outside the former house of an old girlfriend, where he went into the fine points of rock bands he'd once loved, like KISS and Boston; to the cemetery, where we scrubbed bird droppings and dust off the headstones of various family members, and he told me jokes he'd gotten off the Internet; to a bowling alley that one of his uncles had owned, where we ate microwaved pizza and he told me that some of the poems he'd been working on were set in the bowling alley. Most of the poems were about his "sexual awakening," he said. He'd been thinking a lot lately of the first girl he'd slept with—she still lived in town, he told me, though he believed that she was married. "Maybe we could look her up, though. What harm would it do?"

"Dad," I said. "I don't think so."

Still, he seemed so happy that week, very calm, and I didn't want to ruin the mood. Even his drinking seemed better; not less, necessarily, but more festive and less depressed, and it was nice to see him so cheerful and talkative.

So on Friday, when he said, "I'm sure you remember this place, don't you?" I nodded my head as if I did. "Of course," I said, though in fact, I hadn't had any idea where we'd been driving for the last half hour, through anonymous mazes of fields and hills and telephone poles. We'd stopped at an empty crossroads where two gravel roads met.

"Hard to believe," my father said. "But this is Delano!"

And then I realized that we were at the edge of the ruins of a tiny town—I remembered that much at least, putting together fragments of things he had told me. It was a place from my father's childhood, the site of his grandparents' old house, which had disappeared along with the rest of what had once been, long ago, a dot on a map. The little town had been fading away for decades and now, apparently, entropy had taken over completely. My father pointed out the places in the field where there had once been a grain elevator, and a set of houses, and a meeting hall where there had been dances. The last time we had been here, the red brick schoolhouse had still been standing. Now, all that was left was a single dead tree.

"Is this the place?" I said, and watched as he wandered along the edge of the road.

"Of course," he said, and motioned me to look at a spot in the dirt where he was kneeling, where the cement foundation of the schoolhouse was partially plowed over. "I used to come out here all the time when I was a kid," he said. "I ought to remember."

I nodded as he brushed dirt away from the squares of cement. "Weird," I said. I looked out at the line of horizon, that strangely distinct division of sky and land that made it look like there was a bowl sealed over us.

"Well," I murmured. "Progress marches on, I guess."

But he just looked up at me vaguely, smiling as if I'd said something funny. I watched him pick up a rock from the edge of the road. "You know a strange thing about getting older?" he said. "It's very strange, because you start to realize that all these people were once your own age. It takes a while for it to really sink in. But then it becomes kind of fascinating to think about. To try to put yourself in their place."

"Uh-huh," I said, and nodded as if I, too, thought it would be fascinating.

Driving back to Lois and Dick, my father wanted to talk about Delano. He wanted to talk about the sweep of time, the passing of generations, the terrible swiftness of it. "Your great-grandma was raised in a sod house near Delano," he told me. "She came there as a pioneer, in a covered wagon. Can you imagine what that must have been like?"

"Sort of like *Little House on the Prairie*," I said. "I imagine."

"Yes," he said. "I suppose." He thought for a moment, trying to think of a story. "She met your great-grandpa at a dance in Delano. Your great-grandfather Mooney was a fiddler in the band that was playing there."

"Yeah," I said. "I know." It was another story that I'd heard a number of times—something that was supposed to connect my interest in music with the people of the past.

"Hey," I said lightly. "Do you know what the name of the band was?"

He looked stern, because this question had never occurred to him, or me, before. "Ah," he said, and thought for a moment. "Well, I don't know. I don't know whether bands had names then like they do now. I do know that he studied music for a while, at Oberlin College in Ohio, before he went West."

"Oh," I said, and I tried to add this to the store of trivia I already knew. But we grew quiet. I didn't really think it was possible to imagine the people of the past—to understand the mind-set of someone who had lived in my great-grandfather's time. Why would you go West, I wondered, to such a barren place? And why would you stay there, why would you try to build a town that would rise up and vanish within less than a century? What could you have been thinking? It must have been something very different, I imagined—and I thought of the cities I would be touring: Tokyo, and Seoul, and Bangkok. What would such cities make of a place like Delano? Of the tilted, crumbled sod houses, of the abandoned gas station on Highway 30, which looked like some ancient ruin?

But my father didn't say anything. I watched as he tipped his sunglasses over his eyes. He drove into the sunset, as his pioneer ancestors must have done, following a two-lane highway that ran parallel to the railroad tracks, passing through these shriveled little villages, these outposts built by pioneers. What an odd sense of progress they must have had—what hopeful vanity and stubbornness. Which they had passed down, I thought. Though it didn't do my father any good.

When we got back, Lois was cooking, and Dick was sitting in the garage, drinking beer and watching flies stick themselves onto the helixes of flypaper that hung from the rafters. "Howdy, howdy," Dick called as we got out of the car, and the barking dogs converged on us once again. Though we'd been there for days, they still behaved as if they'd never seen us before, every time we drove up.

"You dogs!" Dick yelled. "Shut up!" And we moved sheepishly toward the lawn chairs where he was sitting.

"Ye gods, Harry," Dick said as I followed my father into the garage, with Maple behind me, her muzzle snuffling the seat of my pants. "I can't get over it," Dick said. "You're turning into a giant!" He appreciated this for a moment, gazing at me, and then he shook his head at my father. "I never would've guessed," he said.

I don't know what they once thought of me. My impression is that I was considered tiny and sprightly and funny. A "character," in the way kids sometimes are without knowing it themselves. My father used to tell his girlfriends stories about me, and one of his favorites, which he told again to Lois and Dick that night, was about how I had behaved at my grandfather's funeral. I was six, and didn't seem to know that anything bad had happened. My father described me as skipping along through the milling crowd of funeral well-wishers at the house after the graveyard services. I tasted from various pies and relish trays and covered dishes, humming to myself, completely self-possessed. He remembered standing there, comforting my grandmother as she wept, watching as I sat in a chair with a boiled egg yolk up to my eye like a monocle.

"Look at my beautiful golden eye!" I said to no one in

particular. "I can see the future!" I waved the yolk through the air as if it were flying, then bit into it. "Arrgh!" I cried. "I'm eating my own eyeball!—It tastes—good!" All the while my grandmother continued to cry against my father's shirt and people filed solemnly past me as I chattered away.

I could never figure out why he found this so hilarious or memorable, or even what the point of the story was, exactly. I didn't remember the event at all, but that was true of most of the stories my father told about me. There was a version of me that he held in his mind, one that I didn't quite recognize.

The next day was the day the cousins were supposed to come out to visit us, but things began to fall apart as the day wore on. Cousin Monte phoned in the early afternoon to say that he wouldn't be able to make it—some family problems, he said, as my father and Dick were busily pounding in stakes in the back-yard, preparing for a game of horseshoes. Then another, around three: Jared, who worked for the electric company, had been sent out to fix a downed wire, and didn't think he'd make it until later, if at all. About an hour later, Cousin Arleen called to beg out, too, and I kept my eye on my father, thinking this might send him into a decline. But it didn't. He and Uncle Dick were going beer for beer pretty steadily, and Aunt Lois was drinking gin and cranberry juice, and they all seemed blissfully unfazed by the news that the cousins were standing them up.

"They've never been reliable," Aunt Lois said as we sat around the kitchen table. "They've done this to me before, and you know what? I don't really care. That Monte, he always got on my nerves," she said, and took a sip of her drink. "His wife, she's a Sioux from up to the reservation, and you know what those people are like. Very standoffish."

"More food for us," Dick said.

"Damn right," Aunt Lois said. "Harry, do you want me to fry you up a second steak? I've been noticing that you don't eat all that much for such a big boy. But these are good steaks—thick and marbleized, right off the cow!"

"Well," I said, and my father grinned at me humorously as he dealt another hand of gin rummy to Uncle Dick. "Well," I said. "To tell the truth, I'm kind of a vegetarian."

"Oh," Aunt Lois said solemnly, taking this in. "I didn't know that!" She turned to look at my father, uncertainly. "Is that religious?" she asked.

"No," I said. "It's just something, you know . . ." But it didn't seem appropriate to go into the whole thing.

"Oh, they all do it now," my father said, looking at me from over the tops of his cards. He laughed, as if he were telling them something outrageous. "All these kids his age, none of them eat meat!"

"Huh," said Uncle Dick. He glanced at his cards, then stared at me for a minute, stunned by the news of this fad that was sweeping the youth of the East. "As big a muscles as you've got, I would've thought you'd eat three steaks!"

"Well," I said. "I just work out, that's all."

"Uh-huh," he said. "Well, as long as you don't have any problem with me having my steak, you go right ahead and eat your salads and greens and such. If you lived out here where you got some decent beef, you'd probably change your mind."

"Maybe so," I said, and smiled. If I lived out here, I thought. Then what? They seemed so foreign to me. I used to tell my father that they all seemed vaguely like country singers, like the type of people they sang about in country and western songs, good timing and hard lucking and honky-tonking people. "No, no," my father said, wrinkling his nose, and I knew that I was presenting him with a cliché. But still, here was Uncle Dick with his cowboy boots and his chestnut-colored, leathery skin and dyed black hair; here was Aunt Lois with her tight Western-style blouse and enormous breasts and large pouf of gray-blond hair. I had heard of the large parties when my father was a child, where everyone drank, and danced, where someone played the fiddle and another played the harmonica or guitar and another sang. I don't know whether someone played on a washboard or a Jew's harp, but it seemed likely. It was always hard to picture my father among them, let alone myself. I understood why he'd left.

Still, he seemed very comfortable and jolly, despite the fact that the rest of his relatives had blown him off. He and Lois and Dick gossiped about the absent cousins, and weather, and the crops. Then they remembered again for a while—stories of my grandparents, of my uncle, and the rest: a fishing trip where Uncle Dick and my grandfather had danced around the campfire in their underwear, singing old navy songs; the way my grandmother used to whistle when she wanted her children to come home, putting her index fingers in her mouth, and you could hear her for miles; the way Uncle Stu would always get up on Saturday mornings to watch cartoons, drinking beer and eating cereal, never marrying or even dating a girl.

I ate a salad and a baked potato and a sliced tomato from Dick and Lois's garden while they feasted on their steaks.

• • •

The night wore on, and I sat listening as they talked, watching as they raised cans of beer out of a cooler full of melting ice, smoking cigarettes. I sat in my lawn chair, fading in and out, thinking of what it would be like if my dad got lung cancer, or cirrhosis of the liver. I thought of various ways that he would possibly kill himself, after I left, imagining a number of horrible scenarios in detail. When the talk turned to me, I hardly noticed.

As I tuned back into the conversation, I realized that my father was trying to explain the concept of moshing to Lois and Dick. He had been to a few of my shows, had stood back by the bar, observant and out of place in his button-down shirt and khaki pants.

"They get quite a crowd around the stage," he was saying. "People dancing. And some of them climb up on the stage and just sort of ... dive into that mass of people. And the people catch them—all these hands come up and then the divers pass along on the hands, like they are riding a wave. It's really kind of pretty to watch, in a way."

"I'll bet," said Aunt Lois, observing me with polite alarm, and I ducked my head, blushing.

"We haven't ever heard you sing yet, Harry," Uncle Dick said. "Are you going to do us the honor?"

"I actually don't have my guitar with me," I said. I gave my father a pleading look, but he only smiled hazily. "I'm not really a singer," I said. "I'm just a bass player, you know, and backup vocals."

But Uncle Dick was already out of his seat, headed into

the house. A few minutes later he emerged with an old, cheap, six-string acoustic guitar, which he handed to me. He showed me his harmonica, putting it to his mouth, playing a quick glissando. "Come on," he said. "I'll play with you. Maybe Lois will climb up onto the tool counter and jump off onto your dad."

I took the guitar, a little uncertainly, and strummed it. "I don't know any songs really," I said. "I'm a terrible singer."

"Bullshit," said Uncle Dick. He rubbed the harmonica across his lips, making a sad, train-wail sound. "Play me a song, damn it. Any song. I'll follow along." He put his hand on the counter for balance and I looked over to my father, who was watching expectantly.

I strummed again. "I know a few folk songs," I said. "Do you know 'I Can't Help But Wonder Where I'm Bound'?"

"Play it," Uncle Dick said.

"Play it," said my father, and I began to pick at the strings.

" 'It's a long and dusty road, and it's a hard and heavy load . . .' " My voice felt raspy as I sang, awkwardly formal, but my uncle began to play his harmonica as I sang the chorus. " 'Lord, I can't help but wonder where I'm bound, where I'm bound,' " I murmured, and I could see my father nodding along, expectant and serene. For a moment, my voice—which had never been very good—seemed to come from somewhere else, humming perfectly with my uncle's harmonica, and a chill went up my spine. For a minute, it seemed beautiful.

•   •   •

"Walk with me," my father said, much later. Dick and Lois had gone to bed, but he and I were still up. "Walk with me," he said, and Flossie and Maple followed us down the driveway, out to the road. This had been a kind of town, once upon a time, though it was bordered on all sides by fields and edged, in the distance, by hills. The houses were mostly abandoned, turned into sheds or shacks, but people had lived in them once. We walked, and the moon shone down on us.

"I think I'm going to move back here," my father said, and tripped for a moment along the edge of the ditch. I caught him by the nape of his shirt, steadying him. We had come to the little house where he'd grown up, where his family had lived, where his mother, and then his brother, had spent their last days. The dogs clicked their black nails delicately on the dirt road in front of us, and my father put his hand hard against my neck. "We could stay here," he said. "We could make a new life, Harry. You could play your music—you could start a new band here, you know. I own this house."

"Dad," I said, but he didn't let go of me. We stumbled together into the yard of the house where he grew up, and the darkened windows stared at us, the bats dipped down from the branches of the apple trees, the dogs grew alert and rushed out after some prey. His fingers dug into my arm as if he were falling.

"Dad," I said, and the sky was full of more stars than I'd ever seen before, the long strip of the Milky Way above this empty place.

"Don't leave me, Harry," my father said in a soft voice, with an intensity that made my spine stiffen. "Please don't go. We can stay here. I know there's something we can do together, you and me. We can . . . we can . . . you know! We can work it out."

He caught my hand and held it. Looking over my shoulder from the future, I knew that I'd have to remember him this way ever afterwards—his eyes holding me hopefully, always expectant, the moon and the dewy grass and the old empty house, waiting there, waiting for me to say good-bye.